One look, and sh... change her life....

Hailey couldn't stop the shivers that ran up and down her spine. Never in her life had she been so physically aware, so instantly attracted to a man.

"I'm here on behalf of my client, who was the recipient of your father's letter," Sean Cassadine said.

"I see," she said, not really seeing at all. "And who is that?"

"According to the letter, Alan Palmer, my client, is your biological father."

Her eyes widened. "*The* Alan Palmer? As in Palmer Publishing?" He was one of the richest, most powerful black men in America. "So, after all this time, Alan Palmer wants to play daddy?"

"He would be quite ecstatic if you really were Susan Palmer."

Hailey shook her head. "I'm not interested in playing daughter. He and his wife gave me up for adoption. He's going—"

"Adoption?" Cassadine looked at her as if she'd grown two heads. "Susan wasn't adopted. She was kidnapped."

ABOUT THE AUTHOR

Maggie Ferguson has always been an avid reader with a strong desire to write. Her writing experience was limited, however, until a close friend started penning a romantic suspense novel and encouraged Maggie to do the same. *Looks Are Deceiving*, her first Harlequin Intrigue title, was the result. Maggie says she loves writing stories with a special twist, and that's exactly what you'll find in all her novels. *True Hearts* is no exception.

When she isn't writing or reading, Maggie enjoys watching Alfred Hitchcock movies, horror movies, attending the theater and weekends in St. Louis.

Maggie loves to hear from readers. You may write to her at: P.O. Box 5397, Springfield, IL 62705.

Books by Maggie Ferguson

HARLEQUIN INTRIGUE
284—LOOKS ARE DECEIVING
347—CRIME OF PASSION
408—FEVER RISING

Don't miss any of our special offers. Write to us at the following address for information on our newest releases.

Harlequin Reader Service
U.S.: 3010 Walden Ave., P.O. Box 1325, Buffalo, NY 14269
Canadian: P.O. Box 609, Fort Erie, Ont. L2A 5X3

True Hearts
Maggie Ferguson

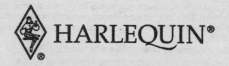

TORONTO • NEW YORK • LONDON
AMSTERDAM • PARIS • SYDNEY • HAMBURG
STOCKHOLM • ATHENS • TOKYO • MILAN • MADRID
PRAGUE • WARSAW • BUDAPEST • AUCKLAND

To my dear friends Layle Giusto and Margie Walker.
Thanks for your support and encouragement.

ISBN 0-373-22474-5

TRUE HEARTS

Copyright © 1998 by Anita Williams

This edition published by arrangement with Harlequin Books S.A.

Printed in U.S.A.

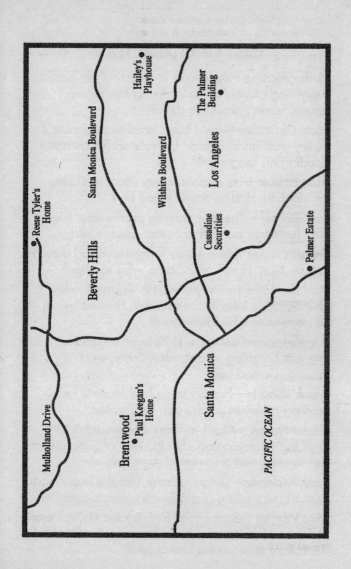

CAST OF CHARACTERS

Hailey Monroe—A woman in search of her past. Everything pointed to Hailey being the missing heiress Susan Palmer. Or did it?

Sean Cassadine—He'd been hired to determine if Hailey was Susan Palmer, but was sexual attraction clouding his judgment?

Alan Palmer—He'd spent twenty years searching for his child. Had he finally found her?

Lara Palmer—The devoted wife and mother. It was after her tragic death that Susan disappeared.

Senator Reese Tyler—Lara's former love had reason to hate Alan. How badly did he want revenge?

Paul Keegan—Lara's brother. He was next in line after Susan to inherit Lara's money. How far would he go to ensure his inheritance?

Eric Keegan—Paul's son. He'd been a teenager, away at boarding school, when Susan went missing. Or had he?

Frank Roberts—Hailey's uncle had reasons for wanting Hailey to put the past behind her.

Gloria Falcon—Alan's mistress. She wouldn't let anything or anyone stand in the way of getting what she wanted, and she wanted Alan Palmer.

Lacy Anderson—Susan's nanny. Did she know more than she was telling about Susan's disappearance?

Mac Warren—Sean's chief investigator. He was one of the best investigators in the business, but would the Palmer case get the best of him?

Chapter One

Her whole life had been a lie!

Hailey's knees buckled, and she sank into the chair next to the bed. Her heart was pounding. It couldn't be true.

"You're not my daughter... you're not my daughter...."

The words reverberated through Hailey Monroe's brain before she could reject them. She grappled for some rational basis to explain her father's shocking pronouncement. He was delirious. He didn't know what he was saying. How could he? She fought back tears as she looked at him lying motionless on the hospital bed, fighting for his life.

His nut-brown face was drawn and tense. A plastic tube fed oxygen into his nostrils. Several feet of tubing hung from an IV bag and fed into a needle positioned in his right arm. Adhesive electrodes were attached to his chest and led to a televisionlike oscilloscope displaying his electrocardiogram.

She bit back a sob. Seeing him like this terrified her. And she had every reason to be scared. His condition was grave. He had a concussion, several broken ribs, a broken leg, a punctured lung and internal injuries. The automobile accident that had killed her mother instantly had brought him to this.

An image of her mother's smiling face appeared before her. She squeezed her eyes shut as a moan escaped her lips.

Oh, Mom. She wanted to scream, to shout, to hit someone or something. It wasn't fair. She'd been doing so well on this latest Alzheimer's drug therapy. She was almost her old self again. They'd made so many plans....

Tears blurred her vision as she stood and laid her hand against her father's arm. "Don't worry, Dad. Everything is going to be all right."

At the sound of his daughter's voice, Jack Monroe slowly opened his eyes. Hailey managed a weak smile. "There is so much I want to tell you," he said.

"Not now," she said gently. "We'll talk later, when you're stronger."

He shook his head. "You've got to listen to me. There's not much time."

His words frightened her, but she tried not to show it. "Dad, just calm down. Dr. Willis says you're not to overtax yourself. I know—"

"You've got to listen to me," he repeated, struggling to sit up.

Perhaps it would be best to humor him. "Okay, Dad, I'm listening. Just lie still."

He drew a deep, raspy breath then lay against the pillow. "Your mother and I wanted to tell you, but the time was never right. We kept putting it off...." He paused and drew another deep breath. "This is very hard for me to say, but you need to know the truth. Your mother and I are not your parents."

"Of course you are," she said firmly. "It's the medication. It's confusing you."

"No, no," he moaned, his head rolling from side to side on the pillow. "I'm not confused. I know exactly what I'm saying."

"Now, Dad—"

"Please, Hailey! If you interrupt, I may lose my nerve and not be able to tell you this." Jack Monroe closed his eyes as if summoning an inner strength. "We should have said something," he continued after a moment. "We knew it, but we—we couldn't give you up." His brown eyes left Hailey's and fastened on some point in space. "We tried a long time to have a child. We were about ready to give up when Abby got pregnant. We were so happy, but…we lost the baby." He swallowed hard, and tears welled in his eyes.

She took his hand in hers and held it tight.

"The doctor said we shouldn't try again, that Abby would never be able to carry a child to full term. We had to accept that we would never have a child of our own."

Hailey went rigid. Had she heard right? They couldn't have kids? No, it couldn't be true. She wanted to cover her ears, not hear any more, but his eyes held hers, forcing her to listen.

"It wasn't fair. Everyone else seemed to be able to have children. Why not us? Everywhere we turned there was a woman with a baby. In the supermarket, the department stores, they were there, a constant reminder of what we would never have. Then one day, a miracle happened." He looked at her, eyes brimming with love. "You came into our lives."

"What are you *saying?*" she asked, her voice little more than a whisper. "I'm adopted?"

"May twenty-first, 1976," Jack Monroe continued, as if she hadn't spoken. "That's the day we became your parents."

Hailey was too stunned to speak. She'd been trying to cope with the loss of her mother, and now this. It was too much.

"My will's in the top desk drawer in the study. Along with it, there's a letter." His voice was unsteady and laced with pain. "You've meant everything to your mother and me. We loved you so. We didn't want to lose you. That's why we didn't tell you, couldn't tell you."

Tears welled in her eyes. "I love you and Mom. Nothing will ever change that, even if I am adopted. You've been the best parents in the world."

His brown eyes locked with hers. "I love you," he

gasped. "Remember that." Jack Monroe's eyes rolled into their sockets, and his head lolled to the side.

She grasped him by the shoulder. "Dad?" she cried, shaking his arm. "Dad?"

For a moment, Hailey was paralyzed. Then she grabbed the nurse's call button and pressed it repeatedly. The charge nurse appeared almost immediately and pushed past her. Several other hospital personnel rushed into the room.

"Code blue," a young black intern barked. "We need a crash cart, now!"

The nurse at the foot of the bed sped to the intercom and yelled for the clerk at the nurses' station to call code blue. The intern was bent over the bed, listening to her dad's heart.

"What's wrong?" Hailey cried, terrified by the scene playing out in front of her. She had no idea what was happening, but she knew it was bad.

"You have to wait outside, miss!" someone said. As she was escorted from the room, she saw the intern pull the pillow from beneath her dad's head and begin to compress his chest. That was the last thing she saw before the door was shut in her face.

Her uncle materialized at her side. "What's going on?" Frank Roberts asked.

"I don't know," she cried. "We were talking, then Dad started gasping like he couldn't catch his breath. That's when…" Her voice trailed off at the sound of heavy footsteps approaching from behind. She turned to see a slightly overweight man coming toward them. It was Dr. Willis, her father's physician. He'd know what to do.

He didn't stop to speak but brushed past them hurriedly, swinging open the door to her father's room. On his heels, two nurses followed, pushing what she presumed was the crash cart. Through the opened doorway, she saw Dr. Willis and the intern position the crash cart next to the bed.

"Get the board under him!" she heard someone shout. Then, once again, the door was closed.

"He's going to be all right," her uncle said reassuringly. "Dr. Willis is a fine doctor, and Chicago Memorial is one of the best hospitals in the city." He placed an arm around her shoulders and led her to the visitors' lounge. There, he pulled out a chair for her, but she shook her head, electing instead to stand. He sighed and sank into a straight-back chair next to the lumpy couch.

"Uncle Frank, he said they weren't my parents." She could hear the hysteria in her voice and wrapped her arms around her body in a defensive gesture as she began pacing. "He said I was adopted."

"Adopted?" he said, frowning. "You must be mistaken."

She paused in her pacing and looked at her mother's younger brother. He was staring at her, clearly concerned.

"That's what Dad said," she told him, trying to stem her rising fear. "Is it true? Am I adopted?"

"Of course not."

She shook her head. "I don't understand," she said hoarsely. "Uncle Frank, why would he say something like that?"

"It must be the medication they're giving him," he replied guardedly. "It's affected his thinking."

"You're right," she said, jumping on his words like a lifeline, "that must be it." And yet she couldn't get out of her mind the way he'd looked, the way he'd sounded when he'd talked about how much they had wanted a child. Drugs couldn't produce that kind of emotion. She bit back a sob. God, it was true. She was adopted. Why hadn't they told her?

She looked at her uncle. Normally, his tobacco-brown face was animated and his brown eyes twinkled with merriment. But at the moment, he looked tired and drawn and every one of his fifty-seven years. He'd lost a sister today, and his brother-in-law was fighting for his life. This was just as hard on him as it was on her.

"Don't let Jack's words eat at you," he said, breaking into her thoughts.

"I'm not!" she insisted, but her words had a hollow ring even to her own ears. "What's *happening* in there? Why doesn't someone come out and tell us something?"

Frank Roberts stood and walked to her, then pulled her into his arms. "I'm sure they will as soon as they know something. Come on, let's sit down." He led her to the lumpy couch and took her hands in his. They sat in silence, each locked in his own anxiety.

A few minutes later Dr. Willis appeared in the doorway, a somber expression on his face. Hailey's heart skipped a beat. Please, God, let him be all right, she prayed.

"I'm sorry," he said gently. "We did everything we could, but we couldn't save him."

For a moment, the room swam around her as tears blinded her. She couldn't speak, couldn't respond. "I want to see him," she whispered finally.

"Of course," the doctor replied. "If there's anything I can do, please call me."

Hailey nodded vaguely then looked at her uncle. She saw the same pain she was feeling reflected in his eyes. "Could you give me a few minutes alone with him?"

"Sure, go on in," he said softly, giving her shoulder a reassuring squeeze. "I'll wait here."

Hailey walked stiffly into the room and approached the bed. She laid her hand on her dad's arm and stared at him. He looked so peaceful, as if he was asleep. But he wasn't asleep. He was dead.

She closed her eyes as a wave of grief washed over her. They were gone. Her parents were dead. *But they weren't your parents,* an inner voice whispered. She stared at the man she'd called Dad for twenty-five years. *God, how could you do this to me? Why tell me now? You were my father. You and Mom were all I had, and you took that away.* A sob tore from her throat as gut-wrenching sorrow squeezed her heart. One tear fell, then another and another.

Once the floodgates were opened, she couldn't stop. She slumped on the bed, rocking as she yielded to the compulsive sobs that shook her small frame.

She grieved for her mother, for her father and for the other person that had died that day. She may not have been in the automobile accident that had taken her parents' lives, but for all intents and purposes, Hailey Monroe had also died that day. No, she thought bleakly, she hadn't died. She had never existed. Her whole life had been a lie.

The room was misty and pristine white. Like heaven, but very noisy. She peeked around the doorjamb and saw a beautiful lady in a long white dress talking to someone. She couldn't see who she was talking to. Mommy said she wasn't to listen to adult conversation, but she couldn't help it. They were talking awfully loud. Suddenly, a hand grabbed the lady by the arm, twirled her around, causing her to lose her balance. The lady fell to the floor with a heavy thud. But before she could move to help the lady, he stepped out of the shadows. For a moment he stood there, looking at the lady, then he slowly turned and looked at her. But the face that stared at her wasn't a person. It was something horrible, evil, a monster.

Terror. Primitive. Primeval. Sweeping over her like a forest fire. She bolted out of the room. The monster was right behind her.

Hide. She had to find a place to hide. Ahead there was a room. She ran inside and slammed the door, only to discover it was the same room she'd been in before. Her eyes flew to the door. It was too late to leave. The monster was coming. She could hear it as it drew nearer, calling her name.

Her eyes darted about the room, looking for a place to hide. She ducked behind a large chair as the door flew open and the monster stepped inside. She held her breath, afraid to move. She could hear it prowling about the room. Her heart was thumping so loudly, she thought the monster would hear it.

The minutes ticked by, and she heard nothing. Had it left? It had been quite a while since she'd heard movement. She had to look, make sure the monster was gone. Slowly, she shifted her head just enough so she could peek around the side of the chair.

Her eyes grew round as saucers at the sight that greeted her. Where everything in the room was white before, it was now a bright, vivid red. As far as the eye could see, everything was red—the walls, the floor, even the lady lying on the floor. And the monster was standing next to the chair, staring straight at her!

Before she could move, run, huge hands were reaching for her, grabbing her, then dragging her across the room. She tried to scream but the monster clamped his hand over her mouth. She bucked, kicked, tried to get away, but his hold tightened. His fingers dug into her skin, hurting her. But she refused to give up. She kicked at his legs and she heard a groan, but he didn't let go. She kicked again, but instead of connecting with a leg, the floor disappeared...and then she was falling. The scream that had been clawing at her throat finally broke free. She screamed again and again. Mommy! Mommy!

Hailey jerked to a sitting position, cold sweat beading on her skin. She pressed her hand against her chest, against the hammering of her heart. Her eyes flew to the doorway. There was no one there. Morning sunlight streamed through the lacy curtains, casting a warm inviting glow on the bedroom furnishings. She was safe, in her bedroom. It had been a dream. Yet it had seemed so real, but then, she thought, pushing back the covers, it always did.

She tried to shake off the dream as she showered then made breakfast, and for a while she was successful. But as she sat at the kitchen table, sipping coffee, once again the dream invaded her thoughts. It was all jumbled, and she could only remember bits and pieces—the monster, the lady in white, the pristine white room that turned red, the sound of running water, the sensation of falling, and fear, overwhelming fear of the monster. As a child, the dream had terrified her. She shuddered. It still did.

She took another sip of coffee. Funny, she had all but forgotten her years of childhood fright, how she had awakened often in the night, drenched with sweat and screaming in terror, calling, *Mommy! Mommy!* Always Mommy.

It had been years since she'd had the dream. Now, in the space of three weeks, she'd had it four times. But it didn't take a rocket scientist to figure out what had triggered the nightmare that had plagued her childhood. Losing both parents and then discovering everything you thought about yourself was a lie—that you weren't who you thought you were, that you didn't even know who you were—could easily throw anyone into an emotional tailspin.

She swallowed the lump that had formed in her throat. She didn't know what she would have done if Uncle Frank hadn't been there for her, especially in the days immediately following her parents' death. It had been rough, but Uncle Frank had helped with funeral arrangements and creditors, going through her father's papers and just being there to talk. He'd tried to convince her that being adopted didn't change anything, that she was still the same person she'd been before.

Intellectually, she knew he was right, but it still didn't make coming to grips with the fact that she was adopted any easier or ease the hurt she felt toward her parents for not sharing that information with her. Nor did it quell her anger at her birth parents for giving her up. Why hadn't they wanted her? Did she have any brothers or sisters? Had they kept them? A million questions ran around and around in her brain. Questions to which she was unlikely to ever get any answers. In the blink of an eye, not only had her whole world been turned upside down, but her sense of who she was had been altered.

When she thought about it, she had no doubt that she

was adopted. It explained so many little discrepancies. The lack of any baby pictures of her, for one. Her parents had said they'd been destroyed in a house fire years ago, but she hadn't remembered any fire. Then there had been the striking physical differences between herself and her parents. Jack and Abby Monroe had both been tall, with dark brown skin and dark brown eyes. She was small, with honey-colored skin and gray eyes. Her mother had explained the physical differences by saying she took after her maternal grandmother. She'd accepted that because skin color variations were common in African-American families. As for her eye color, she'd assumed she'd inherited it from her maternal grandmother, as her mother had said. But now she knew that wasn't the case. Who did she look like? Her birth father? Her birth mother? She had so many questions.

God, she wished she could find that letter. Uncle Frank had helped her look for it, but it had not been with the will. They'd searched her parents' house from top to bottom but hadn't found it. She frowned. Her dad had been an accountant and, like most people in that profession, he'd been a meticulous record keeper. It was totally out of character for him to misplace or not remember where he put something. But then, she thought, he'd been under severe emotional distress—grieving for his wife and having to tell his daughter she was adopted. She sighed. It was probably somewhere in his files in the attic. She still had the things up there to go through. Maybe she'd locate not only the letter, but her adoption papers, as well.

That was another oddity. If she had been adopted, there should have been adoption papers and a birth certificate. She frowned, remembering the birth certificate she'd found. It had raised even more questions. The document was smudged to the point of being almost illegible in certain spots, but it didn't look like normal wear and tear or age. It looked as if it had been tampered with. Things had gotten stranger when she'd called the Bureau of Vital Statistics in

Springfield to request another copy. She'd been told they had no record of her birth. It was the same with the hospital. There was no record of her birth there, either.

Her birth certificate was obviously a fake. But why? The Monroe family was no stranger to adoption. Her cousin Olivia was adopted. No one had made a big deal about that. Had they thought she'd go looking for her birth parents when she came of age? They needn't have worried about that. She had absolutely no interest in parents who hadn't wanted her.

She let out a deep sigh. All this speculation was getting her nowhere. She looked at the clock on the wall above the kitchen stove. Seven forty-six. Normally, she would be on her way to the Baylor Gallery, where she worked as an art restorer. But this morning she had a meeting with the lawyer. She'd better get a move on, or she'd be late.

For the life of her, she couldn't imagine there being anything left to discuss. The only thing her parents had left behind was a string of creditors. So she'd been more than a little surprised when David Forbes had called and asked her to stop by.

God, she hoped he hadn't found yet another creditor. There was barely enough money in the estate to pay off the ones they'd already identified. Oh, well, there was no point in worrying, she thought, heading into the bedroom. She'd find out what this was all about soon enough.

An hour later she stepped out of the elevator and walked down the plush-carpeted corridor toward David Forbes's law office.

The secretary, a handsome young man in his early twenties, looked up as she approached the reception area.

"Ms. Monroe." He smiled. "It's nice to see you again. I'll let Mr. Forbes know you're here."

She watched as he dialed David Forbes's number then spoke into the receiver. "Hailey Monroe is here, sir."

"Send her in! Send her in!" boomed a loud, raucous voice.

She smiled at the receptionist, then walked into the inner office.

"Good to see you, Hailey," David Forbes said, standing. He was a warm, friendly man, and his deep baritone voice was in direct contrast to his stature. He was short and hefty, with gray hair surrounding a bald dome so shiny it looked polished. He was wearing a navy blue three-piece suit, cut to minimize his girth, and a wide welcoming smile. He came around the desk and took both of her hands in his.

"Mr. Forbes," she said, then took the seat across the desk from the rotund little man. "I was a bit surprised to get your call yesterday. I thought all this business with Mom and Dad's estate was finished."

"Ah, well, it seems another matter has cropped up," he said vaguely, then looked at his watch. "We'll get this meeting started just as soon as Mr. Cassadine arrives."

Her brow wrinkled into a frown. "Cassadine? Is he another creditor?"

"Oh, no," the lawyer answered. "It's nothing like that."

"Then I don't understand—"

The phone rang. He gave her an apologetic little smile as he lifted the receiver. Hailey was puzzled. He seemed relieved by the interruption.

"Ah," Mr. Forbes said loudly as the door to his office opened, "here he is now."

Hailey turned and looked up as a tall man entered the room. Her breath caught in her throat at the sight of him. In a word, the man was *gorgeous*. There was no other way to describe him. His features were chiseled perfection, his hair wavy and jet-black, his skin a smooth, golden bronze. His eyes were so dark, they were almost black. His mouth was finely molded with full, sensuous lips above a cleft chin.

He was tall, over six feet, with a lean, athletic build. His hips were narrow, his shoulders broad and his chest wide.

But it wasn't just good looks that brought the sensitive hairs all over her body to attention. He exuded a virility that was all male animal. She felt a tug of attraction that went right to her toes.

"Hailey Monroe, I'd like you to meet Sean Cassadine."

"Ms. Monroe," he said. His voice was warm and velvety.

She couldn't stop the shivers that ran up and down her spine at the sound of his sexy drawl. Never in her life had she been so physically aware, so instantly attracted to a man. It was as if an electrical current were running between them. She wondered fleetingly if he felt it, too. Almost without realizing it, she checked for a wedding band. He wore none. She was irritated with herself for feeling relieved. For all she knew, he could be from the IRS. That thought brought her up short. Had she been drooling over an IRS agent? And, worse, had he noticed her reaction?

She gave him a sideways glance then sighed in relief. Good, he hadn't noticed. In fact, he barely glanced at her as he took the seat next to her. Instead, his attention was focused on Mr. Forbes. Her eyes followed his gaze. Forbes was shuffling through the papers on his desk. He was tense, nervous, on edge. Something was coming, she thought, something she wasn't going to like, and whatever it was, it had to do with this handsome stranger.

"Mr. Forbes?" she said hoarsely, then wanted to kick herself. She had no reason to be nervous. "Is there a problem?"

The look he threw her could only be described as pity. Now she really was scared.

"What's going on?" she asked, unable to disguise the tremor in her voice.

"I, uh—Hailey," Forbes stammered. "I don't know where to begin. You know I was your parents' lawyer for many years."

She didn't like the way he'd started the conversation, but she wouldn't allow herself time to think about it. Instead she nodded twice, then waited for him to continue.

"About a year ago, your father came to see me," the

lawyer went on. "He was very concerned about you, concerned that his failing business and the increasing cost of your mother's health care would wipe them out completely. He wanted to make sure that if something happened to them, you would be taken care of."

She hadn't known. Tears welled in her eyes. She felt oddly comforted by the thought that even after death they wanted to protect her.

"At that time he gave me a letter, to be mailed after his death or your mother's, whichever came later."

Hailey blinked back her tears. A letter? Was it the letter he'd told her about?

"Per his instructions, the day after the funeral I posted the letter."

She turned and looked directly at the man seated next to her. "Does this letter have anything to do with your being here?"

"Yes, it does," Sean Cassadine answered smoothly. "I'm a security consultant, and I'm here on behalf of my client, who was the recipient of your father's letter."

"I see," she said, not really seeing at all. "And who is that?"

For a moment he hesitated, as if surprised by her question. "Alan Palmer," he said finally. "The letter Jack Monroe had Mr. Forbes mail was addressed to Alan Palmer."

Her eyes widened in surprise. "*The* Alan Palmer? As in Palmer Publishing?" He was one of the richest, most powerful black men in America. Born dirt poor, he had single-handedly built a publishing empire, amassing a small fortune along the way. Why on earth would her father have written to him?

As if he had read her mind, Sean Cassadine said, "According to Jack Monroe, Alan Palmer is your biological father."

Her jaw dropped. "My father!" she exclaimed when she could speak. "Is this some kind of sick joke?"

"I'm not laughing and neither is Alan," he said grimly.

Alan Palmer was her father? No, she thought, rejecting the idea. She looked at David Forbes, then at Sean Cassadine. "Th-there must be some kind of mistake."

Cassadine slowly shook his head. "Not according to your father."

"I know this must come as quite a shock," David Forbes said gently. "I was just as shocked when I got Mr. Cassadine's call yesterday and he told me about the letter."

She shook her head. "I don't believe it. They would have told me."

Cassadine's dark eyes narrowed slightly. "I think you should take a look at this." He took an envelope from the inside breast pocket of his suit jacket and handed it to her.

She stared at the envelope and then at the two men who watched her with varied expressions—the lawyer's held pity, while Cassadine's was wary. She took a deep breath, then yanked the letter from the envelope. With shaky fingers, she unfolded the paper and began to read.

Almost instantly tears welled up in her eyes. Her father's handwriting was unmistakable. It wasn't long before a quick frown pulled a tiny furrow across her forehead. It was right there in black and white, in his handwriting. Alan Palmer was her father.

"I don't understand," she said, her mind refusing to register what she'd just read.

Cassadine looked at her coldly. "What's there to understand? Your father's claim that you're Alan's daughter, or how quickly you can get your hands on his money?"

"Wh-what? I don't know what you're talking about!"

Cassadine rolled his eyes. "Oh, spare me the protestation of innocence. I'm talking about you and your father's pathetic attempt to pass you off as Susan Palmer."

"That's a lie!" Hailey jumped up, crumpled the letter into a ball and threw it at Sean Cassadine's chest. "I don't know what kind of game you're playing, but this letter is obviously a forgery." She turned accusing eyes on the lawyer. "I can't believe you'd be a party to this, Mr. Forbes."

"Now, Hailey," he began in a placating tone, "you know better than that. I have no reason on earth to lie to you."

"Then why are you doing this?" she shouted. She leaned forward slightly, planting both hands on his desk. "I'm not Alan Palmer's daughter. My parents are Jack and Abby Monroe—" Her voice broke, and she quickly looked away. She refused to let either man know how deeply her father's letter had affected her.

"Would it be so bad if you were Alan Palmer's daughter?" David Forbes asked gently.

She swallowed the lump that threatened to choke her. She didn't know what to say. She'd accepted the fact that she was adopted, but she wasn't ready for a birth family, whoever that family might be. She made her hands into tight little fists. How could they do this to her? Tell this man he was her father and not tell her? She had no desire for a relationship with her birth family. They hadn't wanted her when she was a baby. She didn't want them now. No doubt Dad had been afraid that would be her reaction and had taken matters into his own hands. He'd wanted to build a bridge between her and her birth family. She knew that was what he had wanted—probably what they'd both wanted—but it wasn't what she wanted. Maybe in time, but not now.

Out of the corner of her eye, she saw Sean Cassadine lean down and pick up the crumpled letter. She crossed her arms over her chest and stared at him. "So, after all this time, Alan Palmer wants to play daddy." Sarcasm tinged the panic she was trying to hide.

"I assure you, Alan has no desire to ignore his daughter," he replied coolly. "Quite the contrary. In fact, he would be quite ecstatic if you *were* Susan. He'd welcome you with open arms."

She shook her head. "Well, tell him I'm not interested

in playing daughter. He and his wife gave me up for adoption. He's going—"

"Adoption?" Cassadine looked at her as if she'd grown two heads. "Susan wasn't adopted. She was kidnapped."

Chapter Two

"Kidnapped!" Hailey Monroe gasped.

Sean watched the color drain from Hailey's face as
shock, then disbelief, then pain chased over her lovely features. For a moment she stood there, obviously stunned.

She was off guard. Now was the time to apply pressure,
before she recovered. He knew that, yet he hesitated. His
heart went out to her. She looked so lost, confused. Maybe
he should back off. Instantly, he was furious with himself
for feeling sorry for her. He was here to do a job, and he
damn well was going to do it.

"If you're Susan Palmer, as your father's letter claims,"
he said with deliberate harshness, "then there's only one
way in hell that's possible. Jack Monroe would have been
involved in the kidnapping. Maybe his wife even had a
hand in it."

"No," she said, shaking her head vehemently. "They
couldn't…" Her voice trailed off as her legs gave way.

Sean caught her before she hit the floor.

He lifted her in his arms. She was as light as a feather.
She felt good in his arms, too good. He shifted her to secure
his grip, but in doing so, his hand inadvertently touched
the smooth silken skin of her creamy thighs. His mouth
went dry.

"Here, lay her on the couch," Forbes said. "Why didn't
you tell me about the kidnapping? She worshiped Jack

and Abby. And—" he looked sharply at Sean as he gently lowered Hailey's limp body onto the black overstuffed leather couch "—I don't care what you say, Jack and Abby Monroe were a fine couple."

"I'm sorry, but Monroe's letter suggests he was anything but a good, upstanding citizen," Sean said dryly. He pulled a white linen handkerchief from his suit jacket pocket. "Here, dampen this for me," he ordered.

Forbes quickly crossed the carpet to his private bathroom, then returned and handed the moist cloth to Sean. "This is horrible," he said as he continued to hover. "Hailey just learned she was adopted, and now you're accusing her father of having kidnapped her."

"I'm simply telling you what his letter implies," Sean replied guardedly. "At the very least, it would suggest Jack Monroe had knowledge of, if not direct involvement in, the kidnapping. However, I'm not quite ready to declare Ms. Monroe to be Susan Palmer. There are still a lot of questions that need answering." He looked at the woman lying on the couch. Again he felt a pang of remorse for his behavior, but it was the only way to find out if she had known of and participated in her father's scheme. He wished he could have handled things differently. He gently ran the cool, damp cloth across her forehead and down her neck. Her skin was incredibly soft, like a baby's.

Her eyelids fluttered, and a soft moaned escaped her parted lips.

"Ms. Monroe...Hailey," Sean called as he gently moved the cloth across her forehead and down her cheek, trying to wipe away the pain.

When she didn't respond, he found himself tenderly pushing the soft black curls from her face in search of a bump or bruise. He bent so close to her, he could smell her perfume. It was a sweet, delicate scent, like the woman herself. It wrapped around his mind and tugged. "Hailey," he called again.

This time she heard him. He watched as her silver-gray

eyes slowly opened. For a moment, her eyes were dazed, unfocused. He braced himself for what he feared was coming. His fears were confirmed when Hailey spoke.

"Don't touch me," she said, knocking his hand away.

He straightened and walked to the wing chair he'd vacated. He moved it so he sat squarely in front of Hailey. He watched as she pushed herself to a sitting position on the couch, then swung her legs to the floor.

"Perhaps you should lie down for a moment," Forbes said quickly. "You've had quite a nasty shock."

"And I can thank *you* for that." Her eyes flashed with anger, and her breath came in shuddering gasps. "You were my father's friend. How could you do something like this—"

Forbes held up his hand, stopping the angry words she hurled at him. "Your father asked me to mail that letter. I had no idea what was in it."

"You should have told me about it."

Forbes flushed, then turned toward Sean. "Perhaps we should continue this discussion at another time," he said. "When Hailey is feeling better."

Sean looked at Hailey. Her color was better. He'd caught her off guard earlier, but she seemed to have recovered.

She met his gaze without flinching. "I'd just as soon let Mr. Cassadine have his say and get this over with."

He had to admire her guts. "I'm sorry. I didn't mean to upset you, but you're right. We need to get this matter resolved. Your father's claim that you're Susan Palmer is a very serious allegation."

"As is your charge that he was a kidnapper," she fired at him. "You'd better have something to back up that claim."

Now it was Sean who flushed. He knew Jack Monroe hadn't been involved in the kidnapping. He'd just said that to get a reaction. But he didn't want her or Forbes to know that, not yet. "You misunderstood me," he said smoothly.

"I said *if* your father's claim is true, that would be the only way."

"I disagree," the lawyer interjected. "There's at least one other possibility." He leaned back in his chair, crossing his hands over his large stomach. "I didn't put it together until now, but I remember the kidnapping. It happened about twenty years ago."

Twenty-two years ago to be exact, Sean thought grimly. But it could have been yesterday. The event was forever ingrained in his mind. He rubbed his hand over his forehead as it all came rushing back.

It had happened about six months after Lara Palmer died. Lara's death hit everyone hard, especially Susan. She'd been with her mother the night she'd drowned. It was a miracle that Susan hadn't also drowned. As it was, she'd been in severe shock, almost catatonic for quite some time. She hadn't spoken for months, but gradually she'd come out of it. But she hadn't been the same vibrant, happy three-year-old she'd been before the accident. She was shy, almost timid around everyone except for nine-year-old Sean, whom she had always adored. And while he generally didn't mind her tagging along, there were times when she was a nuisance and he didn't want her around.

And that's how it happened. His parents, who were close friends of Alan, had gone out of town for a few days and left him in Alan's care. He and Susan had been outside playing when Susan's nanny had asked him to keep an eye on her, but he hadn't. He'd left her alone while he had gone to check out Cook's new golden retriever. He'd only been gone a few minutes, but it had been long enough for the kidnappers. She'd been snatched from the backyard of the Palmer estate in broad daylight.

It had all been his fault, the kidnapping and—he swallowed—what had happened next. But Alan had never blamed him—not then, not now. He blamed himself, though, and he would until the day he died. He was so lost in thought, it took him a moment to realize the lawyer was speaking.

"As I recall, there was a ransom demand," Forbes said. "It was quite large for its day."

Sean nodded slowly. "That's right. They asked for a quarter of a million dollars."

Hailey frowned. "What about the police?" she asked. "Weren't they brought in?"

"Yes," he said, weighing his words carefully, "but not right away. It was the next day. By then the trail had gotten cold. Several weeks later, a child's bloody sweater was recovered from a wooded area about a mile from the Palmer estate. The child's nanny identified it as the one Susan was wearing the day she was abducted."

Hailey stared at him, her soft gray eyes edged with dread. "And the little girl, Susan Palmer. What happened to her?"

"The ransom was paid, but Susan wasn't returned. We never saw her again."

"Oh, my God." Hailey gasped.

"But she could be alive," the lawyer added quickly. Sean could see the wheels turning in Forbes's head as he considered various scenarios to explain how the kidnapped child had come to be with the Monroes. But it was Hailey's reaction that surprised him. He'd given her the opening to make her pitch for being Susan Palmer. But instead of trying to advance the argument or bolster her father's claim, she just sat there, looking slightly dazed. Maybe she hadn't known about her father's scheme.

"What about the kidnappers?" Mr. Forbes asked. "Did they catch them?"

Sean looked at Hailey as he answered. "Ultimately, the kidnapping was linked to the family's chauffeur, Ryan Vanover, and his friend Denny Hanson. Vanover eluded authorities, but Hanson was apprehended, along with forty thousand dollars of the marked ransom money. Hanson claimed the money wasn't his, that he was holding it for Vanover."

"I take it the police didn't buy it?" Forbes asked dryly.

"Not for a second," he said. "It was only after Vanover's bullet-ridden body was found in the trunk of Hanson's car that he admitted his part in the kidnapping. But he maintained that he didn't kill him or know Susan's whereabouts. He claimed some guy called Sarge was holding her."

Hailey paled visibly at the mention of a third man. "There was another man involved?" she whispered.

Sean leaned forward, watching her carefully. "That was Hanson's story. During his trial, his lawyer tried to make a lot out of a handwritten note and some phone calls that were made to the Palmer residence after he was apprehended. His lawyer claimed it was evidence of the existence of the third man, but there was never any real evidence supporting his claim. Until now, that is." He let the implication sink in.

Her chin rose a fraction. "I was adopted, not kidnapped."

"So they tell me," he replied. "Which brings us back to the matter at hand. Your father's assertion that you're Susan Palmer."

Forbes issued a frustrated sigh. "Adopted. Kidnapped. You talk as if they're mutually exclusive, but they're not." He glanced at Hailey, then Sean. "I think it's pretty clear what happened. Jack and Abby adopted Hailey in good faith, but Jack must have come across information, probably quite recently, that led him to conclude that Hailey was Susan Palmer."

"That's possible," Sean conceded. "Naturally, my client requires more proof than a letter proclaiming Ms. Monroe to be his daughter," he said carefully.

"I'm sure Jack left something that we can use to support his claim," Forbes said reassuringly. "At the very least, the adoption decree will dispose of this kidnapping nonsense." He looked at Hailey. "Can you get me a copy of it?"

She looked decidedly uncomfortable. "I haven't been able to locate it," she said quickly.

She's lying, Sean thought grimly. So much for her not knowing what her father had been up to. What *she* was probably still up to, he amended. He didn't know why he felt as if a rug had been pulled out from under him, but he did.

"No matter," the lawyer said with a dismissive wave of his hand. "I'll put one of my clerks on it right away. It was probably an Illinois adoption, so with a little digging, I should be able to get my hands on a copy of the decree."

Hailey wet her lips. It was a nervous gesture on her part, but to Sean it was sensuous and erotic. He swore as a jolt of heat shot through him. "I was going to suggest a blood test," he said in a slightly strained voice. "That's the most effective way of resolving the matter."

Forbes nodded. "That's a good—"

"Wait a minute!" Hailey cried. "You're both moving too fast. Despite my father's claim, I have no interest in pursuing the matter."

He should have been glad she was backing off, but instead he found himself shaking his head. "I'm afraid it doesn't work that way. Your father opened a Pandora's box with his letter. I'm not about to let the matter drop only to have it thrown back in my face in six months when you have a change of heart. I want some answers and I want them now."

"Answers? Answers to what? I'm not Alan Palmer's daughter, case closed."

"You're afraid," he challenged.

She stared at him, her eyes cold, her mouth a thin, straight line. "What would I be afraid of?"

Sean met her gaze head-on. "The truth. That you'll discover your adoptive father was a kidnapper, perhaps the third man."

She bristled. "I'm not afraid of anything, especially anything that pertains to my dad. He would never have been involved in something like that. I don't know why he thought I was Susan Palmer, but we both know that's not the case. She's dead, isn't she?''

He leaned back in his chair, regarding her steadily. ''Yeah, she's dead. But her body was never found, which has led Alan to cling to the belief that one day he'll be reunited with his daughter. It's also led a number of women to claim to be Susan Palmer over the years.'' He gave her a pointed look. ''And why not? She was the heir to her late mother's estate and the Palmer fortune.''

''Well, I'm certainly not interested in money,'' she said coldly, ''and neither was my father.''

''If that's the case, then you shouldn't have any problem with cooperating in my investigation of your father's claim. You can begin by taking a blood test.''

Mouth agape, she stared at him. ''What would be the point? We both know I'm not—'' Her voice broke off as realization dawned. ''You think my father was trying to extort money from Mr. Palmer.''

''I don't think so,'' he countered. ''I know so.''

''That's what this is all about, isn't it?'' Her voice was laced with anger. ''All this talk about kidnapping was just a ruse to get me to admit that my father was trying to extort money from Mr. Palmer and that I was helping him. You thought if you accused my dad of kidnapping, I'd break down, admit it was extortion and plead for mercy.''

He shrugged. ''It was worth a try.''

She threw him a withering look. ''Well, my father had nothing to do with Susan Palmer's kidnapping or trying to extort money from your client, and neither did I.''

''Prove it. Take the blood test.''

''I don't have to prove anything. I know the truth, and that's all that matters. If you think you've got a case against my father or me, then go to the police.''

God, she was beautiful when she was angry. He shook his head. ''That's a pretty little speech, but I'm not buying it.''

She tossed her head like a proud mare. "Frankly, I don't care if you buy it or not," she said coldly. "This meeting is over."

He shrugged offhandedly. "Suit yourself. I'm staying at the Hilton on Michigan Avenue. I'll be there for another couple of days. Call me if you change your mind."

"I won't." In a slow, dignified manner, she stood.

Forbes also stood. "Hailey, I'm really sorry this was dumped on you," he said. "If there is anything I can do..."

"I think you've done more than enough." She walked over and picked up her purse from the floor where she'd dropped it earlier, then headed for the door.

"Ms. Monroe, you really surprise me," Sean called after her. "I guess I had you pegged wrong."

She paused and slowly turned. Their eyes locked and held.

"What do you mean?"

He cocked his head, studying her. "I'm surprised by your attitude. Maybe you didn't know about your father's letter, which I believe was an extortion attempt, but his claim is going to haunt you. Cooperating with the investigation would at least answer the question that has to be uppermost in your mind. You do want to know who you are, don't you?"

SEAN CASSADINE'S QUESTION did indeed haunt Hailey. After she left the lawyer's office, she drove to her parents' house. But instead of going in, she sat in her car, her thoughts in turmoil, thinking about his question. It had gone around and around in her brain until she wanted to scream. Yes, she wanted to know who she was, but she'd lied when she told him she wasn't afraid of what she might find out about her adoptive parents.

She was more than afraid—she was terrified. She thought she had known them, but they hadn't told her about being adopted. Or their belief that Alan Palmer was her father. What else hadn't they told her? Instantly, she thought of the missing adoption papers. Maybe they weren't missing. Maybe they had never existed. That's why there was a phony birth certificate. That's why there was no record of her birth. That's why her dad had seemed…

No, she thought, shaking her head. No matter how desperately they had wanted a child, her dad would never have taken someone else's. But how else could she explain his assertion that she was Alan Palmer's daughter?

It certainly wasn't because he'd been trying to extort money from Alan Palmer, like Sean Cassadine thought. Or had he? Mr. Forbes had said he'd wanted to make certain that if something happened to them, she'd be taken care of. But extortion? She chewed her lower lip. Dear God, she didn't know what to believe. If she could find his letter to her, it might explain everything. It had to.

She looked at the house where she'd grown up. It was a very well-kept, spacious, white, two-story colonial with black shutters and a front door painted a glossy red. Tears welled in her eyes. She had so many happy memories of growing up here. In her mind's eye, she saw scenes from her childhood. She and her mother baking cookies, her father teaching her to ride a bike, the three of them sitting around the Christmas tree singing carols…

She wished briefly, fiercely, that she could drive away, forget about the issue of her parentage. She felt the tears slipping down her cheeks. She bent her head, blotting her eyes on her shirt sleeve, then gazed again at the house, trying to summon the courage to go in and look for the letter and the adoption papers. She had to know the truth, if for no other reason than to clear her father of an extortion charge.

She drew a deep breath then stepped from the car. She walked the short distance to the door, turned the key in the lock and stepped inside. A dozen memories assailed her. She closed her eyes, pushing the memories away. The sound of her pumps echoed off the polished hardwood floor as she walked quickly through the foyer, not stopping until she reached the stairs.

There was no point in checking the downstairs and upstairs rooms. She and Uncle Frank had already done that. The only place they hadn't checked was the attic. She gazed at the curved staircase broken by the second-floor landing. She drew a deep breath, then slowly began to climb.

SEAN'S CONSCIENCE was giving him fits. He had returned to his hotel and tried to put Hailey Monroe out of his mind, but it was no use. He paused in his pacing and stared sightlessly at the street. She was nothing like he'd thought she would be. Instead of finding some money-grubbing female, he'd found a warm, very vulnerable young woman still grieving over the loss of her parents. And totally in the dark in regard to her father's extortion scheme.

He groaned when he remembered telling her about her dad's extortion attempt. She'd put up a brave front, but she had been in pain. Pain he had deliberately caused, and there had been no reason for it.

He jammed his hands in his pockets and resumed pacing. He'd handled it all wrong. Instead of playing some damn cat-and-mouse game, he should have come right out and told her he believed her dad had tried to extort money from his client by claiming she was his daughter. Hell, he didn't have any evidence to suggest she had known, let alone participated in her father's scheme. And after meeting her, he was sure she hadn't known.

He raked his hand over his hair in frustration. What the hell was he doing here, anyway? He didn't conduct investigations of this nature. This sort of thing was generally handled by his chief investigator, Mac Warren. And it wasn't like he didn't have a million other things to do in L.A. Cassadine Securities, which he had started four years ago, was growing by leaps and bounds. His company designed and maintained high-tech security systems for corporations and individuals and offered a wide range of investigative and security-related services.

Instead of being here, he should be at home. The new security system his company had installed at Olsen Electronics needed to be checked out. The plans for Senator Tyler's security detail during his Washington trip next week had to be finalized. And he still had to work out the kinks in the security programs he'd designed for the Lindley estate. He let out a weary sigh. He couldn't remember feeling so ambivalent about a case. Maybe he should let Mac handle the investigation.

He was certainly tempted. It was not good policy to handle a case you were emotionally involved with, and if there was ever a case that pulled at his heartstrings, it was this one. It had haunted him for years and led him from a promising legal career to opening Cassadine Securities. It had led him to violate his company's policy against handling missing-person cases. Yes, he was emotionally involved. But the moment he'd read Jack Monroe's letter, he'd known he would personally handle the investigation. He owed it to Alan Palmer, his father's lifelong friend, and to himself.

He walked to the cocktail table and picked up the letter Alan had received three weeks before. He really didn't need to read it, he thought, as he took a seat on the sofa and settled against the cushions. He'd read it so many times in the last fifteen days, he practically knew it by heart. The letter was short, a couple of paragraphs. It wasn't Monroe's claim that Susan was alive that had thrown everyone into an emotional tailspin—it was the black-and-white photograph that had accompanied the letter. The child in the picture appeared to be about four and could have passed for Susan's twin. More than that, she was wearing Susan's locket, or at least, he amended, what appeared to be. That picture had shaken Alan to the core and sent him running to Sean's office.

It had thrown Sean for a loop the first time he'd seen it.

He remembered how he'd sat looking at the picture. The thought, *Susan is alive,* ran through his mind.

Reason had finally prevailed. No matter how much he or Alan might wish it, there was no way in hell Monroe's claim could be true. Everything in the letter could be explained. There was nothing in it that a highly motivated person couldn't have uncovered, even the existence of the locket. He again looked at the necklace around the little girl's neck. It looked authentic, but there wasn't much a skilled graphic artist couldn't do with a computer—including making a picture lie. Unfortunately, the photo analyst Mac had consulted hadn't been able to confirm that it was a forgery.

He set the letter aside and picked up an eight-by-ten color glossy of Hailey Monroe that Mac had taken. God, she was lovely. Her hair was a rich, mahogany brown, her skin the color of warm honey, and her eyes were the most incredible shade of charcoal gray he'd ever seen.

Theoretically, having only Hailey to deal with should have made things easier, but her striking resemblance to Lara Palmer, Alan's late wife, was going to make things hard. Alan would take one look at her and see what he wanted to see, just like he had with Margaret Williams. Sean's eyes clouded as he recalled the incident. It had occurred a little over a year ago. Margaret Williams had claimed to be Susan Palmer. Alan had fallen for her scam hook, line and sinker. She'd taken him for twenty-five thousand dollars before Sean had been able to convince him she wasn't Susan.

Alan had been devastated, not just emotionally, but physically, as well. He'd suffered a heart attack. Thankfully, he'd made a complete recovery, but he was sixty-two years old, and he wasn't the vital, healthy man he'd once been. A confrontation with another would-be daughter so soon after the last one might be too much for him. The quicker Sean got evidence proving Hailey wasn't Susan, that Jack

Monroe's sole intent was to extort money from Alan, the better.

But getting that evidence was easier said than done. There wasn't a snowball's chance in hell Hailey would co-operate with his investigation, let alone agree to a blood test. They were going to have to rely on good, old-fashioned investigative work, which to date hadn't gotten them very far. While Mac had found holes, inconsistencies in Jack Monroe's claim, he'd been unable to come up with the kind of hard evidence Alan would demand. A frown marred Sean's brow as he thought of the years, the money Alan had spent searching for his daughter. A search everyone knew was fruitless. Why couldn't Alan accept it? Susan was dead.

Against his will, his eyes were once again drawn to Hailey's photograph. She had such an expressive face. It pulled him, drew him. From the moment he'd laid eyes on her picture, he hadn't been able to get her out of his mind. She haunted his dreams, his thoughts. Meeting her in the flesh hadn't made things a damn bit easier. If anything, it made them worse. He remembered her beautiful mouth, her scent, the way she had felt in his arms.

He tossed the picture on the table. Hell, it was going to be hard enough investigating this case without the added complication of sexual attraction. Was that all it was? Sexual attraction, or something more?

He tried to shake off the thought, but couldn't. This case was really getting to him. No, he thought, not the case—Hailey Monroe. He'd handled hundreds of cases in his five-year career as a Los Angeles attorney, then later as a security consultant, but he couldn't remember a single one that made him feel so nervous, so on edge. What was there about Hailey Monroe? Why couldn't he get her out of his mind?

HAILEY'S SEARCH of the attic turned out to be a messy, exhausting job that took several hours, but she didn't find the letter or the adoption papers.

With a heavy heart, she slowly walked down to the first floor. At the foot of the stairs, she paused. For a moment, she considered searching the house again. But she quickly rejected the idea. She and Uncle Frank had searched it thoroughly. Dad had said the letter was with his will. They'd found the will in his study, and the study was where he had kept his important papers. If there was anything in this house, it would be there. Maybe she should check the study again.

Even as the thought crossed her mind, she was moving in that direction. This time she'd check every nook and cranny. She removed the five dozen or so books from the bookcase, giving each a shake before placing it back on the shelf. She looked behind the watercolor paintings on the wall. She even got down on her hands and knees to look underneath the furniture, but she didn't find anything.

She moved to her father's desk. She didn't just sort through the items inside. She took everything out, upended each drawer and checked the inside back wall of the desk. She checked the top middle drawer and all but one of the side drawers but found nothing. Her heart sank. She'd been so sure the letter was somewhere in this room.

She was working on the last side drawer and feeling more than a little down at her failure to find the letter or the adoption papers. She was so caught up in her thoughts that she almost missed the tiny key taped to the bottom of the drawer. She picked it up and studied it. It wasn't the key to the house or the car. It looked like a safe-deposit-box key. She frowned. Her parents had never mentioned one, and Mr. Forbes hadn't said anything about one. But her father had been a very meticulous and careful man. He wouldn't have used a locker at a bus or train station to hide—

Her eyes clouded. She didn't like the word. It seemed to imply subterfuge. But it was an accurate description of what her dad had done. He'd wanted a secure place, like a safe-deposit box, to store something—something he hadn't wanted her and Mom to know about. That's why he'd hidden the key. *Stop it,* she scolded herself. She was letting Cassadine's talk about extortion and kidnapping get to her, causing her to imagine all kinds of crazy things. Just because he'd hidden the key didn't mean he was hiding something terrible. More than likely, it was something he considered important—like the adoption papers and the letter. That had to be it!

She looked at her watch. It was almost noon. Mr. Forbes might still be in his office. She'd call him, tell him about the key. Maybe somewhere in the list of her father's assets, he'd come across a reference to a locked box. She slipped the key into her purse, then lifted the telephone receiver and dialed his office.

She was put through immediately. The lawyer listened carefully to her narrative. However, he was unable to shed any light on whether her father had a safe-deposit box. Perhaps because he was feeling guilty about what had happened that morning, he promised to do some checking and get back to her in a few hours.

There was nothing more for her to do, she thought, as she lowered the receiver into the cradle. She might as well go home and wait for his call.

When she arrived at her apartment, she retrieved her phone messages. There were two messages. One from her uncle, reminding her that he was taking her to dinner that evening, and the other from Henry Granger at Fidelity Mutual Insurance Company. Mr. Granger's high-pitched voice advised her that he was still processing her claim and would get back to her in about three to four weeks.

Three or four weeks! She needed the insurance money to pay her parents' creditors. They'd been patient, but they wouldn't remain that way forever. Why was it taking so long to process the claim, anyway? And why hadn't they released the annuity her dad had set up for Martha Harris, his assistant and secretary? Was there some problem they weren't telling her about?

A deep depression settled over her, and for a moment she stood immobile. Then she slowly walked to the sofa and sank into its soft cushions. They were stalling. She knew it, but for the life of her, she couldn't figure out why. It didn't make sense. Dad had never missed a payment on either the life insurance policy or the annuity. And it had been a one-car accident. So what was the problem?

She drew a weary sigh and leaned into the sofa cushions. She really didn't need this added worry, not now. She had to focus her energy on clearing her father's name. But what if she couldn't? What if she was wrong about the contents of the safe-deposit box? What if it didn't contain information exonerating him?

That thought made her pace. She didn't know what she would do if it turned out she was wrong or, for that matter, if Mr. Forbes couldn't locate the box. She didn't have a clue how to find something like that. And she doubted Uncle Frank did, either. But there had to be a way to locate the box. Or people who knew about such things.

She thought of Sean Cassadine.

The image of his handsome face and gleaming black eyes appeared with shattering intensity in her mind. For all his arrogance, he inspired confidence. He'd know what to do. Before she could stop herself, she walked to the desk in the corner and picked up the phone book. Where had he said he was staying? It had been some place in the Loop. She searched her memory. The Hilton. She quickly flipped to the yellow pages, but just as she got to the hotel listings, she began having second thoughts. What kind of fool was she, anyway? How could she consider working with a man who accused her father of being an extortionist? And who was trying his level best to make the charge stick?

But how could she not? She didn't know the first thing about conducting an investigation and she didn't have the money to hire someone who did. Sean Cassadine was a trained security consultant. No doubt that was like being a private investigator. If she hoped to discover the truth about her parentage and clear her father's name, she needed help—the kind of help Sean Cassadine could provide.

That was the only reason, she assured herself, that she would consider cooperating with him in his investigation. That and the fact that her participation would ensure the investigation was conducted fairly. But she couldn't deny the rush of heat that coursed through her at the prospect of seeing him again.

Swearing under her breath, she ran her finger down the hotel listings until she found the number for the Hilton on Michigan Avenue. She lifted the telephone receiver and punched in the number before she could talk herself out of it. A moment later she was being put through to his room.

"Cassadine."

Suddenly, she was seized by doubt. What was she going to say? Her mind was a total blank. Frantically, she tried to retreat. "Ah...uh, sorry," she stammered and dropped the receiver into the cradle. Calling him had been stupid. What on earth had she been thinking? Just because she hadn't found anything that exonerated her dad after a few hours of searching didn't mean she should go running to Sean Cassadine. She didn't know anything about him. And yet she knew instinctively that she could trust him.

For the next twenty minutes she seesawed, trying to decide what to do. She came to the conclusion that no matter how abhorrent it might be, she needed his help. Gritting her teeth, she called his hotel again. This time when she was put through to his room, she got no answer. Great, now he was gone. She'd try again later, she thought, as she headed toward the kitchen. She had missed lunch and was starving.

The telephone's shrill ring startled her. Had Mr. Forbes found something already? she wondered as she grabbed the phone next to the sofa.

"Hello?"

"Hailey? It's Martha Harris."

Her shoulders slumped as an image of the rail-thin woman who had been her father's secretary for more than two decades appeared in her mind's eye. She'd hoped the insurance company would have something definite to say before she spoke to her. She didn't know what to tell Martha about her retirement benefits. Was that why she was calling? To ask about the annuity? Or, even worse, to advise that another creditor had been located? She hoped not.

"Martha," she said with as much heartiness as she could muster. "I'm really glad you called. I stopped by your house last week to thank you for the lovely floral arrangement, but your niece said there was a family emergency and that you'd be out of town until the end of this week."

"I was, but my sister Bernice is doing so much better that I decided to come back early. I hear you're planning to transfer Jack's active cases to Iocca and Associates. Your father would be pleased."

"That's one of the things I wanted to talk to you about. I was wondering if you could help me sort and catalog the files."

"Of course I will." She chuckled. "In fact, I'm at the office right now. Can you get over here say, in about an hour?"

"The office? What are you doing there?"

"Frank called me last night. He asked if I would box up the case files. He wanted to save you the trouble."

She smiled. He was such a thoughtful man.

"Hailey?"

"Yes, I'm still here."

"Can you come by the office?"

The last thing she wanted to do was talk about case files. "Could you give me some idea what this is about?"

There was a pause. When Martha spoke, her tone was grave. "I'd rather not go into it over the phone. I wouldn't ask if it wasn't important. Can you get over here?"

She nearly said no. She couldn't leave—she had to wait

for David Forbes's call. On the other hand, Martha was not the kind of person to make such a request unless it was important. She issued a weary sigh. "Sure, I'll come down."

"Good. I'll see you in about an hour."

She quickly dialed David Forbes's office and advised his secretary that she would be at her dad's office for a few hours and could be reached there. Then she hurried into the bedroom, where she changed into a light blue silk shirt and slacks.

Ten minutes later, she picked up her purse and sweater and headed to the apartment's parking garage. As she drew close to her red Ford Taurus, she saw that the front tire was almost flat. Great, she thought with a sigh. That was all she needed. She glanced at her watch and hurried out of the underground garage.

On the street, Hailey paused. People streamed past. Traffic crawled along bumper-to-bumper. It was a Wednesday afternoon, and although it wasn't quite rush hour, the booksellers' convention downtown and the festival in Grant Park had traffic backed up for miles. Getting a cab would be difficult. She'd probably make better time if she took the train.

She shivered and slipped her sweater on. Technically, it was summer, but spring was still lingering. A cool breeze off Lake Michigan blew straight at her, but that wasn't the only reason for the chill she felt. Uncle Frank and Martha were good friends. He'd probably told Martha about her being adopted. Could she face a barrage of questions? The thought was daunting. Maybe she should cancel, pleading a headache. And it wouldn't be totally untrue. She'd had a headache since this nightmare began. But she would only be putting off the inevitable.

She walked the few blocks to the train station like a condemned criminal going to the electric chair. The station was brimming with people, all waiting for the train. Holding her purse close to her body, she made her way through the crowd to the platform. In the distance, she heard the whistle of a train. She leaned over and looked down the track. She could just make out the light of the train. She moved closer to the edge as it neared the station.

The platform was so crowded and her attention was so focused on the coming train that she almost didn't feel the strong hands grab her and shove her off the platform into the path of the speeding train...until it was too late.

Chapter Three

The first thing Hailey was aware of was darkness. It was dense, unlike anything she had known before. All around her there was darkness. A deep, rumbling, rushing sound began to fill her ears, and then she was moving forward through the darkness.

So this is what it's like to be dead, she thought. Common sense told her she should have been terrified. All her fears of death and the afterlife should have risen up. But within this black mass, she felt a profoundly pleasant sense of well-being and calmness. She felt she could have stayed in this wonderful state forever.

As she moved through the darkness, she became aware of other people, but at a distance. She couldn't see them, but she could feel their presence. She felt no personal connection to them and knew that they represented no threat to her while she was wrapped in this safe cocoon. Contentment filled her, and she sank more deeply into the blackness, the comforting warmth, rejoicing in her security and peace. She had never felt greater tranquillity in her life.

In the distance, she saw a pinpoint of light. As she drew nearer, a man's face appeared. Light radiated outward from his face like a halo. But it wasn't the brilliant, overwhelming bright light she'd read about in near-death accounts. In those accounts, the light had been described as brilliant beyond belief—even more brilliant than the sun, so bright that no earthly eyes could look upon it without being destroyed.

She frowned. The light in the distance wasn't at all like that. It was more of an irritating brightness, like having a flashlight beamed in her face, and the light wasn't pulsating. As she thought about it, she realized there'd been no tunnel, either. Her frown deepened. And where were the familiar faces of her loved ones? Weren't they supposed to be here to greet her in the afterlife? Maybe she hadn't gone to—

"Stand back," a warm, velvety voice said. "Give her some air."

She knew that voice.

"Hailey, can you hear me?" The voice slowly penetrated her subconscious. She opened her eyes and found herself staring into Sean Cassadine's concerned face.

"Now I know I'm not dead," she moaned. At her words, the look on his face changed from concern to confusion.

"What? Are you all right?" His eyes anxiously searched her face.

"I'm fine," she said. It was then that she noticed the small crowd surrounding them and the curious faces that peered at her. There were several paramedics in the crowd, a transit security person and a police officer. As the fog that had engulfed her mind slowly receded, she realized she was being cradled in Sean's arms on the train platform.

She shot straight up.

She thought she heard a soft chuckle, then Sean said over his shoulder, "She's okay." He said something to the paramedics and the guy from the transit authority that she couldn't hear. The man from the transit authority looked at Sean then at her. "This is highly irregular," he said, "but if you say she's all right and you're willing to accept full responsibility, then I guess it's okay." He said something to the paramedics, then the trio turned and walked away.

"Okay, the show is over," the cop said. "Move along." The crowd slowly began to disperse.

"I thought you were a goner for sure." This came from a young, pockmarked man who was staring at her. "This fellow jumped down there and pulled you back just in the nick of time."

"C'mon. Move along," the cop said. He poked the man in the ribs with his nightstick to get him started.

"What happened?" she asked, gingerly touching the back of her head. She felt a small lump.

"You fell off the platform into the path of a train." Sean's voice was tight and strained.

"What?" She rubbed the bump on her head. It all came rushing back—the jostling, the hand that shoved her. "I didn't fall. I was pushed."

"Pushed?" He looked at her incredulously. "It was pretty crowded on that platform. Someone must have bumped against you." He tried to inspect the back of her head.

"I wasn't bumped," she said. She slapped his hand away and tried to stand. Her legs were a little wobbly, but she made it with some assistance from Sean. "I was pushed off that platform."

"Did you see anyone?" he asked. His eyes were searching the area.

She shook her head, then winced. "It all happened too fast. One minute I was standing there, then the next thing I knew, I was falling, and then…nothing."

"You took a nasty tumble. You sure you're all right? Maybe I should have had the paramedics check you over after all." He ran his hands up and down her back. His touch felt good. He made her feel safe and protected, and she wanted nothing more than for him to hold her forever.

She realized now the warm feeling had been Sean as he'd carried her from the train tracks to the platform. "You saved my life." It was a statement, not a question.

He nodded. "I was about to call out to you when I saw you tumble off the platform."

"You risked your life to save mine," she whispered. She

felt a little shaky as she realized how close she'd come to being killed—how close Sean had come, as well. At the same time, her face flamed with heat. Thank God he didn't know what she'd been thinking as he'd carried her. "Thank you." The words sounded so inadequate.

He gave her a warm smile. "You're welcome."

For a moment they stood there staring at each other, both wanting to say more but afraid to speak—afraid to break the fragile thread that connected them.

"What are you doing here?" she asked, finally breaking the silence.

"You called me. That *was* you that called, wasn't it?"

"Yes, it was. How did you know?"

"Only a handful of people know I'm in Chicago, and none of them would hesitate in the least to call me." He shrugged. "The only other person I could think of was you."

"You didn't even call me back to make certain," she pointed out quietly.

He shrugged. "I thought I'd better hightail it over to your apartment. Since you were having such a hard time talking on the phone, I thought you might do better in person. The doorman told me he'd seen you leave and that you were walking in the direction of the train station." He cocked his head and grinned at her. "So, what did you want to talk about?"

Suddenly, she was a bundle of nerves. "I've had the opportunity to think about your proposal," she said, choosing her words carefully. "I'd like to help with the investigation. Not because I think my dad did anything wrong," she added quickly, "because I don't. I'm doing this to help clear him."

Sean didn't say anything. He looked at her with those dark, penetrating eyes. His expression gave no indication of what he was thinking. "Okay," he said after a moment, "but I think for now I'd better get you home. You've had quite a shock." He took her arm. "Come on. Let's get out of here."

Just then, she remembered her meeting with Martha Harris. "I've got to go to my dad's office," she blurted, then wanted to kick herself.

"What's down there?"

She hesitated, not sure if she should tell him. What if Martha said something that could be construed as incriminating? Did she want him to hear it? Did she want him to know about the locked box? Wouldn't it be best to keep both a secret until she talked to the secretary and knew the contents of the box? Probably, but something told her she could trust him. It was totally irrational to feel that way, but she did. She briefly told him about the call from Martha Harris and about finding the key.

As she talked, the look on his face became cooler. The eyes that had blazed at her with warmth and concern were now like chips of ice, and his lips were stiff and unyielding.

"My, how very convenient." His tone was wary and suspicious. "Your father's secretary suddenly wants to talk to you, and you just happen to find a key to a locked box. Let me guess. Both will, no doubt, result in information that exonerates your father."

Hailey bristled. He didn't believe her. He thought she had cooked the whole thing up. "I guess I had you pegged wrong," she said, throwing his words of that morning back at him. "I thought you were interested in the truth, but I guess it's a witch-hunt you're on."

"You backing out?" he said, raising one eyebrow.

"No, but if you're going to doubt my every word, question every piece of information I bring to you, then this is going to be a very long and difficult investigation."

"I don't doubt it."

She looked him squarely in the eye. "I'm going to the office. You can do whatever suits you."

Sean returned her stare. "Oh, I wouldn't dream of letting you go alone," he said. "Lead the way."

BY THE TIME they reached Jack Monroe's office, Sean's anger had faded. He knew he had overreacted. It was just that Hailey's words had jolted him to reality from the warm, comfortable cocoon that had enclosed them. He'd suddenly remembered why he was there, and he'd felt a twinge of guilt. Not once had he given a thought to Alan or the investigation.

His behavior had been totally unprofessional. It didn't matter that she hadn't known about her father's extortion scheme, he still needed to maintain a professional distance. After all, his job was to prove that her father had tried to extort money from his client. And that meant they were adversaries, of sorts. He didn't want to deal with her as an adversary, but as a man to a woman. And for a brief moment, on that train platform, he had.

His eyes clouded as he recalled how his heart had jumped into his throat when he'd seen her tumble off the station platform. He'd given no thought to his safety but had reacted instinctively. Thank God he'd reached her in time. But he'd been so afraid, more afraid than he'd ever been in his life, that he wouldn't. He sighed. He was just getting his jumbled emotions under control when she'd told him about the phone call and finding the key. It was like having a bucket of cold water thrown over him, and he'd lost it. He had lashed out, attacking her veracity, saying things he had known weren't true. He'd never done anything like that before, but neither had he felt this kind of emotional connection to another human being before, either.

He glanced at the woman who walked alongside him. He had to admire her courage. She was nervous about what they would find, despite her attempt to appear otherwise, but she was willing to face it head on.

They were greeted by an attractive, middle-aged woman sitting behind a large oak desk. Her salt-and-pepper hair was worn loose and long, unusual for an older woman, but on her it looked nice.

"Hailey," she said, coming around the desk and taking her hands. "I'm so sorry about your parents. They were fine people."

"Thank you. Martha Harris, this is Sean Cassadine," Hailey said by way of introduction. "Martha was Dad's administrative assistant."

"It's nice meeting you, Mr. Cassadine." Martha smiled and offered her hand. "Please sit down." She motioned to two comfortable-looking chairs, then sat behind the desk. "Hailey, I don't want you to worry about anything. Like I told Frank, I'll do whatever I can to get things in order."

"Martha, I can't tell you how much I appreciate your help," Hailey said with a grateful look.

The older woman waved her hand dismissively. "It's nothing. I just wish I could do more."

"You've done more than enough." She looked at her hands for a moment, then at Martha. "That's why I feel so horrible about this problem with the insurance company."

Sean sat up straighter. There was a problem with the insurance company? He wondered what that was about.

"It's not your fault," Martha replied. "They're just dragging their feet, but they've got to pay the claim." She made a rueful face. "It just may take a while."

Hailey smiled, clearly relieved by the other woman's attitude. "Thanks, I appreciate your understanding. I should be able to tell you something by the middle of next month."

"Don't worry about that. Oh, Hailey, I almost forgot, David Forbes called. He wants you to call him right away."

Hailey's smile faded, and her eyes flickered from Martha to Sean.

He could see the uncertainty in her eyes as she pondered the advisability of leaving him alone with the secretary. "You'd better call him," he prompted. "He may have located the box."

She nodded. "You're right. I'll call from the conference room. I'll just be a moment." She walked down the hall.

"She's a very lovely girl," Martha said when Hailey was out of hearing range. "How long have you known each other?"

He could see the matchmaking wheels turning in her head. "Not long," he said easily. "How long did you work for Jack Monroe?"

"For over twenty years. He was a fine man. I couldn't have asked for a better employer or friend. I really miss him." She became misty-eyed. She took out a tissue.

He wondered if she hadn't been in love with her boss. "I gather the last few years were pretty rough, with business slacking off and Monroe's money problems."

She nodded. "The last year was especially hard."

"I understand his business had dwindled to almost nothing. Was that because people were unhappy with his work?"

"No," she said, frowning. "And if anyone told you otherwise, they didn't know what they were talking about," she said. "Jack was one of the best CPAs in the city. He had a very solid practice. Why, at one time he handled accounts for some of the richest families in the city, as well as a number of corporate accounts. It was only after Abby became ill that things got a little rough, and that was because he cut back his practice so he could take an active part in Abby's health care. He was absolutely devoted to her and Hailey."

"So, this problem with the insurance company isn't due to any irregularities in his business?"

"Of course not!" she snapped. "That agent is just giving Hailey a hard time. You know how insurance companies are. They want your money, but just try to collect on a claim." She gave him a knowing look. "That's when you find out how compassionate they really are."

This line of questioning wasn't getting him anywhere.

He decided to change tactics. "Did you know Hailey was adopted?"

She shook her head. "No. It came as quite a shock when Frank told me. I've known Jack and Abby for over twenty years, and not once in all that time did they even hint that—" She broke off as they heard Hailey approach.

"I'm sorry I took so long," she said, again taking the chair next to Sean.

From the flushed, excited look on her face, he knew Forbes had located the safe-deposit box. "That's all right," he said. "Ms. Harris was just telling me about your father's business. I hadn't realized his practice was so extensive."

Her chin rose a fraction. "There's a lot you don't know about my father."

"Have you decided what you're going to do with the business?" Martha asked, then quickly added, "Winton and Associates expressed an interest in buying it."

"I really haven't had a chance to give it much thought," she answered cautiously. "For the time being, I'm going to leave things as they are."

Martha looked at Sean and grinned. "She's definitely her father's daughter. Slow and steady."

He felt Hailey shift uncomfortably in the chair next to him. "You said you had something to tell me," she prompted.

"Not so much tell you as show you," the other woman said. She stood. "Come with me."

She led Sean and Hailey into a large room that he presumed was Jack Monroe's office. The room was comfortably furnished and looked out onto a pleasant inner garden.

"Jack kept his confidential records and papers in here," the secretary said, pointing to a series of file cabinets that lined one entire wall of the office.

He had that many confidential cases? Sean couldn't believe it. His face must have betrayed his thoughts, because Martha Harris added, "That's not all work in there. Jack was also a pack rat. He couldn't bear to throw anything away. I bet he still has Hailey's report cards from grade school." She smiled then. "Well, anyway, as I was going through the files, I came across something curious. It struck me as a little odd, so I thought you should see it."

She walked to one of the file cabinets, opened the top drawer, took out an accordion folder and set it on a table. "See what I mean?" She pulled open the folder so they could look inside.

It was stuffed with newspaper clippings, all on the same subject—the kidnapping of Susan Elaine Palmer.

Next to him, Sean felt Hailey stiffen. This was not what she had expected, but it was exactly the kind of evidence he'd been looking for, he thought, paging through the newspaper clippings. Proof that Jack Monroe's aim had been to extort money from Alan.

"I—I guess Dad found this case interesting," Hailey said weakly.

The secretary frowned. "It's odd," she said, oblivious to the undercurrent swirling around her. "I never knew him to be interested in crime stories."

"Well, something about this case must have intrigued him," Sean said, then punctuated his words with his best smile. "Hailey and I will go through the folder, see if there's anything else in here."

"All right. If you need me, I'll be in the other room."

The moment the door closed behind the secretary, Hailey whirled to face him. "This doesn't prove anything," she said.

"I'm sorry, but it proves your dad not only knew about the kidnapping, but knew about it for years, judging from the dates on these clippings." To illustrate his point, he pulled several articles out of the folder and laid them on the table. "Look at the dates—July 6, 1976, September 12, 1976, January 7, 1977. If you were really Susan, as he claims, why didn't he come forward earlier with this information?"

"There's no way we can tell how long he had these articles," she countered.

He shook his head. "You don't believe that any more than I do," he said gently.

She looked at him mutely, all the fire, all the spirit drained from her body. Her gaze focused on the pile of clippings on the desk.

"I know this is not what you expected to find, but if it's any consolation," he continued in that same gentle tone, "I think under normal circumstances he would never have done such a thing. I think he was desperate. He wanted to provide your mother with quality health care, and he also wanted to make sure you were taken care of. He just went about it the wrong way."

She crossed her arms and glared at him. "You've got it all figured out, haven't you? But you didn't know my father. He was a good man. He was honest. He would never have—" Her voice broke. She turned away, but not before he saw the glazed look of despair in her eyes...and the tears.

He studied her for a long moment, noting the determined tilt of her head and the stubborn set to her shoulders. He'd gotten what he came for. He'd unmasked her father for what he was—an extortionist. So why did he feel so lousy?

He walked to where she stood and paused directly behind her. He was standing so close that he could smell the scent of her hair—clean and sweet and intoxicating. Sunlight streaming through the window brought out its glorious chestnut hues. He wanted to reach out and run his fingers through those shimmering strands. His hands began to move toward her. He was making a mistake. He knew it, and yet he couldn't help himself. He placed his hands on her shoulders and turned her so she faced him.

She didn't pull away. She stared at him with those big gray eyes of hers, and he almost lost it. She looked so small, so fragile, as though a strong gust of wind might blow her away.

"I'm sorry," he said softly.

"I know this looks bad," she said, tipping her head so she could see his eyes, "but it's not how it looks. There's a logical explanation for the clippings. I just know it."

The tears she'd tried to wipe away were glistening on her lashes. He had a sudden, crazy yearning to touch her face, to wipe away the tears. And with that yearning came another, just as insane, a man's hunger to know the taste of her lips, the feel of her body against his.

It took all his willpower to restrain himself from wrapping his arms around her, enfolding her in his warmth. He cleared his throat. "Hailey, you may be right about your dad's innocence, but you should also prepare yourself for the possibility that he tried to extort money from Alan Palmer."

Stubbornly, Hailey shook her head. "No, you're wrong. Why don't you wait until we've checked out the safe-deposit box before you string my father up?"

"So he did have one?"

She nodded. "Mr. Forbes was able to locate it. He was also able to get a court order so we can check it out as soon as we leave here."

She was grasping at straws. He knew it, but he also knew it was fruitless to argue with her. "Okay, let's go check it out."

TED KURTIS, the bank manager, had received the court papers by the time Hailey and Sean arrived. He escorted them into the vault, where he removed the safe-deposit box from its locked chamber in the wall. After a cursory inspection of the box, which he explained was for probate purposes, he directed them to a small room containing a table and two chairs, then quietly left.

Sean noticed that Hailey's hands were unsteady as she lifted the lid on the metal box. The box contained four large manila envelopes. The first one held the deed to what he presumed was her parents' house. She gave it a quick once-over, then set it aside. The next envelope was full of money—twenties and fifties.

Hailey dropped it as if it were a hot potato. For a moment he looked at her stricken face, then he picked up the envelope and counted the money. There was five thousand dollars. That surprised him. If Jack Monroe had been so strapped for cash, why hadn't he used this money? Unless…he'd been afraid to. Could this money be part of the ransom Alan had paid the kidnappers?

A chill of foreboding washed over him. He was getting a bad feeling about the contents of the safe-deposit box.

He looked at Hailey, wondering if she felt it, too. He was sure she did, judging from her dazed expression as she looked at the money.

"Hailey?" he prompted. "Aren't you going to check out the other envelopes?"

"Ah, yes," she said in a shaky little voice. She drew a deep breath then picked up the third envelope.

He watched as she opened the flap then looked inside. A flash of pain appeared on her face. She squeezed her eyes shut, fighting back tears.

"What's wrong?" Sean asked. "What's in there?"

Hailey didn't say anything. Instead, she dumped the contents onto the tabletop.

It contained newspaper clippings, stories about the kidnapping. Even though he'd been prepared for this, Sean still felt sick. He would have given anything to make this easier for her, but he couldn't. All he could do was be there for her.

"You okay?" he asked, giving her hand a reassuring squeeze.

She swallowed, then nodded. "I'm all right."

"There's one more," he said gently. "Do you want me to open it?"

She shook her head. "No, I'll do it."

He watched as she drew a deep breath, then picked up the last envelope and dumped the contents on the table.

For a moment they both sat staring, stunned by the documents lying on the table. There were two passports, two Social Security cards and a driver's license. Sean picked up the passports. They had been issued more than twenty years ago. While the pictures inside were of Jack and Abby Monroe—or at least he assumed they were, and Hailey's stricken expression pretty much confirmed that fact—the passports had been issued to a Dan and Kathy Hauser. It was the same with the rest of the documents. They were all more than twenty years old and had assumed names. Clearly, Monroe had planned to leave the country and take his family with him.

The kidnapping had occurred May 15, 1976, and the passports had been issued in August of that year. His heart began to slam against the wall of his chest as he scanned the tabletop looking for the third passport. It wasn't there. Obtaining fake papers for him and his wife would have been difficult, but not impossible. But getting them for a child—a child without identification and whose picture had been plastered all over the newspapers—it would have been extremely risky. Was that why the Monroes hadn't left, because they'd been unable to get a passport for the child?

"What's going on?" Hailey asked. He could hear the fear in her voice.

He couldn't bring himself to voice his own fear, so instead he asked, "Is there anything else in there?"

Hailey picked up the envelope, turned it upside down and gave it a little shake. A tiny gold locket fell out. It looked like the one the child in the photograph had been wearing.

Sean picked it up. With his fingertip, he traced the letters engraved in the gold locket. "SEP," he said softly.

"Susan Elaine Palmer," she whispered.

"It was one of those things the police kept hush-hush," he said flatly, "because only the kidnappers would know that Susan had been wearing it when she was abducted, and it could, therefore, prove he or she actually had her."

Hailey looked at him, her eyes wide, stricken. "No," she said, shaking her head, "he couldn't have been involved."

But everything pointed in that direction—the false documents establishing new identities for Monroe and his family, his obvious plans to flee the country, and the locket. Most of all the locket.

He looked at it again, studying it, trying to determine the probability of it being a forgery. It had been over twenty years since he'd last seen the locket. Alan would have to authenticate it. He was trying to decide how best to break the news to Alan when out of the corner of his eye he saw Hailey take a small yellowish-brown oblong rock out of her pants pocket and rub it between her thumb and forefinger.

His heart stopped. He didn't move, didn't say anything. He couldn't. His eyes were riveted on the tiny object.

"What's the matter?" she asked, noting his expression.

"Where did you get that?" His eyes slid from her face to the object in her hand.

"What? This?" she asked, surprised. She held out her hand, palm up, and looked at him quizzically. "My good-luck charm."

"It's the sun." It was a statement, not a question.

"Yes," she said carefully, cautious. "How did you know?"

Sean cleared his throat. "Where did you get it?" he asked again.

"I don't know." She shrugged. "I've had it for as long as I can remember."

He looked at her then—really looked at her, as if seeing her for the first time. "I gave Susan a rock just like that one," he said in a strangled voice. "She always kept it with her. She had it when she was kidnapped." Oh, my God, he thought, she *was* Susan!

Chapter Four

Hailey barely remembered the drive to her apartment or inviting Sean in, but she must have. Or he wouldn't be here, she thought, as she looked up from her seat on the sofa. He was pacing back and forth, deep in thought. But while she was struggling to come up with a plausible explanation for the things they'd found, she knew he'd already made up his mind. Her father had gone from being an extortionist to being Sarge, the third man in the Palmer kidnapping.

She didn't believe it. Her dad could no more have participated in a kidnapping than he could have tried to extort money from Alan Palmer. There had to be another explanation for the things in his safe-deposit box. And yet she was having difficulty coming up with one.

Sean, on the other hand, was having no such difficulty. He was sure Jack Monroe had been involved in the kidnapping. Everything pointed that way, and to—he swallowed—to Hailey being Susan.

When he began this investigation, he thought he was looking into a simple case of extortion. Instead, he found himself looking at a two-decades-old kidnapping. He was going to have to rethink everything he'd ever thought about the kidnapping in light of this new information, adding Jack Monroe to the equation.

First thing tomorrow morning he'd call Mac, tell him what they had found and get him started on a background check on Jack Monroe. Then he'd call his friend, LAPD homicide detective Tate Wells. He knew Tate wouldn't be able to reopen a twenty-year-old closed case based on what he'd found today, but it might intrigue him enough that he'd be willing to provide some assistance in the investigation of Jack Monroe.

Even with Tate's assistance, it was not going to be an easy investigation. Memories would have faded, and facts would be hard to come by. Also, dredging up the past was going to be painful, not just for Alan, but for Hailey, as well. Maybe even more so in her case.

He looked at her, seated on the living-room sofa, hands clasped tightly in her lap. Her face was pale. God, he hated this. He had to tread lightly. He had to find a way to get to the truth without hurting her any further. He swore when he thought of Jack Monroe. If he'd been the loving father Hailey claimed he was, why hadn't he told her about the newspaper clippings or the things in that damn safe-deposit box?

He knew from the medical report that, unlike his wife, Jack hadn't died instantly. There had been time for him to make a clean breast of things. But he'd said nothing. Leaving it to others to break the news to his daughter that he was a kidnapper, allowing her to face this mess alone.

Hell, it wasn't his job to care about her feelings. Alan was his client and friend. He was supposed to be looking out for his best interests, not hers. But telling himself that didn't do a damn bit of good. He did care, and not just because of the case.

"It's a setup," Hailey said, breaking into his troubled thoughts.

Sean paused in his pacing and looked at her. "What?"

"That stuff in the safe-deposit box. It was planted. It's the only explanation."

He shook his head. "There was only one name on that signature card—Jack Monroe. He was the only person who had access to that safe-deposit box."

She looked as if she wanted to cry. "None of this makes any sense," she whispered.

Unfortunately, Sean thought grimly, it made a lot of sense. He looked at her and chose his words carefully. "Denny Hanson always maintained there was another man involved in the kidnapping, but no one believed him. Not the police, not the media, no one. They thought he'd made up the whole thing to minimize his role in the kidnapping. But it looks as if he may have been telling the truth all along." At her stricken look, he added gently, "I'm sorry, but it looks as if your father may have been involved in the kidnapping."

She stared at him, her expression bleak, then shook her head vigorously. "I refuse to believe that. There's got to be some other explanation for the things we found."

He massaged the back of his neck. "Hailey, I know this is hard, but you can't pretend those fake documents, the passports and the money don't mean anything. Your dad had knowledge of—if not direct involvement in—the kidnapping. There's no other way to explain how he came into possession of Susan's locket and that rock you're rubbing."

She stared bleakly at the object in her hand. "How do you know it's the same one?" she challenged. "You gave it to her more than twenty years ago. How can you be so sure it's the same one?"

"Because there's no other one like it on the planet." His mouth curved into a wry smile. "It's a moon rock."

"As in, from the moon?" she asked, frowning at the object in her hand.

"Yeah. My uncle was with the space program. He was part of the team that designed the lunar module that took the astronauts to the moon. When he retired from NASA, they gave him two nuggets from rocks Neil Armstrong brought back from his moon voyage. He knew how much I loved collecting rocks, so when he died, he left them to me. One rock was yellowish-brown, and I called it the sun. The other was grayish-brown, and I called it the moon."

Hailey could tell this was an emotional subject for him and remained quiet as he continued his narrative.

"Susan was fascinated by the idea that they'd come from the moon and was always pestering me to let her hold them. At first I was reluctant. I thought she'd put them in her mouth, and I would get in trouble. But she said she wouldn't, and she didn't. She'd just rub them for a while then put them in her pocket. After her mother died and she stopped talking, I gave her the yellow one. I told her it was a good-luck charm and that it would protect her from harm."

"This isn't just a routine assignment for you, is it?"

"No," he said quietly. "It was my fault that Susan was kidnapped." He explained how he'd been asked to watch her but hadn't.

"It's wasn't your fault," she said firmly. "Those men were bent on taking Susan. Even if you'd been there, you couldn't have stopped them. God knows what they would have done to you if you had tried."

Sean didn't say anything. He looked at her, his expression bleak.

Hailey swallowed. "Do you think I'm Susan Palmer?" she asked.

Sean didn't know what to say. He'd been wrestling with that question for the past hour. It certainly looked as if Monroe had had some involvement in the kidnapping. But what if, instead of killing Susan as everyone had thought, he'd kept the child and raised her as his own? Apparently, he and his wife had always wanted a child. Hailey was the right age and had the right look. He knew from his years as a defense attorney that criminals often kept as souvenirs personal items belonging to their victims. That would explain why Monroe had the locket and the moon rock. All those things taken together certainly suggested that she *might* be Susan. But they didn't mean she was.

She could just as easily be who she purported to be—Jack and Abby Monroe's adopted daughter or, for that matter, their birth daughter. His eyes narrowed. They only had Monroe's deathbed statement that she was adopted, but he'd seen no evidence, like adoption papers, to support that claim. Possibly, faced with mounting financial problems, Jack Monroe had planned to pull off the ultimate con—passing off his own child as Susan Palmer.

And yet there was something about Hailey that pulled at him. Maybe it was an old memory of his childhood friend. Or maybe it was sexual attraction clouding his judgment. He didn't know what it was, just that it was there, in the depths of his soul. And it caused him to want her to be Susan. It was totally irrational. He knew that. And for that reason, he couldn't trust his instincts on this one.

"Sean, do you think I'm Susan?" Hailey asked again.

He drew a weary breath, then shrugged. "I think there's a good chance, but I'm not sure."

"But you believe my father was involved in the kidnapping," she said, her voice rising. "Don't you?"

"I think you're scared," he answered, and heard her sharply indrawn breath. "And I think you're mad. But you don't know for certain who to be mad at—me or your father."

Hailey ignored the pain in her chest and blurted, "Thank you, Dr. Freud."

"Hey, I'm not the bad guy here. I want to get to the bottom of this just as badly as you do."

She issued a weary sigh. "I know. I'm sorry I snapped at you like that. We need to work together to try to make sense of the things in the safe-deposit box. Any idea how we should proceed?"

He nodded. "The first thing we do is get you lined up for a DNA test. The test is about ninety-nine percent accurate and will tell us if you're Susan or not. Fortunately for us, there's a very good genetic testing laboratory right here in Chicago. I'll give them a call first thing in the morning and arrange for you to give a blood sample. That sample will be sent to a lab in L.A., where it'll be tested along with Alan's blood.''

"How long before we know the results?"

He shrugged. "If we're lucky, maybe a month from the date the lab gets both samples. In the meantime, I'd like to check out the things in the safe-deposit box. I want to know when those passports were issued and if that money is part of the ransom payment.''

She frowned. "If the DNA test is ninety-nine percent accurate, why is there a need for any further investigation?''

"Because the blood test only answers one question—if you're Susan. It won't tell us how you came to be with the Monroes, or if your father was one of the kidnappers.''

She swallowed the lump that had formed in her throat. "I see. What do you want me to do?" she asked.

He gave her a wary look. "I understand your desire to help, but under the circumstances, I don't believe it's a good idea. When I suggested it earlier, I thought we were looking into an extortion, not kidnapping and murder.''

Her chin rose a fraction. "Either you include me in the investigation or forget about using the things from the safe-deposit box.''

His eyes locked with hers and held, and for a moment she thought he was going to call her bluff, but then he said, "I hope you don't live to regret this decision.''

She hoped so, too. "I'll take my chances," she said. "I think we should begin by talking to Denny Hanson.''

"Yeah, that's a good starting place, but it'll take a few days to set up a meeting. He's serving time at the federal prison at San Quentin. I'll have to contact his lawyer and see if he'll let us talk to him. I'm also going to have to talk to Alan.''

"What are you going to tell him?"

He grimaced. "As little as possible. Naturally, I've have to tell him about finding the locket in your dad's safe-deposit box, to get him to authenticate it and to justify scheduling him for a blood test. But nothing more than that.''

"You're not going to tell him about the other things we found?"

He shook his head. "There's no point letting him get his hopes up when I can't say conclusively that you're Susan." He gave her a pointed look. "And I don't want you talking about this case or anything we find to anyone, either."

She looked at him incredulously. "You think I want people to know my father is suspected of kidnapping a child?"

He flushed under her scrutiny. "Then we're in agreement," he said gruffly. "We don't say anything to anyone about any of this."

She was about to nod in agreement when something occurred to her. "Of course, I've have to tell my uncle, but you have my word I won't say anything to anyone else."

He looked at her, frowning. "Why you do have to tell him anything?"

"Because he's always been like a second father to me. I don't feel right keeping information from him. Besides, he was Dad's best friend. Maybe he can shed some light on this."

He agreed reluctantly. "Okay, but make sure he understands he's not to say anything about this to anyone. I think keeping things under wraps until we know something definite is the best course of action. The last thing we need is to have the media breathing down our necks."

"THAT'S INCREDIBLE!" Frank Roberts said, then looked quickly around the restaurant, checking to see if he'd been overheard. Luckily, they were sitting in a secluded spot near the back of the restaurant away from the other patrons. He leaned across the table and stared into Hailey's troubled eyes. "Jack actually had the little girl's locket?" His voice was intense, but discreetly low.

"Well, Mr. Palmer has to authenticate it," Hailey answered, "but Sean seems pretty certain that it's hers."

He shook his head. "I don't know what to say. None of this makes any sense."

"I know," she said bleakly. "I keep thinking this is just a horrible nightmare, that I'm going to wake up and everything is going to be all right, but it keeps going on and on."

He nodded. "I know things look bad, but we can't give up."

"The locket would be bad enough, but Dad also had those fake documents and all that money. I downplayed things with Sean, but I'm certain Dad knew something about the kidnapping." She chewed her lower lip. "What do you remember about the fall of '72, around the time I was born, to the fall of '76?"

He shook his head. "I'm afraid not much. For a lot of that time I was overseas, primarily in Southeast Asia."

Not just Southeast Asia, she thought, in Vietnam. After that he'd been laid up in a V.A. hospital, first in Germany then in the States, recovering from injuries sustained at a little village in Vietnam called Hue.

"I think you were nearly four when I moved to Chicago."

She nodded slowly. "That was the summer of '76, about the time Mom and Dad thought about leaving the country. Do you remember anything unusual happening that summer?"

He frowned. "Unusual? In what way?"

"I don't know. Did they seem different? Maybe worried?"

He shook his head. "Not that I recall, but I was busy getting settled. And I'd just gone to work for the Department of Children and Families Services. I was tied up with my new job."

"Dad planned to leave the country." She chewed her lower lip. "They never said anything to you about leaving?"

Frank Roberts blinked, taken slightly aback by her question. "No, of course not."

"They kept you in the dark, too."

He leaned across the table, covering her hand with his. "Let's not start doubting your dad or jumping to conclusions. You know as well as I do this doesn't sound like Jack or Abby."

She drew a deep sigh. "If anyone had told me this story a month ago, I wouldn't have believed it, but now..." She shook her head. "I'm so confused, I don't know what to believe anymore."

"There's only one thing you need to believe and that is what your heart tells you."

"How can I?" she wailed. "There's just so much Dad didn't tell me...or even you, and you were his best friend."

"He must have had his reasons," Frank Roberts answered cautiously. "Damn good ones, I would imagine."

"I want to believe that, but I can't forget the way he sounded when he talked about how much they'd wanted a child. There was such envy, such longing in his voice."

"Sure, they wanted a child, but not at the expense of participating in a kidnapping. Besides, there was no reason for them to resort to such a drastic measure. Adopting a black child, even a newborn, wouldn't have been difficult, not even twenty-five years ago."

"Are you sure?" she asked, jumping on the idea like a lifeline. With his background in child welfare, he'd know about such things.

"Yeah, I'm sure. There are more black children eligible for foster family homes and adoption than there are black families to take them. It's been that way since the mid-sixties, when the pregnancy rate among black teenagers went through the roof. Add to that the number of women losing custody of their children due to drugs, child abuse and neglect. And until about two years ago, there was a prohibition against cross-racial adoption. All those things taken together have put a lot of black kids into the nation's child welfare system.''

What he said made sense, but.... She looked at him, her eyes troubled. ''I haven't been able to find the adoption papers.''

He shrugged. ''If they weren't in the safe-deposit box, then they must be somewhere in the house. I'm sure they'll turn up.''

''But the fact that they're misplaced is odd. You know what a meticulous record keeper Dad was.''

He shook his head. ''Hailey, he wasn't infallible. Everyone makes mistakes. He must have just misplaced them.''

''Like he misplaced that letter he left for me?'' She looked at her hands, then at him. ''I also found my birth certificate. It looked like it had been tampered with, so I called the Bureau of Vital Statistics in Springfield to request another copy, and they said they had no record of my birth.''

For a moment he didn't say anything. ''Honey, I wish I could give you the assurance you want, but I can't tell you that you aren't Susan Palmer,'' he said quietly. ''I can tell you this—they didn't steal or kidnap you.''

She gave him a wan smile. ''Thanks. I guess I just needed to hear you say that, but I...I don't think the adoption was legal. Something must have come up to make them question its legality. Something that couldn't be easily corrected. That would explain the forged documents and why they might have considered leaving the country.''

He looked at her, his eyes troubled. ''And you think that something was the fact that you're Susan Palmer?''

''I don't know what else to think.''

''I suppose that could be the case,'' he answered slowly, ''but if you're right, aren't you asking for trouble by looking into it? Maybe you should back off, just drop the whole thing.''

''I can't. I have to know the truth. Not just because I want to know if I'm Susan Palmer or not, but also to clear

Dad's name." She shook her head. "Sean Cassadine thinks Dad was involved in the kidnapping, and he's bent on proving it."

"But if you don't help him, if you refuse to cooperate, how far can he get in any investigation?"

She shook her head. "He's not going to back off. He's made that plain. I'm going to have to prove to him that he's wrong about Dad."

"How do you propose to do that?"

"By helping him find the real kidnapper."

He let out a deep sigh. "I wish there was some other way."

"So do I." She took a sip of water. "I asked Mr. Baylor for a month's leave of absence from the gallery, starting next week."

He frowned. "Are you going to be able to manage financially?"

"I've got a little money saved."

The waiter brought their dinners, and they ate in silence. After a moment, Frank Roberts leaned across the table. He cleared his throat. "How chummy are you with this Sean Cassadine?"

"What do you mean?" The question jolted Hailey out of her reveries.

"I couldn't help but notice you're on a first-name basis with him. And you get this sort of dreamy glint in your eyes whenever you talk about him. Are you falling for him?"

She flushed. Was she that transparent? "Of course not," she answered, willing herself to sound nonchalant. "I barely know the man."

He smiled then, his first real smile of the evening. "It doesn't take that long to fall in love."

"Well, I'm certainly not interested in getting involved with Sean Cassadine." Hailey decided now might be the time to change the subject. "Was your source at Fidelity

Insurance able to find out why it's taking Granger so long to process the claims?''

He nodded, then let out a weary sigh. "It isn't good. As you know, both life-insurance policies contained a double-indemnity provision meaning, in the event of an accidental death, they pay double. So, instead of getting a hundred thousand on each policy, you'll get two hundred thousand." He sighed again. "Apparently, Granger thinks the automobile accident that took Jack and Abby's life may not have been an accident."

"What!"

"He thinks it may have been a murder-suicide," Frank answered grimly.

She stared at him, speechless. She thought she'd heard everything, but this was too much. Had everyone gone mad?

"Granger has this theory," he continued. "He thinks Jack was depressed about your mother's Alzheimer's. Because of her failing health and his declining business, he deliberately caused the accident. He seems to have arrived at that theory because the police report attributed the accident to a broken brake line, which caused Jack to lose control of the car. He thinks Jack tampered with the brakes."

"Th-that's the most ridiculous thing I've ever heard," she spluttered. "There's absolutely no proof that the brakes were tampered with."

"I agree, but Granger isn't going to release any funds until the matter has been resolved to his satisfaction."

"That could take forever," she said, her voice laced with frustration. "I need to pay the creditors now. I also want to get started on this investigation as soon as possible, but I can't do that with this insurance problem hanging over my head."

"You don't have to handle all of this alone," he said, giving her a reassuring smile. "I'll deal with Granger. You concentrate on clearing Jack." He spent several minutes laying out how they should proceed, starting with notifying David Forbes and getting him involved, but Hailey was only half-listening. She was still reeling from the latest bombshell.

As if Sean Cassadine's assertions weren't bad enough, now this. What else go could wrong?

SEAN SLAMMED the morning newspaper on Hailey's desk with a loud thud that sent pages fluttering and inserts sliding out.

"Have you seen this morning's paper?" he demanded, glaring at her.

She glanced up from the phone she was speaking into. From her startled expression, Sean knew he was the last person she'd expected to see. Well, if she thought she was going to get away with this, she could think again.

She quickly placed her hand over the phone receiver. "Please lower you voice and sit down. I'll just be a minute."

His mouth tightened, but he sank slowly into the chair in front of the desk and glared at her while she concluded her phone conversation. From bits and pieces of her conversation, he gathered she was talking to her uncle.

"Okay, I'll get back to you," she said a few minutes later, then lowered the phone into the cradle. She stared at him for a moment, then picked up the paper. He'd circled the story in red, but even if he hadn't highlighted it, she couldn't have missed it. The *National Banner*'s front page proclaimed in bold headlines, Alan Palmer's Daughter Returns From Dead.

There was a picture of Susan as a child and one of an adult Hailey, apparently taken with a telescopic lens. There were also several pictures of Alan. The story was short, only a couple of columns. It alleged that Alan Palmer's daughter, who'd been kidnapped and presumed dead, had been found alive, then went on to recount the story of the kidnapping, the murder of Ryan Vanover and the subsequent arrest of Danny Hanson and his claim of a third man involved in the kidnapping. Then the story shifted to Jack Monroe and how he'd contacted Alan to tell him that his daughter was alive. The article concluded on a speculative note, suggesting that Jack Monroe may have been the third man in the kidnapping, but that somewhere along the way he'd decided to keep the child and raise her as his own. Supposedly, "sources" close to the investigation had established conclusively that Hailey was Susan.

He didn't know which was worse, the fact that she'd broken her promise or the fact that she had the gall to sit there and feign innocence. For someone who didn't know if she were Susan Palmer, she'd wasted no time trying to capitalize on the situation.

"I heard about this," she said, dropping the newspaper on the desk, "but this is worse than I imagined."

His mouth tightened. "I thought we agreed we wouldn't discuss this matter with anyone or go public with any of this until we knew something concrete."

She looked at him, surprised. "Are you accusing me of leaking that story to the tabloid?"

"Well, didn't you?"

"Of course not!"

"What about your uncle Frank?"

A flash of anger appeared in her eyes. "He wouldn't do something like that."

"Then how do you explain this story?" Sean's voice rose. He drew several deep breaths as he tried to hold onto his temper. "Someone sure as hell leaked it to the press. What about a boyfriend?"

"I just told you, I didn't tell *anyone*," she snapped.

"Of course you didn't." Sean laughed bitterly. "You really had me fooled. I thought you were different, that you really wanted to get to the truth. What a joke. You're just like the other Susan Palmer imposters, out for what you can get."

All the color drained from her face. The light in her gray

eyes dimmed, and the corners of her lovely mouth turned down. A flash of remorse blindsided him, but he shook it off.

She swallowed. "What about someone at the bank? A secretary or teller. They could have leaked the story."

He shook his head. "No one had access to that box but the bank manager and us."

"What about him? He saw what was in that safe-deposit box—the newspaper clippings, the money. And he had a copy of the court order. He could have surmised what was going on and leaked the story to the press."

Sean shook his head again. "He has too much to lose."

She looked at him, incredulous. "And I don't?"

Sean ran his hand over his hair in frustration. "All I know is, only two people knew the actual contents of that safe-deposit box—you and me. And, to a lesser extent, Alan and your uncle. I know neither Alan nor I said anything to anyone."

"Why would I give the story to the papers?" she challenged. "It doesn't make sense. Just think about it. I want to get to the bottom of this kidnapping as much as you do, but not by implicating my father, labeling him a criminal, a kidnapper."

What she said made sense, or maybe it only made sense because he wanted it to. She was confusing him. *No, she wasn't,* an inner voice whispered. He'd simply gone off half-cocked and overreacted, the way he had the day before. He drew a deep breath. "I'm sorry. I should have known you wouldn't do something like that."

"Apology accepted," Hailey said. She drummed her fingernails on her desktop. "Maybe no one leaked anything to the *Banner,*" she suggested. "Perhaps they were working on the story all along. The *Banner* may be a rag, but their reporters are competent. They're perfectly capable of coming up with a story on their own."

Sean shook his head. "Hell, there's no reason for the *Banner* to be dredging up a story that's more than twenty years old. And I don't believe in coincidence. Someone tipped them off.''

"For what purpose?''

"Money.'' He shrugged. ''But we may never know who did it.''

She nodded slowly as she considered his words. ''Do you think this is going to impact the investigation?''

He let out a weary sigh. ''It certainly complicates matters. Instead of being able to conduct a quiet, discreet inquiry, we're going to have the media breathing down our necks, dogging our tails.'' Not to mention Alan, he thought grimly. He'd already fielded several phone calls from him that morning. After reading his advance copy of the article off the AP wire and seeing Hailey's picture, Alan was convinced she was Susan. It was all Sean could do to stop Alan from getting on the next plane and coming to Chicago.

''A few radio and television stations have already picked up the story.'' He fingered the edges of the tabloid. ''By six o'clock, it'll probably be the lead story on the evening news on every major network and the front-page headline in tomorrow's morning papers. I think we can look forward to a media frenzy for the next few days.''

''There must be some way to downplay this.'' She pointed to the tabloid.

''My office is preparing a statement that Alan will release to the press later today, and he's been instructed to defer any questions to his attorney. There'll probably be a gang of reporters camped outside your apartment by the time you leave here. You might want to stay at your uncle's place for a few days. And if you've got the time, you might want to take a few weeks off from work.''

She shifted slightly. ''I've already made arrangements to take some time off, starting next week.''

''Good. However,'' he continued, ''the problem is we've lost the element of surprise. Potential witnesses have been tipped off. People have time to manufacture evidence or fabricate their stories. Even worse, sell their stories to tabloids like the *National Banner*." Sean sighed. "Damn it, what a mess."

She looked at her hands. "I guess now is not the best time to tell you about the other thing."

Something in her voice made him look at her sharply. "The other thing?" he asked slowly. She averted her eyes, refusing to look at him. But before she'd lowered her gaze, he'd seen confusion, anxiety. No, he thought, it had been guilt, but what could she be feeling guilty about? He was convinced she'd had nothing to do with the article in the *Banner*, and she certainly hadn't.... Suddenly it hit him. "You talked to Alan!"

"I know what you're thinking," she said quickly, "but you're wrong. It wasn't like that."

He laughed bitterly. "You couldn't wait, could you? You just had to call him. What did you say? That you were his own sweet daughter?" he asked, mimicking her voice.

She stared at him. "That's a terrible thing to say. I wouldn't do something like that." Hailey bit her lower lip, fighting the tears that threatened to burst forth. "I didn't call him. He called me."

"I don't care," Sean snapped. "I want you to stay away from him."

She shook her head. "I'm afraid that's not possible."

"And why is that?" he asked, but he had a sinking feeling he wasn't going to like what she was about to say.

"Because Mr. Palmer called me about twenty minutes ago. He invited me to come to Los Angeles and stay at his estate while we wait for the results of the DNA test. And I took him up on the offer."

Chapter Five

"Mr. Palmer is expecting you," the butler said, then stepped aside so they could enter.

With a sense of awe, Hailey followed Sean into a foyer that was larger than her entire living room. The floor was black-and-white marble, and the three-story white staircase was covered in black plush carpeting. A spectacular crystal chandelier hung in the center of the foyer. It wasn't just the beauty of the estate that took her breath away. It was also the fact that she was really here. Sean had been totally opposed to her coming. And, surprisingly, so had her uncle Frank. He'd done everything he could to dissuade her. She knew he was afraid she was going to find out things about her dad she might not like.

Well, she was afraid of that, too, but she had to risk it. She had to know the truth, and the only way she could do that was by taking an active role in the investigation. And that meant she had to be here. It wasn't that she didn't trust Sean to conduct a fair and impartial investigation. He'd try. But he wasn't a disinterested party. And therein lay the problem. His interpretation of the evidence might be colored by his personal feelings about the kidnapping. She already sensed a reluctance on his part to consider that someone other than her father could be Sarge.

The more she thought about it, the more she believed that *if* she was Susan Palmer—and she still had some doubt about that—there had to have been another party involved in the kidnapping. It was the only way to explain how she'd come to be with her parents. But she had no idea how she was going to go about proving it—that is, until Alan Palmer had called, inviting her to stay at his estate. It had been the answer to her prayers. It would not only allow her to stay where the kidnapping had occurred, it would also allow her access to the people who had been around during that time. She'd tried to explain this to Sean, but he wouldn't listen. He was too busy casting her in the role of opportunist.

She looked at him. He was helping Niles, Alan's butler, with her luggage. Niles was exactly what you would expect in a butler. He was a very distinguished-looking man of indeterminate age, and he spoke with a slight British accent.

"Mr. Palmer and the rest of the family are in the living room," Niles said once the last of her luggage was brought in. "He's expecting you."

Sean placed his hand around her waist and was about to move in the direction of the room across from the staircase. Niles cleared his throat, then looked at Hailey. "Mr. Palmer is quite excited about your arrival, miss. We all are. It's nothing short of a miracle that you were found...a miracle." He turned beet red, then swiveled on his heels and walked away.

She couldn't help but smile. She glanced at Sean. He was smiling, too. A big, warm smile that made his handsome face seem relaxed and happy.

Her heart did a flip-flop. It was the first sign of thawing in the cold shoulder he had been giving her since she'd told him about accepting Alan's invitation. She couldn't help but hope the thawing would continue. It was going to be hard enough facing these people. It would be nice to know she wasn't totally alone.

Sean must have read the worry on her face, because the hand he'd placed around her waist a moment earlier tightened, and he gave her side a little squeeze, as if to assure her she wasn't alone. She knew the gesture was meant only as a show of support, but she could feel the heat from his hand through her dress, all the way to her skin. Her awareness of him was heightened as he walked beside her. She could feel the sexual magnetism that made him so self-confident. It pulled at her, drew her. She shivered.

"Don't worry," he coaxed. "You're going to be just fine."

She searched her mind for something to say, anything to block the sensations he aroused in her.

Before she could respond, her attention was caught by the sound of voices raised in argument. One of the double doors opposite the staircase was wrenched open, a harsh, furious voice shouted, "Eric, come back here!" and a tall, slender, light-skinned man in tight jeans and a polo shirt erupted from the room. He slammed the door behind him with a vicious thrust, then caught sight of Hailey and Sean and froze.

With his long, wavy black hair pulled into a ponytail and gold studs in each ear, he looked androgynous. He appeared to be somewhere in his mid to late thirties. She guessed he was no more than five foot eight or so, but he looked taller because his body was almost all legs. Without a doubt, his most striking feature was his steel-gray eyes. Though at the moment, they were shooting daggers at her. If looks could kill, she'd be a dead woman.

Hailey felt Sean stiffen beside her, then take a step forward in a protective stance, shielding her. She was glad for his presence. The fury emanating from the man who stood before them was so strong it was almost visible, like heat shimmering off the sunbaked pavement.

"Ah, the prodigal daughter," the man said, sneering. "I wish I could say welcome, but I don't want you here, and I'm not going to pretend otherwise." He stalked past them.

She hadn't realized she'd been holding her breath until she heard the front door slam behind them.

"If you're wondering, that's Eric Keegan. Alan's nephew."

She should have known. Only a relative would exhibit such hostility. "I guess you want to say, 'I told you so,'" she said.

He looked at her, surprised. "My concern is with the impact your presence may have on Alan. But now that you're here, I expect you to be treated with courtesy and respect. I'll speak to Alan. I don't condone that kind of behavior, and neither does he."

"Please don't. I don't want to cause any trouble. Besides, I didn't expect to be welcomed with open arms." That wasn't entirely true. She'd hoped for the best.

"Come on, let's go meet the family."

Family? It was a strange way to think of these people, she thought, as they moved in the direction of the living room. From the sound of angry voices coming from the other side of the door, Eric Keegan wasn't the only one who didn't want her there. Sean threw her one last look before pushing open the double doors.

There were four people in the room—two men standing near the fireplace, and a man and an auburn-haired woman seated on one of two long sofas in the room.

"Darling," the woman was saying, "Eric's right. This is nothing more than a scam to obtain money from you, just like the others were. Jack Monroe was a liar and, quite possibly, a murderer. What makes you think for one moment that horrible man's letter contained a shred of truth? Susan is dead. We all know that—"

"Maybe I should have knocked," Sean said smoothly.

Conversation ceased as four sets of eyes swung in their direction. You could have heard a pin drop. The silence that followed was strained and awkward. It seemed to stretch for painfully long minutes, but Hailey knew it was probably only a few seconds. The only person who didn't seem affected was Sean.

Taking her arm in a light grasp, he led her across the room to the taller and older of the two men standing in front of the fireplace and said simply, "Hailey Monroe, I'd like you to meet Alan Palmer."

Sean squeezed her hand then let it drop. She tried to ignore the feeling of loss.

Hailey drew a deep breath as she stared into the face of the man who might be her birth father. Alan Palmer was not a handsome man, probably never had been. He was very distinguished-looking, though. A couple of inches over six feet, broad-shouldered and powerfully built, he was a man who inspired confidence. His salt-and-pepper hair framed a mahogany-brown face, and his dark brown eyes gleamed like black coals.

"Hailey," he said, and then he seemed unable to say anything else. She could feel the powerful emotions that emanated from him as the small, slender hand she extended was engulfed in both of Alan's big, leathery hands. She knew if she'd given him the slightest encouragement, he would have swept her off her feet in a bear hug.

"It's nice meeting you, Mr. Palmer," she told him as she gently drew her hand free of his grasp. "I appreciate your letting me stay here while we wait for the results of the DNA test."

Before Alan could respond, the man seated next to the auburn-haired woman did.

"We all call him Alan," he told Hailey, and when she looked at him, he offered her a slightly strained smile. "I'm Paul. Paul Keegan. Your mother's brother."

Like his son, Paul Keegan was light-skinned and gray eyed. But that's where the similarity ended. Where his son was slim, he was soft looking, on the pudgy side, though his well-tailored suit did much to hide a slightly protruding stomach. Not a strand of his perfectly groomed, swan-white hair was out of place. At one time he was probably quite handsome, and though a lifetime of temper and indulgence had ruined his once-handsome features, he was still an attractive man.

He stood and came toward her, a forced smile on his

lips, arms outstretched. "There are no words to express our joy at your being found. So I'll just say, welcome home...niece."

From his words, Hailey drew two conclusions. One, that Alan had made it plain to his family he considered her to be the real McCoy until proven otherwise, and expected them to behave accordingly. And, two, that Paul Keegan was too smart to openly defy him—as his son had—despite any reservations he might have about her being Susan.

Hailey took a step away from Alan and offered her hand to Paul Keegan. "It's nice meeting you."

"That's not much of a welcome," he said with forced joviality before enfolding her in a bear hug.

"Thank you," she said, carefully extricating herself from his arms. "Ah...Mr. Keegan."

"Please, you must call me Uncle Paul."

The woman sitting on the sofa rolled her eyes and laughed. Color rose in Paul's face, but he continued to smile at her.

"Gloria, come and meet Hailey," Alan said, trying to cover the awkward moment.

The auburn-haired woman rose slowly from the sofa and stepped forward. From what Sean had told her, she knew this was Gloria Falcon, Alan's longtime mistress. Younger by about ten years than Alan, Gloria was five foot seven and so thin she looked as if a slight breeze might blow her away. She was dark chestnut in coloring and had large features. At fifty-two, her face contained only a smattering of wrinkles. She carried herself with confidence and poise.

"I hope you'll forgive me for that comment you overheard," Gloria said lightly. "It was quite tactless of me. Although I'm sure you understand why we might feel some reticence about embracing you with open arms. We only have your—"

"Gloria! That's enough." Alan's voice broached no argument.

She batted her eyes at him and gave him a guileless look.

"Did I say something wrong? I just want her to understand this is all something of a shock." She looked at Hailey. "I'm certain this isn't the welcome you were expecting."

Like Eric, she was coming out swinging, but Hailey wasn't about to let her insult pass. "I wasn't expecting anything, Ms. Falcon," she said smoothly, then added, "except common courtesy."

The carefully shaped eyebrows on Gloria's forehead rose to amazing heights as she let Hailey's words soak in. "Good, then I guess we understand each other."

"I think we do, Ms. Falcon."

"Call me Gloria." Her mouth curved into the semblance of a smile, but her eyes remained cold. "And what do we call you? Susan?"

"Hailey," she replied smoothly. No doubt Gloria was bent on stirring up trouble and thought this might be a sore point.

"Of course, we'll call you by the name you were raised with, although it's not the one you were given at christening," Alan added. He ignored Sean's look of warning as he stepped aside to introduce the man who'd been standing quietly to the side of the fireplace, taking it all in.

"Hailey, this is Senator Reese Tyler. He's a business colleague, as well as a longtime family friend."

Reese Tyler had the kind of face you saw on television anchoring the evening news. He was probably about the same age as Alan, and yet there was a youthfulness, almost a boyish charm about him. He had tawny brown skin and pleasant, even features. Laugh lines fanning out from the corners of his brown eyes suggested he was quicker to smile than to frown. Hailey had an instant impression of someone kind and gentle. There was no forced joviality about this man. She liked him on sight.

For a moment, Reese Tyler didn't say anything. He stood staring at her. Then his mouth curved into a warm smile. "Ms. Monroe," he said, stepping forward, extending his hand in welcome. "You must forgive me for staring. It's just that you look so much like…'' She knew he was about to say *your mother* but caught himself.

Hailey's mouth tightened. She hadn't expected people to assume she was Susan. She thought they'd be more like Sean—receptive to the idea, but unsure.

Alan, who had rarely taken his eyes off Hailey, urged her to sit down, and then he took a seat next to her on the sofa. Gloria and Paul had resumed their seats on the sofa across from them. Sean took up a position at the fireplace, leaning a shoulder against the mantel. She was glad for his presence. He made her feel safe and protected.

She glanced at him. She could have sworn she saw a flicker of something that looked like encouragement in his eyes. But it was a fleeting thing, gone so quickly she thought perhaps she had imagined it.

''So, you grew up in Chicago?'' Alan began, pulling her attention to him. What might have seemed an inane or awkward question was made less so by Alan's tone, which was as intent as his gaze.

He asked a number of questions, all geared to put her at ease. But despite his attempt to make her feel welcome, she felt far from it. Actually, she felt as if she'd just stepped into a lion's den.

''ALAN—''

''Don't say it, Sean.''

''I have to say it.'' Sean watched as Alan went to the wet bar tucked neatly into the corner of the room and poured himself a Scotch. He wasn't supposed to drink, but that hardly mattered. ''Somebody has to say it. You shouldn't have invited her here.''

''That's what I told him,'' Gloria said, ''but he won't listen to me. Maybe you can talk some sense into him.''

Sean doubted it, but he had to try. ''There's not a shred of hard evidence to support Jack Monroe's claim that she's Susan. None at all.''

"What do you mean, no evidence? What about the locket?"

Niles had taken Hailey to her room, with Reese going along to carry the luggage. Paul was on the phone with Eric, trying to convince him to come for dinner, so only Sean and Gloria were left with Alan. The older man's features were set in a stubborn expression that was familiar to everyone who knew him.

"Are you sure it's the same locket?" Sean asked. "You could be mistaken. It's been more than twenty years since you saw it. It would be easy enough for a jeweler to make a copy."

Alan shook his head. "It's the one Lara bought for Susan. She gave it to her the day she died. How could I forget something like that?"

"Even if it is authentic, the locket alone doesn't make her Susan."

"But Monroe knew its significance to me. That's why he kept it. That's why he sent the photograph of Hailey wearing it."

"He had stacks of newspaper clippings, not just on the kidnapping, but on you and Lara, as well. Maybe he saw a picture of Susan wearing the locket in one of the articles, read something about it being Lara's last gift to her daughter, realized its significance and had a copy made."

Alan shook his head. "I'd stake my life on it being authentic. And what about that moon rock you gave her?"

"The one I *supposedly* gave her."

Alan frowned. "Supposedly?"

"All right, it's the one I gave Susan," he admitted grudgingly, "but that doesn't make her Susan."

"What does Hailey have to say about all this?" Gloria asked curiously.

"She was vague," Sean replied. "She said she didn't remember where she'd gotten it."

Gloria snorted. "That's awfully convenient."

"For heaven's sake," Alan said impatiently, "she was

just a baby when you gave her that rock. Maybe she honestly doesn't remember you giving it to her."

"Maybe," Sean said. "But if a piece of rock was my only link to my past, I'd damn well remember where it came from. I can take you to the exact spot where I left Susan that day, tell you what she was wearing, what I was wearing—and that was twenty-two years ago."

There was a moment of silence and then Alan said gently, "Sean, you and I both know why you can't forget it, why it's so clear in your mind."

Sean flushed, annoyed at himself for his emotional outburst. It was unlike him to lose control.

"The point is, while Jack Monroe was probably involved up to his neck in the kidnapping, precious little of his claim that Hailey is Susan can be substantiated." Sean stared intensely at Alan. "Frankly, I don't think we should start getting our hopes up."

"She's got the right coloring," Alan said.

Sean shrugged. "So? That doesn't prove anything."

"But she's the spitting imagine of Lara," Alan insisted. "Not just in facial features, but in body type, as well. You know as well as I do that short stature and small frames are dominant traits in the Keegan family."

"And unusual height and large bones are dominant in yours," Sean reminded him evenly. "Genetically speaking, the real Susan is far more likely to be somewhere in the middle. She'd probably be average height and have a medium frame."

Alan frowned at his glass. "But what about her eyes? They're that same slate gray as Lara and Paul's. And gray eyes are rare among African-Americans."

"Yeah, but not unheard of."

Alan's eyes narrowed. "What are the odds of someone claiming to be Susan just happening to have the right eye color? Slight, wouldn't you agree?"

"I don't play odds," Sean quipped. "I'm interested in what I can prove, and I don't have a shred of hard evidence proving that she's Susan. But I have tons suggesting she's Jack Monroe's daughter.''

"His *adopted* daughter," Alan corrected.

"And that brings up another point. The one lead we should have to go on—the adoption papers—just happen to be missing."

"What are you saying?" Alan asked impatiently. "That she wasn't adopted by Monroe and his wife? Seems to me that would strengthen the case for her being Susan."

"Or it means she's Monroe's birth daughter and this talk of adoption was just part of an attempt to bolster his claim that she's Susan."

Alan shook his head. "I know you're only looking out for my best interests, but I believe she's Susan. Everything you've uncovered points in that direction. The locket, the moon rock, the absence of adoption papers," he said, ticking the points off on his fingers.

"No, they point to Monroe being involved in the kidnapping, but not necessarily that she's Susan." Sean issued a frustrated sigh. "Alan, all I'm asking is for you to take it slow. Don't start getting your hopes up. Wait for the results of the blood test."

"Hell, what do I need a test for? It can't tell me anything that I don't already know."

"Alan—"

"It's her, Sean. I know it. I knew it the minute I saw her picture in the *National Banner*. And any doubt I may have had was removed when she walked into this room today. It was like seeing Lara all over again." Alan's eyes were overbright and charged with excitement. He downed his Scotch in a single gulp, grimaced briefly as the liquid fire settled in his belly, then nodded decidedly. "My little girl's come home."

"You can't be sure she's Susan, not this quickly." Sean knew he wasn't making much headway, but he had to continue to try. "At least give it a little time, Alan. Wait for the test results and, in the meantime, talk to her, question her about her life, her background. I don't want you to get hurt again by jumping the gun on this.''

''Please, listen to him,'' Gloria pleaded.

Alan smiled. ''I appreciate your concern, both of you, but I know my own daughter.'' At Sean's grim expression, he issued a weary sigh. ''All right, all right, I'll take things slow, for now.''

Sean sighed in relief. ''That's all I'm asking for, time to conduct a proper investigation of Jack Monroe.''

Alan nodded. ''You got it, but I won't wait forever.''

''Then I'd better try to get you some answers.'' Sean stood. ''If you need me for anything, I'll be at the office.''

''Come for dinner tonight,'' Alan called after him.

Sean hesitated. He knew he should decline. He had a million things to do at the office. There was no reason for him to come back that evening. No reason at all. There was probably a stack of paperwork on his desk, meetings he needed to schedule, no doubt a dozen or more phone messages requiring his attention. Despite all that, he heard himself accept Alan's invitation.

He ignored the little voice in his head that insisted he come because he didn't want to desert Hailey. That was absurd, of course. If anyone needed protecting, it was probably Alan.

''One more thing, Sean,'' Alan said. ''Thanks for bringing my daughter back to me.''

If that's what he'd done, Sean thought, then why did he feel as though he was waiting for the next shoe to drop?

DINNER WAS A DISASTER.

Despite what she'd said to Sean about not having any expectations, Hailey had hoped things would have gone better. Not that anyone was overtly hostile to her, but the strain of pretending to be unaware of the tension that swirled around her proved to be too much.

The moment dinner was over, Hailey excused herself, pleading fatigue and a headache, and left the others in the living room—all except for Reese Tyler, who had left right after dessert so he could attend a fund-raiser for another political candidate. As weary as she was, she was too restless to go to her room. Instead, she slipped out the front door and walked across the porch to lean against one of the six white marble columns. She stood gazing out on the neat front lawn of the Palmer estate. It was truly a magnificent place. The three-story mansion stood on ten acres of prime real estate about thirty miles outside Los Angeles. Woods bounded the estate, giving it a sense of seclusion and privacy.

Normally, she would have been eager to explore the house and grounds, but her mind was too full of thoughts and questions, all centered on the Palmer household. After that awkward moment in the living room, they'd been all smiles and laughter, but beneath the smiles, she'd sensed anger and rage. A lot of it came from Gloria Falcon. She was a bitter, angry woman who deeply resented her lover's only child. And Paul Keegan wasn't much better. While he spoke fondly of his niece, there was an undercurrent in his voice suggesting he, too, felt a degree of animosity toward her. What Hailey didn't know was if it was because they believed she was an imposter or if they were afraid she was the real Susan.

Alan seemed totally oblivious to the tension that surrounded them. His entire being seemed focused solely on her—almost embarrassingly so. His eyes lit up whenever he looked at her, which, to her consternation, he did quite often. It was apparent he'd already made up his mind she was Susan. And that troubled her. She knew Sean hadn't given him any hard evidence on which to form that belief. No doubt it stemmed more from wishful thinking and her apparent resemblance to his late wife.

She felt a twinge of guilt. Before this meeting, Alan Palmer had been just a name, not a person. Now she realized he was a victim like her, maybe even more so. She knew what it was like to lose a loved one, but in the death of her parents, there had also been closure. To never know what had become of a loved one had to be untenable. No wonder Sean was so protective of him.

For the first time, she understood Sean's opposition to her coming here. Alan might be the head of a multimillion-dollar Fortune Five Hundred corporation, but where his daughter was concerned, he was ruled strictly by his emotions.

She didn't know if she was Susan Palmer, but Alan's constant reference to her as his daughter made her feel uncomfortable, as if she were there under false pretense. She didn't want to hurt him. She was going to have to tread carefully, not encourage him in his belief that she was Susan. That, at least, was one thing she and Sean could agree on.

If only Sean wasn't totally convinced her father was the kidnapper called Sarge. It would make working together a whole lot easier. Well, that wasn't entirely true. There was still the problem of her attraction to him. Every time the man came within an inch of her, her pulse went into the danger zone.

The opening of the front door behind her caught Hailey's attention. She glanced over her shoulder and saw the object of her thoughts cross the porch to stand next to her.

"So this is where you escaped to."

"They're a little overwhelming," she said, returning his smile.

"Not quite the Huxtable family, are they?" He leaned against the column, arms folded across his chest, and stared at her.

"No, they're not," she conceded. "I was surprised you came for dinner," she said, for want of something to say.

He shrugged. "It saved me the hassle of cooking or having to pick up something. Besides, I never pass up a home-cooked meal."

Since he didn't seem to have any intention of leaving, Hailey cast about for a safe subject. "Why do Paul and

Gloria feel so threatened by the prospect that I might be Susan?''

One eyebrow rose. ''You picked up on that? Gloria's been in love with Alan for as long as I can remember. After Lara died they grew pretty close. There was even some talk of marriage, but then Susan was kidnapped.''

Hailey nodded. ''And he put his life on hold and hers with it. So she blames Susan for the fact that he's never married her.''

''Probably,'' he agreed. ''Though, in all honesty, I've never quite understood Alan's attraction to Gloria. She couldn't be more different in looks and temperament from Lara. Lara had a kind, sweet nature and was incredibly beautiful. Heads turned when she walked by, and mouths fell open in awe.''

Her mouth curved into a warm smile. ''You sound as if you were half in love with her yourself.''

''I probably was,'' he said, returning her smile. ''I thought she was the most beautiful woman I'd ever seen.'' His voice lowered an octave. ''Until I met you.''

Their eyes locked and held. She found herself caught in a whirlwind as his eyes slowly moved over her face and settled on her lips.

She swallowed, her mouth suddenly dry. ''Lara sounds as if she would be a hard act to follow,'' she managed to say. ''Perhaps having once been married to such a beauty, he didn't want the same thing.''

''Perhaps,'' he agreed. He still stared at her lips.

''Uh, so what's Paul's story?'' she asked, trying to lessen the sexual tension that threatened to engulf them.

He shrugged. ''The age-old one, money. Lara made quite a bit of it as a high-fashion model before she married Alan and retired. In her will, she left everything to Susan, with the proviso that if Susan didn't live to reach age twenty-six, the money was to go to Paul. Since Alan refused to have Susan declared dead, Paul hasn't been able to inherit.''

Hailey frowned. "I thought once a person was missing for seven years, they could be declared legally dead."

"And the operative word is *could*," Sean said. "Alan has the money and political clout to prevent that from happening. Then, just when it looks as if Paul's about to finally get his inheritance, you show up. Susan's twenty-sixth birthday is in two months."

"I see," she said slowly. "And that's why Eric is also angry. He's feels his inheritance is being threatened."

"It's a little more complicated than that," Sean told her. "Over the years, he and Alan have become quite close. Not only has Alan taken him under his wing, he's also given him a vice presidency at Palmer Publishing. Don't get me wrong, he's a hardworking and smart guy. He deserves everything he's gotten. But if it turns out you are Susan, his position with Alan and the company is bound to change. No matter how much Alan cares about Eric, Susan is his heir."

"That has to be very difficult for Eric. To know that no matter how hard you work, in the end, it's not going to matter."

"Sympathy? Eric would hate that, and it's wasted. Alan won't leave him penniless. He just won't get Palmer Publishing and this." His eyes scanned the grounds.

"But he never had it. I mean—"

"I know what you mean." His voice took on a cool edge. "This house, the grounds, the company, everything belongs to Alan, to give or bequeath as he chooses. And if he changes his will leaving everything to you, there isn't a judge in the state who'd set it aside."

Hailey looked at him for a moment before responding. "This is not about money, that's not why I'm here. All I want is the truth—to clear my father's name and try to find out who I am."

He let out a deep sigh. "I'm sorry. That was a cheap shot. I know you're not after Alan's money."

That was something, she thought. "What I don't understand is why you can't give my dad the benefit of the doubt.''

Sean shook his head. ''There are just too many unanswered questions,'' he said. ''Your dad told you that you're adopted, yet neither you nor anyone else can produce the adoption papers. You have a phony birth certificate. He had Susan's locket and a wad of money stashed away in a secret safe-deposit box. Shall I go on?''

''No.'' She turned her gaze to the peaceful scene spread out before them and wished her thoughts were as tranquil. ''I think you've made your position quite clear.''

''I don't want to hurt you, that's not my intent, but I'm going to get to the bottom of this kidnapping. I believe your father was the man that Hanson called Sarge, and I'm going to prove it.''

She held her head high. ''And I'm going to do everything I can to prove you're wrong. When do we get started on this investigation?''

''I'll be in touch.''

He left without another word, striding across the lawn to his car, a shiny red Corvette, parked in the circular driveway. She watched as he stepped into the car and drove out of the yard.

Hailey didn't move for a long time. She couldn't stop thinking about their conversation or, for that matter, Sean. Despite their differences, she liked him. She even hoped they might become friends. She could certainly use one. But the likelihood of his wanting to have anything to do with her outside of this case was probably slim to none.

That thought depressed her as she walked into the house. She didn't understand it. She shouldn't care what he thought. He was the last man she ought to be thinking about, anyway. But telling herself that didn't seem to do any good. Just thinking about him sent waves of excitement through her. It was crazy.

She paused at the living-room door. Voices inside told her the others were still in there. For a moment she considered joining them. Maybe that would help take her mind off Sean and the case. But then she thought better of it. Instead, she decided she'd get a book from the library and head up to bed.

The library was dimly lit. One sofa lamp cast an inadequate glow from a side table, enough to illuminate a section of the room. Hailey felt a bit like an intruder, so she didn't turn on the ceiling lights.

She moved to the bookcase nearest the door and ran a finger along the volumes. Nearly everything seemed to pertain to business and economics. There was a smattering of books on psychology and, surprisingly, true crime. She grimaced. Given the events of the past few weeks, crime was the last thing she wanted to read about. She sighed, then looked down the spines of the next shelf. Again, the titles were all on business and economics. She turned to the psychology offerings. She began thumbing through the books, pausing when she came to the biography of a renowned psychologist who had advanced the theory that obese people were overweight due to having been rejected by their parents in early childhood. "Albert Manning. His drivel will certainly put me to sleep," she muttered.

Out of nowhere, a voice boomed. "Are you disparaging one of my favorite writers?"

Hailey nearly jumped out of her skin. The book she was holding slipped from her fingers to the carpeted floor. As she knelt to pick it up, a light clicked on. She looked up to see Alan sitting in a soft leather chair, a glass of brandy nestled in his hand.

"My dear, I'm so sorry. I didn't mean to startle you." His voice was low and gentle.

"Oh, you didn't startle me," Hailey lied. "I didn't know that you were there. I—I…" She realized her entire vocabulary had deserted her. She swallowed. "I didn't mean to intrude. It's just that I forgot to bring anything to read with me, and so…"

He waved off her words. "You're free to explore the

house and grounds, use the library and other facilities on the property. I want you to feel comfortable here.''

''Thank you. I'm sure I will,'' she said, backing out of the room.

''Don't leave,'' he said, getting up. He flipped on another light. ''Why don't you come in…sit down. We didn't really get a chance to talk before, did we?''

''No, we didn't,'' she began, then stopped when she caught a glimpse of the portrait hanging above the fireplace. Frowning, she took a step into the room. She moved on instinct, drawn in spite of herself to the woman's image on the lacquered canvas.

''She's lovely, isn't she?'' Alan said quietly, then turned her so she faced the picture.

Hailey's gasp of recognition pierced the silence. ''Oh, my God.'' She felt faint, hot, dizzy. The impossible had suddenly become possible.

''I kept telling myself that this was going to turn out to be a mistake,'' Hailey whispered, and the man standing next to her heard her words. ''I didn't know how, but I kept telling myself it would all work. Now, I don't know. I just don't know.''

She turned and looked at him. There had to be an answer to this nightmare, but there was nothing except the look of sadness on Alan's face.

''That's Lara,'' he said gently. ''She was your mother…'' His voice broke. ''I'm sorry. I shouldn't have said that. I'm just a foolish old man.''

Hailey barely heard and only fleetingly registered the longing in his eyes. She didn't know if Lara Palmer was her mother or not, but the one thing she knew for sure was that Lara Palmer was the woman from her dream!

Chapter Six

She sensed the monster's presence. Hovering in the shadows, coming closer. Hailey's eyes darted to the door as she tried to decide if she should make a run for it. Even if she did make it to the door, she couldn't outrun him. He was too fast. She scrunched down, trying to make her tiny body into a little ball. Her breath came in small, desperate gasps. Beads of sweat dotted her brow. She couldn't stay here forever. A part of her wanted to peek around the corner of the sofa, to see if the monster was gone. But she was afraid.

She looked at the lady lying on the floor. She was hurt and needed help. Maybe if she was very quiet, she could slip out of the room. Out of the corner of her eye she saw his hands—huge, monstrous hands—reaching for her. Before she could move, run, he grabbed her and began to drag her across the room. She tried to scream, but the monster clamped his hand over her mouth. She bucked, kicked, tried to get away, but his hold tightened. She refused to give up. She kicked at his leg and heard a groan. She kicked again, but instead of connecting with his leg, the floor disappeared and she was falling. She screamed again and again. "Mommy! Mommy!"

Hailey bolted upright in bed, her screams echoing off the walls of the dark bedroom. Breathing hard, drenched in sweat, she looked around her, confused, disoriented.

Only a dream, she told herself. *Just a dream. Nothing to be scared of.* But it had been so terrifyingly real. She had all but felt the monster's breath on the back of her neck. It—

There were two sharp raps on her bedroom door, then it swung open and Alan stood in the doorway. "Hailey, are you all right?"

He sounded anxious and out of breath, as if he'd been running. She wanted to sink through the floor. This was so embarrassing. "I'm fine," she said with a shaky little laugh. "It was just a bad dream."

He looked at her as if he didn't quite believe her. "Can I get you anything?"

She shook her head. "No, I'm fine. I'm sorry I woke you."

"You didn't. I was reading when I heard you scream." He continued to stand in the doorway, hesitant, as if he wanted to say something more. But he apparently thought better of it, for when he spoke again it was to say, "Well, try to get some sleep. I'll see you in the morning."

"Good night, Alan."

The moment the door closed, she groaned. Of all nights to have that dream. She let out a deep sigh and wrapped her arms around her knees. As much as she tried not to, she couldn't get the dream out of her mind. It had been so intense.

Was it because she'd seen the portrait of Lara Palmer and recognized her as the woman from her dream? Was that what had prompted the nightmare to come with such clarity, such intensity? Or was it because she now knew that Lara was her—

She swallowed the lump that formed in her throat. She was blowing things way out of proportion. Maybe Lara Palmer wasn't the woman in her dream. Maybe she only resembled her. After all, the library had been dimly lit. She'd seen the white dress, and in her tired and emotionally charged state, her mind may have played a trick on her— made her think Lara was the woman from her dream.

She gave herself a mental shake then slid once again beneath the covers. She was attaching too much significance to a dream. That's all it was, a silly dream, nothing more.

But as she lay there staring at the ceiling, she couldn't stop the other thought that crept into her head—the one that had instantly sprung to mind when she'd seen the portrait. She had pushed it to the furthest recesses of her mind, terrified of giving voice to the possibility. She swallowed. Lara Palmer could be her mother.

HAILEY HAD the nightmare again the next night and the next. Perhaps it was the shock of discovering that Lara Palmer was the woman in her dream, or maybe it was the culmination of events of the past few weeks. Whatever the reason, she found the dream was stronger, more intense than before. Details she had never noticed were clearer, more in focus. Monstrous hands she'd always thought of as huge had only appeared that way because they wore gloves. Also a strong, sweet odor had preceded the monster's entrance into the room.

She had been forced to face the fact that there was only one explanation for Lara's presence in her dream. Lara Palmer was her mother. But she was reluctant to tell Sean she believed she was Susan, because she'd have to tell him about her dream. Assuming he believed her, it might cinch things in his mind regarding her dad being Sarge. He might halt the investigation and wait for the results of the blood test. That was the last thing she wanted. Now, more than ever, she needed to know what had happened all those years ago.

It didn't make sense. If she was Susan, why didn't she remember anything? Susan had been almost four when she was kidnapped. A child, yes, but old enough to retain some memories of her early years, and yet she didn't remember anything.

She glanced at Alan, seated in the chair next to her, and

sighed. He'd been trying to jog her memory. They had spent part of yesterday looking at family photos and Susan's beloved toys, but nothing looked familiar. Well, at least one issue would soon be resolved, the issue of her paternity. She and Alan were seated in the waiting room of Genetic Laboratories. They had given blood samples a few minutes ago and were waiting to see Dr. Price, the lab director.

"Mr. Palmer, Dr. Price can see you and Ms. Monroe now," a nurse said. Alan gripped Hailey's hand as they followed the nurse down a corridor to an office. She wasn't sure which one of them was more tense.

Dr. Clifford Price looked up from a chart over half glasses. Hailey had never met Dr. Price but had heard a lot about him from Alan and Sean. A noted author, teacher and lecturer in the field of DNA, he'd testified in hundreds of criminal cases and was highly respected. He was in his late thirties and exuded that comfortably paternal air that people traditionally associate with doctors.

"Please sit down," he said, motioning to the chairs facing his desk.

"I just want to thank you," Alan began, "for agreeing to personally handle the DNA testing. I realize the testing is normally performed by a staff member, but it's important to me that no mistakes are made." He looked at Hailey and smiled. "And no one will ever doubt the results if you perform the test."

Dr. Price blushed, and his head dropped to his chest in a bashful gesture. "I'm flattered that you have such faith in me and my lab. I'll do my best to live up to your vote of confidence."

"I'm sure you will."

Dr. Price cleared his throat. "There is one thing. My work load is pretty heavy right now, so I won't be able to get to it right away, but if you're willing to wait a little longer, I can handle it for you."

Hailey frowned. "How much longer?" She didn't want to drag things out any longer than was absolutely necessary.

He shrugged. "Maybe a week, two at the most, but I'll do what I can to expedite matters."

Alan stood. "Thank you, Dr. Price," he said, extending his hand.

"Anytime." Dr. Price came around from behind his desk and walked them to the door. "I'll call you as soon as the results are ready."

"I'd appreciate that," Alan replied. He took Hailey's arm and led her down the wide corridor and out the door of the clinic. "I don't know about you," he said, "but I'm glad that's over. We'll have the results soon, and everyone will know that you're my daughter. Not that I need any damn test to tell me I'm your father."

Her father? It seemed odd to think of Alan that way. It wasn't that she didn't like him, because she did. He was a kind and generous man, but her father? She was going to need some time to adjust to the idea, she realized, as she followed him to the limousine parked at the curb.

"I hope you're not in too big a hurry to get home," Alan said as he slid into the back seat next to her. "There's something I'd like to show you."

He sounded so mysterious, and there was a strange gleam in his eyes. She looked at him, her curiosity piqued. "I don't have any plans."

"Good," he said, beaming, then slid the glass partition aside and spoke to the driver.

"Where are we going?" she asked.

"Now, it wouldn't be a surprise if I told you, would it?" he asked, looking like the cat that had just swallowed the canary.

Now what was he up to? she wondered.

"DOES IT LOOK FAMILIAR?"

Hailey heard the wistful note in Alan's voice, felt the tension emanating from his body, and her heart went out to him. This was their third stop since leaving Genetic Laboratories. The first had been the Los Angeles Children's Zoo, then a popular fast-food restaurant, now the playground of a park. All places Susan had obviously loved. Alan had no doubt hoped that seeing them would trigger a memory. Just like he had thought seeing family photos and Susan's old toys would. But if she had been here as a child, the memory was buried so deep she'd forgotten. Just like she'd forgotten Lara Palmer, and Sean, and everything else about her former life.

"I'm sorry," she said. "But it doesn't look familiar."

"Look at it again," he prompted. "You loved this place. Your mother used to bring you here all the time."

She could hear the disappointment in his voice, but she couldn't say the words he wanted to hear. For a moment she considered telling him about her dream and her belief that he was her father, but Alan was so vulnerable. He would latch onto her words, and the investigation would be over.

Alan must have noticed her pensive look. He leaned over and patted her hand. "That's all right. It'll come back. We just have to give it a little time."

She nodded, not sure what to say.

"You're probably just tired. We did leave a little early for our trip into the city."

"I am a little tired," she said. "I didn't sleep that well last night."

Alan looked at her, clearly concerned. "I'm sorry. Is there anything I can do to make you more comfortable at the house?"

"I am comfortable," she said, seeking to reassure him. "I had a nightmare, and after I woke up, I couldn't get back to sleep. But the nightmare has nothing to do with you. I've had them since I was a kid."

He looked at her strangely. He opened his mouth to say something, but then must have thought better of it. Instead, he leaned back in his seat and smiled. "We'll have the report soon, and everyone will know that you're my daughter.''

She felt as if she should say something. But what? She had no idea. She plastered a smile on her face. ''Where to now?'' she asked brightly.

''There's a little dress shop on Rodeo Drive. Gloria loves it. I thought we could stop in there and I could buy—''

She shook her head. ''It's kind of you to offer, but I can't let you buy things for me.''

''Why not? I can afford it. Besides, it would give me such pleasure. You're my daughter, and I want to give you all the things you've missed out on.'' He paused, then added, ''I know I can't make up for everything, but I want to do as much as I can. Won't you let me do that?''

''We weren't rich, but I never wanted for anything that I really desired, and I love my job at the art gallery.''

He took one of her hands, absently stroking it with his thumb. ''There's something I've been wondering about. I haven't been able to work up the nerve to ask you about it, but it's driving me crazy. I've got to know.'' He sounded so serious.

''What is it?'' she asked cautiously.

Alan looked at her, his eyes deeply troubled. ''Were they—the Monroes—good to you?''

''Yes, of course, they were. I loved them very much, and they loved me.''

He seemed visibly relieved by her answer. ''I'm glad. You read about adopted kids being abused. I'm glad nothing like that happened to you. I don't think I could live with myself if they'd hurt you. You have no idea how that fear has weighed on my mind over the years.'' He swallowed then looked to the side. ''I know you loved the Monroes, but do you think you have room in your heart for me?''

''Yes, of course, I do,'' she said, blinking back tears. He'd lost so much. Suddenly, she wanted to do something to take away his pain. So she did the only thing she knew would make him happy. She let him take her shopping, and make him happy it did. It didn't take a rocket scientist to know it was his way of showing her how much he cared about her and how much he wanted to be a part of her life.

He dragged her to several designer stores, where she had all she could do to keep his spending in check. As it was, he bought her several outfits that cost more than she made in three months. Then he took her to a trendy little café, where they had lunch. Then they headed to the estate.

She looked at him. He seemed happier, more relaxed than she'd ever seen him.

He must have felt her eyes on him, because he turned and looked at her, grinning. "Did you enjoy your day?"

"Very much," she said, returning his smile.

"I'm glad." He beamed. He took her hand and held it in his. "We've got so much catching up to do. I want you to tell me everything, starting with what you were like as a child, what your favorite foods are, if you like sports." He smiled. "I want to know everything."

Her smile widened. "That's a tall order. I'd rather you tell me about yourself."

He waved off her words. "It's all boring stuff."

She laughed. "I'm sure it's not, but if you don't want to talk about yourself, then tell me about Lara."

A smile touched his lips and his eyes took on a dreamy, faraway look. "Lara was an amazing woman. She was not only beautiful, but smart. You know, she worked at the publishing house after we got married. And kind. She had a heart of gold. Everyone loved her." He spoke in a quiet, almost reverent voice as he told her about their courtship, their life together. It was clear he'd loved her deeply, probably still did. She was so caught up in his story that before she knew it, they were pulling up in front of the Palmer house.

He looked up, surprised. "You shouldn't have let me go on like that."

"I enjoyed it."

And she had. She felt a sense of connection to him and Lara that hadn't been there before. This feeling of companionship continued until they stepped into the living room. Sean was waiting for them. His eyes narrowed as he took in the boxes she carried.

She knew what he was thinking, but she wasn't going to let him make her feel guilty for accepting Alan's gifts. She raised her chin and stared at him, challengingly.

"Sean, I didn't know you were going to stop by," Alan said, unaware of the undercurrent that swirled around them.

"Niles called the office. He said the electronic sensors out by the stable weren't working. With all those reporters camped outside the gate, I thought I'd better take a look at it."

Alan walked to the bar in the corner of the room. "Thanks. I certainly feel better knowing that all the sensors are working. Any idea what caused the malfunction?"

Sean shrugged. "Probably some animal got tangled in the wires. Everything's in working order now."

"I'm going to have a brandy," Alan said, holding a glass up. "Would either of you care to join me?"

Sean and Hailey both declined.

"Actually, I'm glad you stopped by," Alan continued. "There's something I thought you should know."

He threw Hailey a conspiratorial look and grinned. She blinked. She had no idea what he was talking about.

There was a knock on the door, and Eric Keegan stuck his head inside. "Alan, there's an overseas call for you. It's Ambassador Younge."

Alan gave them an apologetic look. "I'm sorry, but I have to take that. I'll just be a minute. Eric, why don't you keep Sean and Hailey company?"

The glint in Eric's gray eyes told her just what he thought of that idea, but when he spoke, his voice didn't betray him. "Sorry, Alan, I've got a courier waiting to take Gleason the figures we worked up on the advertising budget for next year. Then I've got to dash over to the stable to check on that mare you bought." He turned and followed Alan out of the room.

Sean came and dropped on the love seat next to her. Hailey felt suddenly breathless, aware of her erratic pulse as his thigh pressed against hers.

"Any idea what Alan wants to talk to me about?"

"Not a clue." She tried to sound nonchalant, as if she wasn't bothered by how close they sat. "Did you know he was going to ask Dr. Price to personally handle the testing?"

Sean chuckled. "No, but it doesn't surprise me. This test is very important to him. He going to do everything in his power to ensure its accuracy."

She nodded slowly. "Actually, I was a little surprised that a man of Dr. Price's caliber would agree."

"Dr. Price is no fool," Sean said, draping his arm along the back of the love seat. "It doesn't hurt to help someone like Alan. He can be quite generous."

Damn, he was too close. She could feel the potent energy that radiated from his body. "How's the investigation coming?" she asked, trying to focus on something besides her awareness of him.

He cleared his throat. "Actually, that's the other reason I came by. I'd like your permission to review your dad's bank statements and federal tax returns for the last twenty-two years."

"Like hell you will. My father was not involved in the kidnapping, and I'm not going to stand by and watch you railroad him."

Sean's eyes narrowed. "I'm not trying to railroad anyone. If he's innocent, the investigation will clear him."

"What investigation? I've been here three days, and the only thing you've done is schedule the DNA test. It seems to me the only person you're actively pursuing is my dad."

"We're reviewing the evidence," he said somewhat defensively, "and as much as you don't want to admit it, the only concrete suspect we have at this time is your father."

"That's only because you haven't looked for anyone else. In case you haven't noticed, there are several people connected to this household who could bear some checking out—Paul, Gloria and Eric. If you weren't so fixated on my dad, you'd see that."

"I've known these people all my life. They're not involved," he said firmly.

"Shouldn't you be open to other theories?"

"Theories, yes, fantasies, no."

That was too much for Hailey. She told him what he could do with his theory, then stormed out of the room—and barreled into Gloria Falcon. From the guilty expression on her face, it was clear Gloria had been listening at the door.

"Sorry," Gloria mumbled, then scurried down the hallway.

If she hadn't been so angry with Sean, Hailey might have confronted the older woman, but all her anger was leveled at him. She stomped out the front door, down the walkway and across the neatly manicured lawn.

She was sick and tired of Sean's harping. He was like a broken record, she thought as she walked through the grounds of the massive estate. But even more, she was angry with herself for wanting him to see things from her perspective. She shook her head. Why should she care what he thought? She should let him waste his time, investigate her dad to his heart's content. It wouldn't get him anywhere, because her dad was innocent. *Are you sure about that?* an inner voice whispered. If he was innocent, then why had he been in possession of all those newspaper clippings, those forged documents and Susan Palmer's locket? And why had he sent Alan that letter saying she was Susan? That thought brought her up short. There were so many unanswered questions.

And, damn it, she did care what Sean thought. It didn't matter that she wasn't supposed to care. She did care. If only she could talk to him, tell him about her dream.

She sighed deeply and slowed her pace. There was little chance of that happening. It seemed as if she couldn't be around him for any length of time before they were arguing, or she was getting all hot and bothered. At least he didn't know how attracted she was to him. That was one thing to be thankful for, Hailey thought. She sat next to him, flustered as hell, and all he could talk about was the investigation.

Thank God he hadn't noticed. The last thing she needed was for Sean Cassadine to be aware of her as a woman. Things were complicated enough. It would be untenable if her father's chief accuser suddenly made a pass at her. Especially since she wasn't completely sure she'd be able to resist him.

She continued walking, her thoughts in turmoil. She went past the swimming pool, the tennis court, the stables. The trail became narrower, rougher, overgrown with weeds and underbrush. She was coming close to Alan's property line. She was debating whether she ought to head back when she came upon a small lake. The water was clean and clear, and she spent several minutes enjoying her surroundings. The sun was brilliant in the hazy blue sky, beating down on the lake. The scent of water and plant life was strong, and a light breeze stirred the air. It was a day for lying in the sun, for walking in the woods, for sitting and daydreaming. It wasn't a day for thinking about a kidnapping investigation.

But she had no choice. Much as she'd like to sit by the lake and soak up the sun, she couldn't forget why she was here.

She moved away from the water's edge. Brooding was not going to get her anywhere. Action would. If Sean wasn't going to check out Paul and Gloria, then she'd have to do it herself. She would begin first thing in the morning. She'd go to the public library and review the newspaper stories on the kidnapping. The local papers may have handled the story differently. Maybe she'd get lucky and find something Sean and the police had overlooked. She would also question Niles, discreetly, of course. He had been on staff during the time of the kidnapping. He might be a good source of information.

A flash of lightning split the afternoon sky, followed by the sound of thunder. She looked at the sky. The sun had disappeared, and rain clouds were quickly moving in. If she hurried, she could make it to the house before the storm broke. She turned and began to retrace her steps.

Getting out was just what she had needed. It had cleared her mind. She had to call Uncle Frank that evening and tell him about Lara Palmer being the woman in her dream and what she thought that meant. She also wanted to find out how things were coming with the insurance. Better than things here, she hoped. She could use some good news.

Suddenly, she heard a sound. Someone was on the trail behind her. She paused, her eyes searching the area. She didn't see anyone and resumed walking. It was probably some animal seeking shelter. Or one of the numerous individuals who worked on the estate.

Nevertheless, she quickened her pace. She'd only gone a few steps when the sound came again. She whirled around, her eyes once again scanning the thick underbrush on either side of the trail.

"Is anyone there?" Hailey called. There was no answer. She was totally alone. It was then that she realized how far she had come. She was at least a mile from the house. Totally at the mercy of anyone lurking in the woods. There was a flash of lightning, and she jumped, then wrapped her arms around her middle. She hated storms.

She moved down the road, her gaze searching for movement, something out of place. Aside from the occasional flash of lightning and the rumbling thunder that followed, the area was motionless and still. Imagination could be a wicked thing, and as far as Hailey was concerned, hers was working overtime. Couple that with another sleepless night, and it all added up to a bad case of the jitters. Well, no more. She was taking control. No longer would she sit around waiting for Sean to broaden his investigation.

She was so lost in thought she wasn't watching where she was going. Her foot slid out from under her, sending her flying. She caught herself only by the grace of God and the four-board fence that lined that stretch of trail. A split second later, a gunshot shattered the silence and something struck the fence inches from her head. She ducked, heart pounding, as another shot was fired.

My God, she thought, someone was out there. Someone with a gun. And they were shooting at her!

Chapter Seven

Hailey lay very still for a precious long moment, scarcely breathing. Someone had taken a shot at her—had missed because she'd stumbled. Was that person still there? Her eyes searched the area, but she didn't see anyone.

She slowly began to rise. Immediately another shot rang out, the bullet striking a rock inches from her head. She ducked. Her heart hammered against her chest wall as though pounding to get out. Two more bullets hit the ground near where she lay, spitting dirt into her eyes.

Then, abruptly, the shooting stopped. In the distance, she heard a faint crunching sound, like that of leaves and twigs being broken.

Footsteps! Someone was coming! Was it the person shooting at her? Coming to finish the job? She had no idea who was there, and she wasn't about to hang around to find out. Her eyes darted around the area. There were several large boulders and woods lining either side of the trail, but no real hiding place. She couldn't stay in the open. She'd be a sitting duck.

Crunch! Crack!

The sound was louder. The footsteps were getting closer. She looked again at the cluster of trees and underbrush along both sides of the trail. She could take a chance and stay on the trail or she could hide in the woods where there was less likelihood of being spotted. It was probably the last place her pursuer would expect her to go. She grimaced. She certainly didn't relish the thought of going in there. What if she got lost? Or met some wild animal? No, she wouldn't think about that. If she stayed near the edge of the woods, keeping the trail in sight, she'd probably be all right. She hesitated, wishing she were wearing jeans and sneakers instead of a linen skirt and low-heeled shoes. Well, there was nothing that could be done about that. She drew a ragged breath, then made a beeline for a cluster of trees.

She was immediately engulfed by foliage. She moved slowly through the woods, brushing aside overhanging branches and underbrush all the while trying to keep the trail in sight. She'd only gone a few feet when she heard someone on the trail. She was far enough from her stalker to be unseen, and she had the advantage of being small, so the trees and tall weeds hid her small frame, but she dropped to her knees anyway.

The sound of big feet clumping across hard, dry earth reverberated, deafening her. She stopped breathing. Then she heard nothing but the sound of her heart hammering in her ears. It was quiet except for the sounds of the woods. Maybe he was gone. She crawled to the edge of the trail. Gingerly, she moved the underbrush aside and peeked through the tiny opening she'd made. What she saw made her heart stop.

A man stood on the trail, his back to her. He wore jeans and a green army jacket. He was holding an automatic weapon. From her hiding place, she could only see him from his legs to his rib cage, but she could tell from his movements that he was searching for her. As if her thoughts had brought about her worst fear, he began to move in her direction. She held her breath. He moved closer. Any moment, he was going to find her. Her heart was beating so loudly, she was surprised he didn't hear it. A few inches from where she lay, he paused. He must have decided she wasn't in the woods on this side of the trail, because he turned and headed for the woods on the opposite side. But when he didn't find her, he'd be back.

She had to get out of there. Crouching, Hailey moved quickly from one tree to the next, staying as close to the edge of the woods as she dared. She was aware of stinging sensations along her arms and legs, scratches she'd gotten when she dived to the ground. The sharp edges of rocks and weeds sent new pangs of pain through her hands, arms and legs as she pushed aside tree limbs in her flight.

She didn't slow down until she'd put a reasonable distance between herself and her pursuer. When she thought it was safe, she crept to the edge of the clearing. She pushed back an overhanging branch and peeped out. The man was nowhere in sight. Now was her chance. She ran out of the woods and onto the trail. She didn't look back, just kept running for what seemed like miles. Her lungs screamed for air. Every part of her body ached. But she didn't stop, certain that at any moment her pursuer would catch up to her. She looked over her shoulder, but she didn't see anything. She was so busy looking that she didn't see the man coming down the trail until she plowed into him.

She turned to run, but steel fingers grabbed her arm and held her. She began to flail wildly, instinctively, swinging her free arm, catching the man with a fist.

"Hey!" Strong arms whipped around her. "It's me."

"Sean?" She stared at him. She'd never been so happy to see anyone in her life. She threw her arms around his neck.

"Take it easy," he murmured, pulling her against him. She took a convulsive breath, leaned into him and felt his strong arms encircle her waist. "It's all right, baby," he whispered against her ear. "It's all right." Sean's deep baritone washed over her like soothing water.

She took another deep breath, almost a sob, and he started rubbing her shoulders and back, murmuring to her, soft meaningless words meant to calm and reassure. His touch felt good. He made her feel safe and protected, and she wanted nothing more than for him to hold her forever.

"You want to tell me what happened?" he asked. "Did something frighten you?"

"Not something, someone," she said, looking quickly over her shoulder. "Someone was shooting at me."

She felt him stiffen, instantly alert, on guard. "What do you mean someone was shooting at you?"

"Just what I said. Someone took several shots at me," she explained.

Sean's eyes anxiously searched her face. "You okay?"

"I'm fine," she said, looking over her shoulder again. "I think whoever it was is gone, but let's get out of here anyway."

She began to move, but Sean stood stock-still. His eyes scanned the area. "Where did this happen?"

"It was farther back," she answered, gesturing. "Near that little lake."

His gaze flicked in the direction she pointed, then he took her arm and began to move quickly down the trail. "After I drop you off at the house, I'll check it out." He glanced over his shoulder then at her. "It was probably a hunter. Alan should have warned you. His property is adjacent to some public land that's used by quail hunters. Occasionally, some hunter strays off the public lands onto Alan's. Though this is the first time I've ever heard of anyone actually being shot at."

She looked at him, clearly skeptical. "That was no stray bullet. He fired at me at least three times. Whoever was out there was aiming at me." Her eyes widened as a thought suddenly hit her. "Was Eric at the house when you left?"

"No, I think he left right after you—" He stopped abruptly and stared at her. "Now wait a minute. Don't start jumping to conclusions. Eric may be a little hotheaded, but he wouldn't hurt a fly."

"You said yourself he was threatened by my presence here."

"But not enough to try to harm you. Hell, he doesn't even believe you're Susan. The only person who does is Alan."

"And that's all that counts, isn't it? Gloria, Paul and Eric want me gone. They've made no bones about it."

"Look, I've known these people all my life. They may not want you here, and they may even make your stay uncomfortable, but they certainly wouldn't do anything to harm you."

"What about participate in a kidnapping?"

"Give it a rest." He tried to take her arm, but she shook him off.

"Oh, so it's okay to investigate my father, call him a kidnapper, but when things seem to point to one of your friends, you disregard the evidence."

He planted his hands on his hips and glared at her. "I'm not disregarding anything. Eric couldn't have been involved in the kidnapping. He was fifteen and away at boarding school. Paul and Gloria were thoroughly checked out by the police. There was no evidence suggesting they had anything to do with the kidnapping."

"So Eric is in the clear, but Gloria and Paul could certainly bear a second look." Sean didn't say anything, and that infuriated her. "Okay, if you won't check them out, fine, I'll do it myself." She started to walk away.

"Like hell, you will." He grabbed her arm. "I want you to promise me that you won't do any investigating on your own."

"I'll do no such thing." She tried to pull away, but his hold only tightened.

"Listen, Hailey, you have to promise me that you won't—" His voice broke, and he pulled her against him. "Oh, God," he groaned. "When I think of someone shooting at you…what could have happened…."

She stared at him, about to tell him to let her go, but at the look in his eyes, the words stuck in her throat. Then she was totally incapable of thought as his mouth covered hers in a mind-shattering kiss. The sweetness of it sent warm currents of pleasure through her.

One part of her mind yelled out a warning to call a halt before it was too late. But the other part, the part that was in control, trembled with anticipation. She'd been fascinated with this man since the moment they met. She knew it was foolhardy to think about him in any way other than the other half of the investigation team, knew it was dangerous to get involved with him, but she couldn't stop. Just once, she wanted to see if her fantasies matched the reality.

His mouth moved slowly, sensually over hers, more deeply and hungrily by the second, until the erotic pleasure of it made her strain against him. She moaned, returning his kiss with an ardor that shocked her. In response, his mouth became demanding, intoxicating. She felt her breasts swell, and their sensitive peaks tightened as she burned with desire. She couldn't get enough of the feel and the taste of him. He deepened the kiss.

Fire leaped through her veins and engulfed her as if she were dry tinder. Never had she felt such instant desire, such immediate passion. The investigation, her father, the angry words that had passed between them moments before were forgotten. All that mattered was the man who held her so tightly in his arms.

The kiss went on and on. Hotter, hungrier by the minute.

This is sheer madness, she told herself. She'd never lost control like this. It took all her willpower to draw her mouth away from his and step out of his arms. Lips still tingling from his touch, she looked at him. He seemed as shaken as she felt.

She stared at the ground, appalled by her behavior. Her cheeks burned with embarrassment.

"I—I'm sorry," he said. "I shouldn't have done that."

She couldn't look at him. "Er, that's okay."

"It's not okay," he whispered. "But, God, I've wanted to do that ever since I first laid eyes on you."

She looked at his face. She swallowed at the desire she

read in his eyes. It was crazy, wildly inappropriate for her to fall into the arms of the man who suspected her father of being a kidnapper. That he wanted her just as badly didn't make it any better.

"But you're right," he said. "We can't do this. Not because I don't want to. Lord, it's not that. It's just that it would complicate matters for both of us."

She struggled to find her voice. "I know."

"Maybe when this is all over…" His voice trailed off.

"You think we'll still be speaking to each other?" she asked teasingly, trying to lighten the sexually charged situation.

"We can only hope," he said, following her lead. "Come on. We'd better head back before Alan decides to send out a search party."

They walked in silence for a while, but it was a comfortable silence.

"What brought you out here?" she asked.

"I was looking for you. You were gone such a long time, I got worried and thought I'd better see what was keeping you. It's a good thing I did."

She glanced away, not sure what to say. But a warm glow began to spread throughout her body at the knowledge that he had been worried about her.

"Mac Warren, my chief investigator, is reviewing the case files of everyone connected to Denny Hanson and Ryan Vanover. I suppose it wouldn't hurt to have him review Paul's and Gloria's as well."

She couldn't stop the surge of happiness that coursed through her. It wasn't exactly the face-to-face interview she'd like, but it was a beginning. "That's great," she said, "but why can't we do it?"

"We're going to have our hands full tomorrow. Maybe for the next few days."

She glanced at him. "We are?"

"Yeah. We're going to San Quentin to pay a visit to

Denny Hanson. I don't know about you, but I've got a lot of questions for him.''

Maybe she was reading too much into his apparent about-face, but suddenly she wanted to tell him about her dream.

''What would you say if I told you I've come to believe that I'm Susan Palmer?'' she asked, choosing her words carefully.

His glanced at her and nodded. ''I'd say it's a reasonable conclusion that can be drawn from what we've found thus far. What made you change your mind?''

She laughed nervously. ''You'll probably think I'm just being silly, but I've been having this dream—''

''Yeah, Alan told me.'' At her look of confusion, he explained, ''Susan suffered from nightmares.''

''She did?''

''Yeah, they started right after her mother died. The psychiatrist said she was dreaming about the night her mother drowned.''

Hailey frowned. ''I don't understand.''

''Susan was with her mother when she drowned. Lara was getting ready for bed when she slipped on some water on the bathroom floor. They had a huge sunken bathtub. She hit her head on the side of the tub when she fell in. The police surmised that Susan fell in trying to save her mother.''

Hailey went still as she pondered his words. The pristine white room could be a bathroom. The floor disappearing beneath her feet could have been her falling into the sunken tub. And the monster could have been her fear of the situation.

''Susan was traumatized by what happened,'' Sean said. ''She was in a catatonic state for quite awhile, but she gradually came out of it. However, the memory of what she saw was fixed in her mind and came out in the form of a nightmare.''

Hailey thought about that. "So the dream is actually a recollection of what happened that night."

"More or less. The doctor said it was her way of coping with what she saw. She couldn't face it consciously, so it came out in the form of a dream."

Hailey's head was spinning. If she'd witnessed her mother's death, no wonder she couldn't remember anything. Seeing something like that would be traumatic for anyone.

"I'm curious about something," Sean said, breaking into her thoughts.

"What's that?" she asked.

"If you believe you're Susan, how can you still maintain your dad is innocent?

SEAN GLANCED briefly at Hailey, who was sitting in the passenger seat next to him. She hadn't spoken more than a dozen sentences since he'd picked her up that morning. She had said absolutely nothing to him during the hour flight to San Quentin and only a few words at the rental car agency. She was still angry at him for questioning her dad's innocence.

Well, what the hell was he supposed to think? He had a mountain of evidence pointing to her father, and the more they dug, the worse things looked for him. Take her nightmare, for instance. Didn't she realize it was another piece in the puzzle? The closer they came to proving she was Susan, the stronger the case for her father being the third kidnapper.

If he'd been presented with this evidence in any other case, he'd halt the investigation and wait for the DNA results. But this was not a typical case. He had to go forward with the investigation. So many lives had been affected by Susan's kidnapping. It was time to lay aside the ghosts of the past, and only a complete and impartial investigation would do that.

And then there was yesterday's shooting incident, which

unnerved him. After he had dropped Hailey at the estate, he'd gone and checked out the area. He had found a bullet in the wooden fence where she'd said the shooting had occurred, two empty shell casings and signs of a person on the trail behind her. He had been studying the footprints when it had started to rain, washing away the prints and anything else related to the shooter.

He'd tried to tell himself the shooting incident didn't mean anything, but just in case, he was going to keep a close eye on Hailey. He glanced at her. Things would be a lot easier all around if he wasn't so damn attracted to her. She had him so tied up in knots, he didn't know if he was coming or going. He was losing his objectivity. He shook his head. Hell, he'd lost it. If he had any doubt about that, all he had to do was remember his behavior the day before.

He groaned. He couldn't believe he'd kissed her like that. Afterward, he hadn't known what to say or do, so he'd taken refuge in changing the subject, acting like the kiss had never occurred, talking about the investigation. Hailey seemed to be working hard to do the same.

If he was smart, he'd let Mac handle things. But he couldn't bring himself to do it. This case had consumed far too much of his life to bail out now. But including Hailey in the investigation had been a mistake. He couldn't work around her, at least not with the single-minded dedication and efficiency he expected from himself. And this constant harping at each other certainly didn't help matters.

Sean glanced at Hailey again. "For the sake of the investigation," he said, choosing his words carefully, "I think we should declare a truce. You have my word I'll try to be open and more receptive to your suggestions regarding the investigation. And, in return, I want you to stop jumping down my throat every time I mention your dad."

She gave him a sideways glance, then nodded.

He hadn't realized he'd been holding his breath until then. "I also want to apologize for my behavior yesterday. I shouldn't have said what I did about your dad. I'm sorry."

"You don't have to apologize. Your question was a legitimate one. It's just so hard for me to believe Dad could have had anything to do with the kidnapping."

"I understand," he said softly. "I know you've been concerned about my investigating your dad, but you shouldn't be. This is going to be a fair and impartial investigation. I plan to follow up on every lead. If your dad is innocent, this investigation will clear him."

She looked at him. "That's all I've ever wanted, to know that you're following up on every lead."

He took her hand in his and held it tight. "Regardless of the outcome of this investigation, I want you to know I'm here for you."

"Thanks," she said shyly, and looked to the side. She didn't pull her hand away.

Suddenly, he felt good, real good. Like he'd just won the lottery.

A couple of minutes later, the prison came into view. It was surrounded by a fence at least twelve feet high and crowned with thick strands of barbed wire. In each corner of the grounds was a tower with a glass-enclosed guard station at the top, manned with armed guards. Directly ahead was the entrance to the prison, with the words California Federal Penitentiary on the arch above it.

A big burly female in uniform stepped from the guardhouse under the arch and stared through the window at them. Sean lowered the window and smiled.

"Mornin'," she said. She had a gun on her hip and a clipboard in her hand. Another guard watched from inside the guardhouse. "What can we do for you folks?"

"We're here to see a prisoner," Sean said smoothly, very much aware of Hailey sitting next to him. She'd tensed up the moment they'd stopped. Prisons had that effect on most people.

"Your names?" she said, studying the clipboard.

"Sean Cassadine and Hailey Monroe."

The guard's lips moved almost imperceptibly as she

looked for their names. Finding them, she made a check-mark. "And the prisoner?"

"Denny Hanson. We have permission from his lawyer to talk to him," he added.

The guard wrote something on the clipboard, then reached inside the car and placed a card on the dashboard. "Take a left at the building directly ahead," she said, pointing, "then wind around to the back of that redbrick building. The visitor's center is inside."

Sean thanked her, then gently pressed down on the ac-celerator. He followed her instructions and parked in front of an aging brick building. Inside, they were met by a prison guard who again asked their names and instructed them to sign in. Then they were led to separate rooms, where they were frisked and had their personal effects searched. Satisfied they weren't carrying any contraband, a guard led them down a narrow corridor. Someone some-where must have pushed a button or pulled a lever, because there was a humming noise and the first of two sets of iron bars slid open. They walked about fifteen feet down a nar-row corridor, then stopped as the first set of bars closed behind them. When the first set locked into place, the sec-ond one rolled back, and a short, stocky guard with arms as big as Sean's legs began to amble down the corridor toward them. He had a hard-looking belly and a thick neck, and he wore a bored, jaded look that was common among people in law enforcement. A look that seemed to say he'd seen and heard it all.

"Follow me, please," he said. He led them through an-other gated door into a small room. The room was probably thirty feet long and twelve feet wide, with a concrete floor, bright fluorescent lighting and an aging ceiling fan. The room was divided down the middle by a partition made of brick for the first three feet, then a small counter that pro-vided lawyers with a place to set their legal pads and take notes, then thick, bulletproof glass ran from the counter to the ceiling. In the center of the glass was a metal plate approximately four inches by ten in diameter, filled with tiny holes. Through it they would speak to Denny Hanson.

"I'm gonna lock this door," the guard said as they stepped inside. "When you're ready to leave, just press the buzzer." He pointed to a small button on the wall next to the light switch. "Hanson will be out in a minute."

"Give him this." Sean handed him his business card.

The guard nodded. "Sure thing." A moment later the door slammed, and they were alone.

"When you see prisons on television or in the movies, they don't look quite so cold or intimidating," Hailey said, looking about the gray, windowless room. "This place really gives me the creeps."

"I know," he said, pulling out a chair for her to sit in, then taking the chair next to hers. "That was one of the things I hated about being a criminal lawyer, visiting my clients in prison, especially the ones whom I thought were innocent."

She shuddered. "I can't imagine being innocent and being locked up in a place like—"

A door bolt clicked, and Hailey stiffened next to him. He gave her a reassuring smile before turning his attention to the door on the other side of the partition. It opened slowly, and a young white guard stepped into the inmates' side. Behind him, in a bright orange jumpsuit, hands cuffed in front of him, feet shackled, was Denny Hanson. He glowered around the room until his eyes focused on Sean and Hailey. A second guard entered and pulled at Hanson's elbow, leading him to a spot directly across from them.

The guard pulled out a chair and the first guard sat him in it. He placed Sean's business card on the counter. Hanson stared at them as the guards made their noisy departure. The door slammed, and the dead bolt clicked.

Sean pointed to the card on the counter. "My name is Sean Cassadine, and this is Hailey Monroe."

Hanson picked up the card and examined it front and back. Sean watched his every move. Hanson's fingers were wrinkled and stained brown from nicotine. His face was long, thin and pasty white, as if he didn't get much sun. His hair was long, gray and oily and slicked back severely from his face. Deep furrows crisscrossed his forehead and cheeks, and layers of tiny wrinkles dotted the corners of his eyes. He looked nothing like the man in the videos and newspaper clippings from the 1977 trial. He'd been young then—in the prime of his life. Now he was an old man. Prison had done that to him, made him old before his time. The only resemblance to the man he'd once been was the piercing blue eyes that lifted themselves from the card and stared coolly at them. "Are you a pair of do-gooders? Come to save my soul?" he asked in a slightly mocking tone.

"Afraid not," Sean said, returning the stare.

"Then what do you want?" he asked as he set the card aside. His words were soft, slow, delivered with the patience of a man who'd spent almost half his life behind bars.

"We'd like to talk to you about the Palmer kidnapping."

He looked at Sean and Hailey with decidedly more interest. "You must be the guy my lawyer told me was coming to see me," he said. "I understand you work for Alan Palmer."

Sean nodded. "That's right. I'm a security consultant for Mr. Palmer."

Hanson reached into the pocket of his jumpsuit and removed a crumpled pack of cigarettes and a book of matches. He lit a cigarette and exhaled toward the ceiling. "You wasted your time. There's nothing to talk about. I killed the kid and Ryan, case closed."

Sean stared at him, frowning. "You admit you killed Susan Palmer?"

Hanson smirked. "The jury said I did. The appeals court said the jury was right. That's all that matters, isn't it?"

Sean hesitated as he tried to decide how much to tell him. "We recently came upon information that suggests there may have been a third man involved in the kidnapping." A flicker of interest appeared in Hanson's blue eyes. "We're looking into that aspect of the case. If we're successful in proving that there was another person involved in the kidnapping, it may be grounds for a new trial for you."

"And what do you get out of it? A book deal? A movie of the week?" Hanson's voice was harsh and cynical. He held the cigarette between the index and middle finger of his right hand and casually flipped ashes onto the floor.

"We don't have any ulterior motives, Mr. Hanson," Hailey answered. "We only want the truth."

He smiled without humor. "Yours or mine?"

"There's only one," Hailey told him.

When Hanson remained silent, Sean added, "You've always maintained that you didn't kill Ryan Vanover and Susan Palmer. We're giving you the chance to prove it. I'd have thought you'd want to take it."

"What do you know about me?" Hanson snapped.

"I know everything there is to know about you. I've read every page of the transcript of your trial and subsequent appeals. I've gone over the police reports and exhibits more times than I care to remember. There's nothing I don't know about you or this case. I also know you've already spent twenty-two years in here. The question is, do you want to die here?"

Hanson didn't say anything. He lit another cigarette and stared at something on the counter. He gently rubbed his right temple with his right thumb, the cigarette just inches from his hair. For a long time the only sound was the gurgling of the overworked ceiling fan. The silence was awkward and stretched for long moments.

Sean stood. "Come on," he said, taking Hailey's arm. "We're wasting our time here."

"Wait!" Hanson called. "What do you want to know?"

Sean stared at him for a moment, then sat. "I want to know everything there is to know about the kidnapping,

Ryan Vanover and the third guy, Sarge. Don't leave anything out.''

Hanson began slowly, but as he got into his narrative he spoke with deep passion. The story he told was identical to what he'd told the authorities—that he'd participated in the kidnapping but not in the murder of Vanover or Susan.

Now that Sean had the big picture, he wanted the fine print. "Tell me about Vanover. How did you meet him?''

"We met at a bar about a year before the kidnapping. We started hanging out together.''

"Why don't you tell it like it was? You were helping him fence stolen goods.''

Hanson glanced quickly over his shoulder. "How did you find out about that?'' he whispered. "I never said anything to the cops, and it didn't come up during the trial.''

"There was a notation in the police report. Apparently, several of your neighbors reported seeing all kinds of unsavory-looking people going to and from your house at all times of the day and night. It doesn't take a rocket scientist to know what that kind of traffic means—you and Vanover were either dealing drugs or fencing stolen goods. I didn't know which. You just told me.''

Sudden anger lit Hanson's eyes. "Why, you bastard—''

"Let's get back to the kidnapping," Sean said, cutting off what was no doubt going to be an angry tirade. "How did the subject come up?''

For a moment, he thought the other man wasn't going to answer.

"I'd lost my job a couple of months before," Hanson said. "Money was pretty tight, even with fencing. One night we were sitting around drinking, just shooting the breeze." He shrugged. "I made some comment about being desperate enough to stick up a bank. Ryan said he knew how we could get our hands on a lot of money, and that's when he mentioned snatching the kid. I thought he was kidding." He shook his head. "But the more he talked, I realized he was serious. At first I refused, but he made it sound so easy. We'd snatch the kid, collect the ransom money. No one was to get hurt."

"But someone did get hurt, didn't they?" Hailey asked quietly.

Hanson's head snapped up. "I told you, I didn't kill Ryan or that kid."

"Okay," Sean said impatiently. "Tell us about the day of the kidnapping."

"Everything went just like we'd planned. I waited in the car outside the gates of the estate while Ryan got the kid. When I saw them coming, I taped the ransom note to the gate, then we drove to my place."

"The three of you?" Sean asked.

"Yeah, that was the original plan. The kid was to stay with me. Ryan left, then came back a couple of hours later, real agitated. He told me there'd been a change in plans, that he was going to park the kid elsewhere. That's when he told me about Sarge."

Sean's eyes narrowed. "That was the first time he mentioned Sarge?"

Hanson's head bobbed. "That's right. Until then I thought it was just the two of us." He took a drag on his cigarette. "It really unnerved me. I didn't like the idea that Ryan had withheld the fact that another person was involved."

"What did he tell you about Sarge?"

Hanson shook his head. "Nothing."

"And you didn't question that?" Sean did nothing to hide his skepticism.

"Hell, yes, I questioned it, but Ryan said the less I knew the better off I'd be, and I guess deep down I didn't want to know." Hanson rubbed his temple. "I was getting a bad feeling about things."

"How do you know this man even existed?" Hailey asked, picking up the questioning. "That it wasn't just a ploy to enable Vanover to get the lion's share of the ransom money?"

"Because it all made sense," Hanson said, planting his arms on the counter and leaning forward. "Ryan wasn't the smartest guy in the world. Don't get me wrong," he added quickly, "he wasn't stupid, but he wasn't—what's the word? Analytical. Someone else planned that kidnapping, was calling the shots. And that someone was Sarge."

"Did you ask him where Sarge was keeping Susan?"

"Sure I did, but all he would say was that she was in good hands, that he'd left her with a friend. Some friend." Hanson snorted. "He killed Ryan and that little girl, then framed me."

"Were those his exact words?" Hailey asked. Her eyes gleamed with interest. "He'd left her with a friend?"

Hanson smoked and contemplated the question for a moment. "As near as I recall."

"How did Vanover sound when he talked about Sarge?" Hailey asked.

"How did he sound?" Hanson closed his eyes and thought. "I don't know. Like I said, Ryan didn't really say that much about him, but I did get the impression Sarge was someone he trusted. Someone he'd known awhile, maybe from his past."

"Why do you think that?"

Hanson shrugged. "I don't know. I just remember thinking that."

"Did Vanover ever refer to him as anything besides Sarge?" Sean asked.

Hanson shook his head. "Not that I recall, but it wasn't like he talked about him all the time, either."

"Do you think Sarge could have been a nickname for someone he met in the service?"

Hanson shrugged again. "I don't know. It could have been."

"Did he ever mention the name Jack Monroe?" Sean noticed Hailey flinch at the sound of her father's name, and he cautioned her with a look.

Hanson shook his head. "No."

"Okay, let's get back to the kidnapping."

"The next day I left the second ransom note and prepared for the drop, which was to occur the following evening. The plan was for me to lead the cops off our tail while Ryan recovered the ransom money, which Palmer was to place in a small canvas bag. I thought things went off without a hitch, but Ryan claimed that when he got back to the estate, there had been a problem with transferring the money from the canvas bag to his. The long and short of it was, he only gave me forty thousand dollars that night. He said I'd get the rest the next day. That was the last time I saw him alive."

"So you're saying it was Sarge who killed Vanover and framed you for the murder." Sean did nothing to hide his skepticism.

"That's what I'm saying," Hanson retorted. "I don't know how he pulled it off. But Sarge killed Ryan and stuffed his body in the trunk of my car for the cops to find. He probably killed that little girl, too."

"Then how did Susan's blood get on your living-room carpet? And what about the blood on Susan's sweater?"

Hanson averted his gaze, then mumbled, "Uh, I guess it could have gotten there when the kid fell." He shifted uncomfortably under Hailey's scrutiny. "Uh, the kid had a little accident right after we got to my place. She fell, and I jerked her up. She wiped her mouth on the sleeve. She must have cut her lip or something."

Sean thought about that. "Was she wearing the sweater when Ryan took her to Sarge?"

Hanson shook his head. "No, Ryan made her take it off, and he took it with him that first time. He said the sweater would come in handy, that he was going to use it as proof that we really had the kid."

But that's not what he'd done, Sean recalled. Susan's sweater hadn't been found until several weeks after the kidnapping, lending credence to the belief that she was dead.

Sean looked at Hailey, then back to Hanson. "I'm going

to show you a photograph. I want you to look at it carefully, then tell me if you've ever seen this man before." He reached into the inside breast pocket of his sport jacket and took out a three-by-five black-and-white snapshot of Jack Monroe. He placed it against the glass.

Hanson studied the photograph for several minutes, then shook his head. "Nah, I've never seen him before."

Sean would have been surprised if Hanson said yes, but he had to ask, though from the stormy look Hailey threw him, he didn't think she agreed with him on that score.

"Is there anything else you can tell us about Vanover or the kidnapping?"

Hanson lit another cigarette, took a long drag then sat back in his chair, thinking. "I've been locked up here for a long time," he said. "I've had nothing but time to think. Ryan was an attractive guy, and like a lot of men, he didn't have many male friends. As far as I know, I was—well, Sarge and I were his only male friends. But female friends...he had a ton of them. If I were you, I'd look into that angle."

"Any specific lady?"

Hanson shrugged offhandedly. "Look close to home."

Sean's eyes narrowed. "Are you suggesting he was involved with someone in Alan Palmer's circle of friends?"

Hanson shrugged again. "He was pretty tight with someone in the Palmer household. Whether she was part of the household staff or one of Palmer's family members or friends, I don't know." He leaned forward, his expression intense. "But I do know this. When Ryan snatched the kid, he wasn't gone long, just a couple of minutes. It was like he knew exactly where she would be and just went in to get her. I didn't give it much thought at the time, but now I wonder if it wasn't because someone in there helped him. Maybe that someone is Sarge."

Chapter Eight

"Well?" Hailey drummed her fingers on the arm of her chair and glared across the mahogany desk at Sean. After returning from San Quentin, they had gone to Sean's office.

"Well, what?" he asked.

"Are you or are you not going to check out Hanson's claim?"

Sean pursed his lips and stared at her. "I'm not sure if I believe him."

Neither did she, but this was the first solid lead that pointed to someone other than her dad being Sarge, and she wanted to check it out, no matter how speculative it might be.

"The police looked into the question of whether someone connected to Alan could have been involved in the kidnapping. They checked out the entire household staff, family members and a number of Alan's closest friends and ruled out the possibility."

"They also ruled out the possibility of there being a third man involved in the kidnapping," she countered. "We now know that was probably not the case."

"People talk. We would have heard about a relationship between Vanover and one of Alan's friends or someone on staff. Something like that doesn't remain a secret for long."

She shook her head. "It would if they were extremely discreet. If the woman was one of Alan's friends, she wouldn't have wanted it known that she was involved with a chauffeur. And if it was someone on staff, they may have been concerned about Alan's reaction to that kind of frat-ernization among his employees.''

''Let's stick with the facts. Motive, for instance. Assum-ing this supposed relationship existed, why did she cover for him?''

''For love. Money. And she did more than cover for him. She helped him kidnap a child. That's enough to keep any-one's lips sealed.''

''True, but the problem is there's not a shred of evidence that suggests Sarge is female. This is the first time Hanson has even made that claim.''

She issued a deep sigh. ''Look, I understand your reluc-tance to accept Hanson's claim, but it does make sense.'' At Sean's look of skepticism, she added hurriedly, ''Just listen for a minute. Alan keeps that place tighter than Fort Knox, and yet, by all accounts, Vanover was able to take Susan out of there undetected in a matter of a minutes. Haven't you ever wondered how he was able to do that?''

''It's no great mystery. He worked there almost a year. He was familiar with the house, the grounds and the security. He knew everyone's routine, and he was in a position to manipulate their schedule to his advantage.''

''That's possible,'' she conceded, ''but it's also possible that he was able to slip in and out undetected because he had inside help.'' She sighed again. ''Sean, what harm would it do to at least look into Hanson's claim?''

He shrugged his broad shoulders. ''None. I just think that if there was another person involved, it was more likely a man than a woman.'' He leaned forward. ''Everything points that way—the nickname Sarge, not to mention the fact that it took a strong person to stuff Vanover's body into the trunk of Hanson's car. Vanover was over six feet and weighed about a hundred and seventy pounds. And let's look at the crime itself. He was shot at close range. A bullet in the head and two in the chest." He shook his head. "That's not a woman's style."

"Says who?" she challenged. "A woman is just as capable of committing a heinous crime as any man. You said you were interested in conducting a fair and impartial investigation, that you were going to follow the evidence no matter where it led. Or did you mean only if it led to my father?" The moment the words were out she wished she could take them back.

He recoiled as if she'd struck him. "You know me better than that," he said quietly.

"I'm sorry. I shouldn't have said that."

"Hailey, I know how much you want to clear your dad," he said softly. "I'm just not sure how much credence we should give to Hanson's claim. But, if it'll put your mind at rest, we'll look into it."

Before she could stop herself, she was out of her chair and had thrown her arms around his neck.

Sean's arms went around her waist, pulling her close. "Hey, if I'd known I was going to get this kind of reaction, I'd have agreed in a New York minute."

Her cheeks burned with embarrassment as she stepped out of his arms. "I'm sure it won't take that long," she said, searching for something to say. "We only have to check out the women in Alan's inner circle and those on staff. And I think you have most, if not all, of that information right here in your files."

"Yeah." He grinned. "I've got it. Give me a minute."

She watched as he stood, walked across the room and opened a door leading to a small storage area. It was lined with file cabinets. Her eyes roamed over him as he moved about the room. Broad-shouldered and slim-hipped, his body was that of an athlete, with the lithe grace that was born of ingrained self-assurance and confidence. He was wearing a blue denim work shirt and jeans that fit snugly in the back, molding his long, muscular thighs and tight buttocks in what she found to be a thoroughly unnerving way. She felt her cheeks grow warm and forced herself to look away.

A moment later he turned, a huge stack of folders in his arms. He laid the bulk of them on the conference table where she was standing. A smaller pile he placed on the floor.

"Where do you want to begin?" Sean asked, turning slowly to face her.

"Why don't we start with the background reports on Alan's female friends," she said, shaking off her fantasies.

Even splitting the files, it took several hours to go through the folders. The police investigation had been extremely thorough. They'd interviewed everyone who had been at the estate during the month leading up to the kidnapping—not just friends, but delivery and repair people, as well. She hated to admit it, but it didn't look as if any of the women could have been involved with Ryan Vanover.

"Well, that was helpful." Sean gave her an I-told-you-so look.

"Let's not throw in the towel just yet. We still have the files on the household staff to go through," she said, pointing to the folders on the floor. She knelt to pick them up.

"Here, I'll get them." He crouched next to her, and they reached for the folders at the same time, his fingers lightly brushing against hers.

A jolt of electricity shot through her, curling her toes. She jerked her hand away. From the dazed expression in his eyes, she knew he'd felt it, too.

"I've got them," he said, picking up the folders and straightening.

She also stood, but that was just as bad. He was close, too close. She could feel the warmth of his body reaching out to her.

"There's only about a half dozen files to go through, so why don't we do these together," he suggested.

She watched as he took a photo from each folder and laid it on the table in front of them. Then he placed each file beneath its picture.

Pointing with his finger from one photograph to the next, he said, "We have the cook, Rose Yaeger, the nanny, Lacy Anderson, the housekeeper, Mildred Weiner, and the maids, Jennifer Lloyd and Victoria Nelson." She was surprised by the next picture. It was of a young Gloria Falcon. "Gloria isn't technically part of the household staff," he said, "but since we're looking into women connected to Alan, for the sake of discussion, we'll include her with this group."

She studied the pictures. "We can eliminate the cook and Jennifer Lloyd." She pointed to photographs of two elderly women. "From what Hanson said, Ryan sounds like a guy who was into looks. I can't see him involved with either of them. They're both too old."

Sean nodded. "And they also had airtight alibis. We can also eliminate the housekeeper, Mildred Weiner." He pointed to a stern-looking woman in her mid-forties. "She'd been taken ill earlier that morning and had to be rushed to the hospital."

Hailey frowned. "Didn't anyone question that? Talk to the admitting physician to make sure she was really ill?"

"They did," he replied, digging through the file. "I think I have a copy of that interview. Yeah, here it is." He spent several minutes skimming a document, then looked at her. "According to the admitting physician, she was hospitalized complaining of severe abdominal pain that was later diagnosed as food poisoning. She was questioned extensively, but was eliminated as a suspect."

Hailey thought about that for a moment then asked, "Did anyone else get ill?"

"There's no indication of that in the police report, and I don't remember anyone else being sick."

"And no one thought that was odd?"

"Sure they did, but they weren't able to attribute her illness to Ryan or the kidnapping."

Hailey issued a frustrated sigh. It had seemed like a good lead, but it was just another dead end. Her disappointment must have shown in her face, because Sean leaned over and gave her shoulder a little squeeze. She looked at him and wished she hadn't. His gaze was as soft as a caress.

She flushed. No man had ever ruffled her composure to such an extent. Every time he looked at her, she felt a rush of heat. *This has got to stop,* she told herself. She was a mature woman, not some sex-crazed teenager. Besides which, she needed to focus on the task at hand.

She looked at Sean. His dark head was bent as he studied the pictures. He pointed to Gloria's photograph. "She's a maybe, but she wouldn't have been pretty enough for Vanover. Besides, it was clear to anyone with eyes she was in love with Alan."

"Who would have been pretty enough for him?"

He pointed to a small, raven-haired beauty. "That's Victoria Nelson, but she wouldn't have given him the time of day. She was very religious. She left not long after the kidnapping to do missionary work. And as far as I know, that's what she's still doing."

"What about her?" Hailey asked, pointing to a tall, slender blonde.

Sean cleared his throat. "Ah, that's Lacy Anderson. She was Susan's nanny."

Hailey picked up Lacy's file and read it. "According to the statement she gave the police, she left Susan with you in order to make a phone call."

Sean nodded. "She was trying to reach her boyfriend to confirm weekend plans."

"Did the police check out her story?"

"Initially she refused to disclose the man's name. She said she didn't want to embarrass his wife and kids."

She looked at him incredulously. "And they let her get away with that?"

"I remember Alan was livid. By the time he was able to convince her to disclose the guy's name and they'd taken his statement, the police were onto Ryan."

"Do you have a copy of the statement he gave the police?"

He threw her a warm smile. "Sure, I'll get it."

It took several minutes for her to get her raging emotions under control. By then, he'd returned from the storage room. He handed her a thin folder labeled Matt Gilbert.

Hailey quickly skimmed the report, then glanced at him in surprise. "She couldn't have been on the phone with him that day. It says here he claimed the affair ended two months earlier."

"Let me see that," Sean said. She watched as he quickly read Gilbert's statement. "Damn it, how could I have overlooked something like that?"

"You didn't overlook anything. The police did. Maybe there's nothing here."

"Maybe," he answered, his expression grim, "but I don't like loose ends. I'll have Mac see if he can locate her. I have some questions for her, starting with why she lied to the police."

"I only have one," Hailey said. "I want to know why she left a three-year-old child in the care of a nine-year-old."

IT HAD TAKEN several days, but Mac had finally located Lacy Anderson. After she left Alan's, she had gone to work for the Los Angeles school system as an elementary school-teacher and was now retired.

Sean had called and asked if he could meet with her. He'd gleaned from their brief conversation that she traveled a great deal and that she lived in an upscale area known as Panther Creek, about twenty-five miles west of Los Angeles. The houses and condos were advertised to appeal to the rich, and Sean guessed that most people who lived there were quite well-to-do. He knew he was right when he arrived in her neighborhood and saw BMWs and Mercedes parked in the driveways.

Lacy Anderson's condo was midway around a cul-de-sac, well back from the curving street. He judged the two-story colonial structure to be priced in the $400,000 to $600,000 range. He was surprised she could afford such an expensive place on a teacher's pension.

His next surprise came when he came face-to-face with Lacy Anderson. It had been more than two decades since he'd seen Susan's old nanny. She'd been in her mid to late thirties then, which would make her close to sixty. But a deeply tanned, much younger-looking woman came to the door. Lacy Anderson looked like someone in an ad for a health and fitness club, one of those women who smiled as she did step aerobics. There wasn't a strand of gray in her strawberry blond hair, and her eyes, a deep, clear blue, were as sharp as ever. But when Lacy Anderson extended her hand, it was bony, wrinkled and dotted with brown age spots, confirming his earlier guess of her age.

"Sean, it's so good to see you." Her tanned face crinkled into a welcoming smile. "How have you been?"

"Fine, thanks," he said, returning her smile. "Lacy, this is Hailey Monroe. We're glad you could see us on such short notice, but, like I told you on the phone, we're looking into the Palmer kidnapping."

She gave Hailey a curious glance, then said, "You're the girl that was in that *National Banner* article, the one claiming to be Susan."

"If you read the story, then you know we're trying to determine if Ms. Monroe is Susan. Can we come in?"

Lacy nodded. "Yes, of course." She led them into a tastefully and very expensively decorated living room. Several watercolors hung on the walls, and a number of valuable antiques were strategically placed about the room. A set of Gucci luggage stood near the door. "Please forgive the mess. I just got back from Cancun," she said, waving them toward the sofa. She planted herself on a chair across from them.

Sean wondered again how a teacher's pension paid enough for her to travel and live this well. He looked at Hailey and knew she was wondering the same thing.

"I'm a little surprised to hear you're taking Ms. Monroe's claim seriously." She looked at Hailey. "No offense, but I thought it had been pretty well established that Susan was dead.''

"Well, that's what we'd always thought," Sean said, "but it looks as if we may have been wrong. Like I said, we're looking into the kidnapping. Specifically, the possibility that there was a third person involved."

Lacy frowned. "A third person? But the police discounted that theory."

"Yes, they did, but we now have information that suggests another person may have been involved."

"That's incredible. Do you have any idea who it might be?"

"I really can't go into that with you." He was being deliberately evasive. "I'm sure you understand."

"Yes, yes. Of course."

"Let's start with a few basics. How long did you work with Ryan Vanover?"

"I didn't exactly work with him. I began taking care of Susan when she was two years old. Ryan was hired the following year. So I guess about a year."

"Had you known him before then?"

She shook her head. "No, we'd never met."

"How well did you know Vanover?"

Lacy shrugged offhandedly. "We were just casual acquaintances. We spoke—hello, goodbye. That was about it."

"What about other household members? Do you know if he was close to anyone?"

"He was friendly with everyone, but close?" She shook her head. "I don't think so."

"Do you recall hearing any gossip about Ryan and any of Alan's female friends?"

She looked at him, surprised. "No, I never heard anything like that."

"What about any of the women on staff?"

She shook her head. "No, he wasn't involved with anyone on staff, but there were plenty of women in his life. They were constantly calling him, making a nuisance of themselves.''

''Do you remember if there was a particular woman who called him often?''

''No, I don't. Ryan liked women and women liked him,'' she said with a trace of bitterness. ''But he wasn't serious about anyone.''

Now how would she know something like that? Sean wondered, but aloud, he asked, ''Did you observe any changes or notice anything unusual about him in the months leading up to the kidnapping?''

She leaned forward, clasped her hands together and looked at them for several long moments. ''Ryan had money problems. Serious ones, although at the time I didn't realize it. Ryan wasn't the kind of person you ever worried about. He was so confident, self-assured,'' she explained. ''But he didn't have a clue about managing money. He was in one financial bind after another, but he always seemed to land on his feet. I thought that last time wasn't any different.''

For someone who claimed not to have known Vanover very well, Lacy seemed to know an awful lot about his personal life. ''How did you know he had money problems?'' Sean asked.

She looked at him and blinked, as if for the first time realizing she may have said too much.

''Ah…I remember taking several calls from irate creditors,'' she said quickly. ''Besides, it wasn't a secret. We all knew Ryan lived way above his means. He spent a small fortune on clothes, partying and fancy vacations. He also had dreams of being a rock star. He was always saying that with his looks, he could make it, if he could just get the money to cut a demo record. But I would never have guessed he'd resort to kidnapping to get the money for it.'' Her hand flew to her mouth. It seemed she hadn't meant to say that, or had she?

Lacy cleared her throat. ''I guess living on the estate in

such close proximity, we were all much more involved in each other lives than we realized.''

That was one possible explanation for her amazing amount of information about Vanover, or it could be she'd known him a lot better than she was willing to admit.

"Let's go to the day of the kidnapping," he said smoothly. "Did you see Vanover at all that day?"

"Did I see him?"

Sean's eyes narrowed. It was a simple enough question. He wondered why she was so uncomfortable with it.

Lacy thought for a moment, then shook her head. "No, I'm sure I didn't."

"Was that unusual?"

"Not really. We often went days without seeing each other."

That wasn't possible, he thought. The servants' quarters weren't that large. There was no way for their paths not to have crossed at least once during the course of the day. So why was she trying to downplay that fact?

"I'd like to go back to the nature of your relationship with Vanover."

"We di-didn't have a relationship," Lacy stammered. She clasped and unclasped her hands in her lap. "We just worked together."

"Did he ever ask you out?"

"I—I don't remember. It was a long time ago. But if he had, I wouldn't have gone. I was seeing someone."

"That's right, a guy named Matt Gilbert. You told the police you were on the phone with him when the kidnapping occurred."

Lacy nodded. "Matt and I were going away for the weekend, and I called him to confirm our plans."

Sean shook his head. "Gilbert told the police the two of you didn't talk that day. He said he hadn't talked to you since your breakup two months before the kidnapping. Why don't you just admit it, Lacy? The man you were seeing was Ryan Vanover."

Lacy paled visibly at his words. "That's nonsense!"

"Not according to Denny Hanson. He said you and Ryan were quite chummy." That's not what Hanson had said, of course, but she didn't need to know that.

"Who are you going to believe, a convicted murderer or me?" She licked her lips, her eyes darting from Sean to Hailey. When she realized they weren't buying it, her eyes hardened. "All right, all right. We dated a few times, so what?"

Sean shook his head. "It was more than a few dates. You were having an affair."

"No! You're wrong."

"You helped him kidnap Susan." It was a statement, not a question.

She opened her mouth to deny the allegation, but before she could say anything, Sean added, "I want to remind you, more than a kidnapping occurred twenty years ago. A murder was also committed. If you were involved in any way in that kidnapping, you're just as guilty as Denny Hanson, and you can still be tried for murder. Why don't you do yourself a favor by telling the truth?"

Sean felt Hailey's hand on his knee. She leaned forward and asked softly, "Were you involved with Ryan?"

"Yes, I was involved with him." Lacy laughed, a bitter sound. "God, I thought I was in love with him."

"Did you know he was planning to kidnap Susan?"

"N-no, of course not. I was just as surprised as everyone else."

"But you helped him."

She shook her head. "No! I didn't know what he was planning. He asked me to meet him at the gazebo that day at two o'clock sharp. I'd arranged for Mrs. Weiner to watch Susan, but she was ill, and Victoria refused. There was no one around. I was desperate—"

"So you asked a nine-year-old child to watch Susan." Hailey finished her sentence for her.

Lacy nodded, her expression bleak. "I hadn't planned to

be gone that long, but Ryan didn't come. I waited and waited."

"What was so important that you had to leave Susan with another child?" Hailey asked.

Lacy dropped her head. "I thought Ryan was going to ask me to marry him," she whispered.

"Why didn't you tell all of this to the police?"

Her head snapped up. "Because I didn't think he was involved. Then later, when it came out that he was one of the kidnappers, I kept quiet because I didn't want people to know how he'd set me up, played me for a fool."

Sean shook his head. "I think you didn't say anything because it would have implicated you in a kidnapping and murder."

"That's not true! I adored Susan. I would never have done anything to hurt her."

"That's a very touching little speech, but it doesn't square with the facts. You lied to the police. You withheld information that was relevant to the kidnapping. It seems to me you did everything you could to impede the investigation."

"Not deliberately." Her eyes darted from Sean to Hailey. "I—I wasn't thinking."

Sean looked at her coldly. "On the contrary, I think you were doing a lot of thinking—then and now." He glanced leisurely about the room. "You've done well for yourself, haven't you? I can't help but wonder how you can afford such an expensive life-style on a teacher's pension. Maybe you had some help...say the two hundred thousand from the ransom payment?"

Lacy clasped and unclasped her hands. "It's not what you're thinking. This is all mine. I worked hard for it."

"I don't doubt it," he said coldly, "but not by teaching."

"I don't have to prove anything to you," she challenged.

"You're right. You don't have to prove one damn thing to me. Now the police...that's a different matter."

She licked her lips. "Hey, we don't have to bring the police into this, do we?"

He gave her a measured look. "That depends on what you have to say."

She hesitated. "I knew Ryan and Hanson were fencing stolen goods. After Ryan's body was discovered, I—I went to the storage locker where he kept the merchandise and...and I took it." She gave him a defensive look. "Hey, it wasn't going to do him any good."

So much for true love, Sean thought wryly.

"What else was I going to do? Alan gave me two weeks' notice and three months' severance pay," she said, her voice laced with bitterness. "I'd taken care of Susan for almost two years, and that's the thanks I got. Who was going to hire me?" Lacy wailed. "The child I'd been hired to take care of had been kidnapped. My career as a nanny was over. So I took the merchandise, but I didn't waste my time on the nickel-and-dime stuff Ryan handled. I went for big-ticket items, like art and precious stones, and I'm good at it."

Sean shook his head. "That's an interesting tale, but I think that's all it is."

Her eyes flew to Sean's. "I swear it's the truth."

"Prove it." His voice was cold, and sharp like a whip.

"How am I supposed to do that?" she snapped. "I don't file tax returns on that portion of my income. If you're looking for someone who had a motive for kidnapping Susan, I suggest you talk to Paul Keegan. He was desperate for money. His business was on the verge of financial ruin."

That was the first he'd heard of it. He exchanged a look with Hailey. "Just how did you come by that information?"

"A couple of weeks before Susan was taken, I overheard Paul and Alan arguing. It was hard not to hear them. You know how quick-tempered Alan can be. Well, anyway, Paul must have hit him up for another loan, because I heard Alan say that he wasn't going to bail him out of every financial bind he got himself in the way Lara had. That it was time for Paul to take responsibility for himself and his actions. Paul said he needed money and he needed it fast, that if he didn't have the money in sixty days, he was going to lose everything.''

"You think he arranged the kidnapping and the murder of Vanover to get it?''

Lacy cocked her head and gave him a quizzical look. "He's still in business, isn't he?''

NOT ONLY WAS Paul Keegan still in business, but from the looks of his Brentwood estate and the Bentley parked in the driveway, business had flourished. But at the expense of his niece's life? Sean seemed doubtful of Lacy Anderson's claim, but Hailey wasn't so sure. Paul struck her as a man who loved the good life. And he had been on the verge of financial ruin. He had probably been desperate for money. Desperate enough to arrange for the kidnapping of his niece?

It was possible. That might explain why she had not been killed. It was one thing to arrange for a kidnapping. It was something else to go through with the murder of his own niece.

Hailey glanced about the sunlit room the butler had led them into. She walked to the desk and picked up a silver-framed photo. It showed a smiling Paul, Eric and Alan at Eric's college graduation. Paul had his arm draped around Alan's shoulders. Hailey couldn't help but wonder if Paul felt as kindly toward his brother-in-law as the pose implied. She was sure Alan felt that way, but did Paul truly return the sentiment? Well, that was the sixty-four-thousand-dollar question. Or maybe she should say the two-hundred-thousand-dollar question.

"Just one happy little family," Sean observed.

"Perhaps," Hailey agreed. "But looks can be deceiving."

There was a whisper of noise behind them, and they whirled. Eric Keegan stood in the doorway watching them, tense, alert. Like the first time she'd seen him, he was dressed in tight jeans and a polo shirt. And, once again, his handsome face was scrunched into a scowl. Didn't he ever smile? she wondered.

"I heard you tell Grady you wanted to see Dad."

"We'd like to talk to him about the kidnapping," Sean said.

"That's right," Eric drawled, moving into the room. "You're looking for the elusive Sarge."

"You don't sound as if you believe he exists."

"I don't, and I'm surprised you do."

"It wouldn't be in your best interest if it turns out that he did," Hailey said.

Eric shrugged offhandedly. "I'm not worried, but you ought to be. Oh, I know Alan is convinced you're his precious Susan, but don't sell him short. He's no fool, and neither am I."

Hailey's eyes narrowed. "You don't like me, do you?"

"No, I don't," Eric growled. "And I'm not going to pretend otherwise. You may have bamboozled Alan and Sean, but you don't fool me. I know a gold digger when I see one."

Hailey's eyebrows rose. "Is that a fact?"

"Yes, it is," he said smugly. "You're not the first gold digger I've dealt with."

Hailey's eyebrows rose a fraction higher. "Dealt with? That's an interesting choice of words. Just how do you plan to deal with me? Shoot me?"

Eric looked taken aback, but he recovered quickly. "Alan told me about your *claim* that someone took a shot at you," he said with a sneer. "Trust me, if I'd shot at you, I wouldn't have missed."

Sean stiffened next to her. "I've taken as much as I'm going to from you," he said coldly. "Apologize to Hailey. Now!"

Eric took a step back as Sean moved on him. Hailey grabbed Sean's arm. "Don't. He's not worth it."

Eric threw Hailey a cold look. "Like I said, I'm not worried. You can't keep this act up forever. You're going to slip up, and I'm going to be around when that happens."

"Maybe I am the real Susan Palmer," Hailey suggested.

Eric rolled his eyes. "Oh, please! You're no more Susan than the last one who was here. It's the money, plain and simple, that you're after."

"That's enough!" a voice boomed. Three pairs of eyes swiveled in the direction of the sound.

Paul Keegan stood in the doorway.

Eric stood stock-still, wringing his hands. "Dad, let me explain—"

"I think you've said enough," he interrupted, spearing his son with a cold look. "Maybe you ought to go for a swim to cool off."

"Dad, listen—"

"We'll talk later." There was steel in the older man's voice. Hailey watched as Eric Keegan slunk out of the room.

"I must apologize for my son's behavior," he said, taking a nearby chair. "He's my only child. Naturally he's very protective—"

"Of you? Or his inheritance?" she challenged.

Paul's mouth curved into a slight smile. "Probably both. Alan's treated Eric more like a son than a nephew. Taken him under his wing, even made him one of his VPs at Palmer Publishing. Naturally, Eric would be concerned about his standing with Alan and the company should it be proven that you really are Susan. But Eric loves Alan, and he's only interested in his happiness. He'll come around."

"And what about you?" Sean asked, picking up the questioning. "What are you interested in?"

"Why, I'm interested in what's best for Alan," Paul answered smoothly. "And if that means we go through this farce of a third man, then, by all means, ask your questions."

"I see," Sean said somewhat vaguely. "You know, you're to be commended. A lot of people in your position might not feel so kindly toward Alan."

Paul's eyes narrowed. "Just what are you getting at?"

"Alan stood in the way of your inheriting Lara's estate."

"It was understandable. If you were a parent, you'd see why I couldn't hold that against him."

Hailey didn't agree, but schooled her features so as not to betray her thoughts. "So it didn't bother you that Alan was holding onto what had to be a large sum of money at the same time your business was in trouble?"

That brought a frown to Paul's face. "What do you mean?" he asked.

"It's our understanding that around the time Susan was kidnapped, you were experiencing some financial difficulties. You asked Alan for help, and he refused."

Paul pulled out a cigar, clipped the end with a cigar cutter, then lit it. "Ah, there's nothing like a fine Cuban cigar," he said, leaning back in his chair. He took a drag then said, "Alan thought I should stand on my own."

"And that angered you, didn't it?" Hailey asked.

"Of course," Paul answered smoothly, "but he was right." He took another drag on his cigar. "I was thirty-nine going on twelve," he explained. "I'm not proud of it, but it took a long time for me to grow up. Alan's refusal to help me was the best thing he could have done. He made me stand on my own two feet for the first time in my life. You can't put a price tag on something like that."

Hailey couldn't help but wonder if he was being entirely candid. "I understand that," she said slowly, "but wasn't that the wrong time for him to exercise tough love? When your business was on the verge of going under?"

He shook his head. "I assure you that was not the situation. While it's true I was experiencing some financial difficulties, it was just a minor setback. Nothing serious. My company was not on the verge of going under, as you put it."

"Lacy Anderson says otherwise," Sean told him.

"She's a lying bitch!" Paul erupted.

Hailey blinked, surprised at his outburst. "So it wasn't true?"

"Of course not!"

Hailey and Sean exchanged looks. Could Lacy Anderson have been mistaken about what she'd overheard? Maybe

Paul's financial situation hadn't been as bad as it sounded. But that still didn't answer the question of where he'd gotten the money to save his business. There was no delicate way to ask, so she just came right out with it. "So where did you get the money to bail out your company?"

"I'm not obliged to answer that question," Paul told her coldly.

"No, you're not," Sean answered. "But it does make one wonder, especially when you consider that two hundred thousand dollars of the ransom money was never recovered."

Paul shrugged. "Frankly, I think Denny Hanson probably has it stashed somewhere." When she and Sean didn't say anything, he looked at them coldly, then said, "All right, if you must know, Gloria loaned me the money."

Now that was interesting, Hailey thought.

"Uh, there was a time when we were close," Paul stammered. "I was going through a divorce from my first wife, and Alan and Lara had just gotten married. The affair didn't last long, just a couple of weeks, but we remained friends. So when I had financial problems, I approached her, and she loaned me the money."

Paul and Gloria, lovers? Hailey just couldn't see it. For that matter, how could Gloria have gotten her hands on the kind of money he'd probably needed to bail out his company?

Paul cleared his throat. "I would prefer you not mention any of this to Alan. It was a long time ago."

In other words, Hailey thought, Alan didn't know.

Paul took a drag on his cigar, then looked at her. "You know, I don't believe you're Susan, or for that matter that your father had anything to do with the kidnapping. But I do believe he was trying to extort money from Alan."

"That's interesting," Hailey said. "Do you have any other observations for us?"

"Actually," Paul said slowly, "I do. Not that I have any evidence to support it, you understand. I think Susan is dead, killed by Denny Hanson and Ryan Vanover. But if I was going to look for a third man, I'd looked at Reese Tyler.''

"Reese!" Sean frowned.

Hailey was just as surprised as Sean. "Why Senator Tyler?'' she asked.

"Because if anyone had a reason to hate Alan, it was Reese. Sean, you don't remember this because you were just a baby when it happened, but Reese dated Lara before Alan. Actually, I thought they were pretty serious, but no woman wants to be second best in her man's life, especially a woman like Lara. She decided Reese's first love was politics, dumped him and began dating Alan. Reese didn't take it too well. He even made some threats.''

Sean frowned. "What are you suggesting? That Reese had Susan kidnapped to get back at Alan for marrying Lara?''

Paul leaned back in his chair. "I realize it sounds a little farfetched, but you have to understand the fierce rivalry that has existed between those two men. It goes back to their college days. In many ways, it's probably one of the reasons each is so successful today. But to your initial question, that marriage caused quite a rift in their friendship.''

"If Reese was that angry," Sean challenged, "that bent on revenge, why did he wait years to extract it? Hell, Lara had been dead for months when the kidnapping occurred.''

Paul gave him a sour look. "Reese and Alan only patched things up about six months before Lara died. So you see, Reese wasn't in a position to take his revenge until then.''

Hailey frowned as Paul continued speaking. She couldn't put her finger on it, but something wasn't right. He said all the right things, but... Then it hit her. They'd started off talking about Paul's financial situation, but somehow he'd managed to shift the conversation to Reese Tyler. He seemed to relish the thought that Reese could be the third man in the kidnapping. Was it because he believed the senator was capable of committing such a heinous act, or was it to distract attention from himself?

SEAN STARED out the seventh-floor window of the Palmer Building, one of the most prestigious office buildings in the city. In the heart of L.A.'s business district, it housed Palmer Publishing, a host of other notable businesses and Reese Tyler's suite of offices. It was common knowledge that Reese could only afford such a high-rent area because Alan was cutting him some slack, which seemed to undercut Paul's claim of hostility between the two men. Or did it?

He heard about things today that he would never have thought Reese, Paul, even Alan, for that matter, were capable of doing. Things that suggested none of them were quite who they seemed. Things that, indeed, suggested further investigation. But none of what they'd learned overcame the mountain of evidence they had against Jack Monroe. Although he doubted if Hailey saw it that way. From the way she'd reacted to each new revelation, she thought they were on the road to exonerating her dad. Maybe they were, but at this point all they had were some interesting anecdotes and no hard evidence.

As far as Reese extracting revenge against Alan in such a horrible way, he had found it hard to pose the question to him.

Reese reacted the way Sean thought he would. He blew up. Sean turned from the window and looked at him. Reese was known for being calm and cool under pressure, but at the moment, he looked loaded for bear.

"I know you have to ask questions," he said as he paced back and forth, "but I don't appreciate having my personal life dissected."

Sean massaged the back of his neck. "Reese, you know we're not asking these questions out of morbid curiosity, but as part of the investigation. If Jack Monroe didn't kidnap Susan, then someone else did, someone who is, most likely, intimately connected to Alan."

"It certainly wasn't me."

"We're not suggesting it was," Hailey said in a placating voice.

Reese looked at Hailey, and his face softened. "Thank you, my dear, I appreciate that." He drew in a deep breath, then dropped into a chair across from her. "But, I have to admit, a lot of what Paul told you is true. Lara and I dated, and she dumped me for Alan. It's also true that I threatened them, but they were words spoken in anger. I didn't mean it."

Hailey frowned. "Paul thought you did."

"Well, Paul thinks a lot of things are true that aren't."

Sean looked at him sharply. "Care to elaborate?"

Reese's mouth curved into a humorless smile. "Paul believes that he was the target of my supposed anger. Shortly after Alan and Lara got married, I was elected to the city council. I voted against a piece of legislation that would have benefited Paul financially. He stood to make a bundle. I voted against the bill because I truly believed it wasn't in the city's best interest, but Paul took it personally. He accused me of doing it just to spite him." Reese sighed. "Over the years, we've learned to tolerate each other, but there's no real friendship between us."

Hailey looked at him curiously. "Did Paul have anything to do with Lara's breakup with you?"

"I don't know," Reese answered. "Back then I was a young, struggling lawyer in the throes of my first political campaign. On the other hand, Alan was already on the road to becoming a multimillionaire." He shrugged. "Paul may have encouraged her to see him."

Sean nodded. No doubt a wealthy brother-in-law would have been a welcome addition to the family.

"But," Reese added, "Lara was her own person. I don't think she did anything that she didn't want to do." He looked at Hailey, and his mouth curved into a warm smile. "She was very much like you, my dear—very beautiful."

Sean sat up straighter. Was he flirting with her?

"Were you in love with her?" Hailey asked, returning Reese's smile.

"Very much, and I thought she was in love with me.

That's why I was taken completely by surprise when she dumped me for Alan. Maybe if they had waited, not rushed into marriage, I could have accepted it. But they were married less than two months after we broke up.''

''That must have been horrible for you.'' Hailey leaned over and placed her hand on his. Reese smiled.

The muscle in Sean's jaw tightened. He didn't like the idea of Reese, or any man, touching her. ''What about the threats?'' he asked, bringing the conversation to the matter at hand.

''I was young, and when you're young, you say and do foolish things. I didn't mean it. The three of us put it behind us. The only person who even remembers that silly comment is Paul. I bet Alan doesn't.'' He continued talking about his friendship with Alan.

Sean studied Reese as he talked. He made it all sound so innocent, but it couldn't have been, or it wouldn't have taken more than three years for him to patch up his differences with Alan and Lara.

HAILEY COULDN'T believe it. Yesterday, her father had been the lone suspect in the Palmer kidnapping. Today they had three more people who could be considered suspects. And as far as she was concerned, they were much stronger suspects than her dad. Hailey looked at Sean as he talked on the phone. Having been out of the office for most of the day, he had phone calls that needed to be returned. She tapped her foot impatiently. She couldn't wait to hear his take on what they'd found.

A few minutes later, he lowered the receiver into the cradle and stared across the desk at her. ''Mac's checking out Lacy's claim, but I think she was telling the truth about the money and Ryan using her. I don't think she had anything to do with the kidnapping.''

''Neither do I.'' Hailey leaned back in her chair. ''What do you make of Paul's claim that he and Gloria were lovers and that she loaned him the money to save his business? Do you believe him?''

Sean nodded slowly. "The lovers part, yes, but none of the rest of it. If Gloria loaned Paul money, it wasn't because they were lovers.''

"Blackmail?''

"I wouldn't be surprised at all.''

"But what could he have on her?''

"Beats me. She never struck me as the type to have skeletons in her closet, but after what I've learned today, I guess anything is possible. Anyway, we'd better find out what Paul is holding over her, as well as how she got her hands on such a large sum of money.''

Hailey gave him a thoughtful look. "And why do you think Paul told us that story about Reese?''

Sean shrugged. "Obviously, he's still carrying a grudge.''

"That's for sure. It seemed to me he was doing his best to embarrass Reese.''

Sean pursed his lips, thinking. "Yeah, he did that, all right, but Reese wasn't being entirely candid, either.''

"What do you mean?''

"I think he was trying to downplay the seriousness of the rift in his friendship with Alan. Frankly, I think he was just as angry as Paul said he was.''

"Perhaps,'' she said. "But I don't think he had anything to do with the kidnapping. I think we can eliminate him as a suspect.''

Sean shook his head. "I think removing him is a bit premature.''

"If we can remove Lacy from the list of suspects, why not Reese?''

"That's different, and if you hadn't been so busy letting him charm you, you'd see that.''

"What?'' She looked at him, surprised.

"You heard what I said.''

"Heard it, yes. But I don't believe—'' She smiled. "You're jealous.''

"Why would I be jealous of Reese?" he asked gruffly. "I'm simply pointing out that he had a pretty strong reason to want to hurt Alan. He was in love with Lara. He may even have blamed Alan for her death."

"I understand that, but I think he's a man of integrity."

"You're looking at this too logically," he said. "What we're talking about is illogical, unbridled passion—lust. Something that defies logic." Black eyes gazed deeply into gray ones. "Chemistry is a strange thing."

She shifted uncomfortably under his scrutiny. "Uh, that's true," she said, "but Lara and Reese don't sound to me as if they were all that suited for each other."

His eyes continued to hold hers as he said, "Sometimes we're attracted to people who are all wrong for us. Our minds tell us not to get involved, but our emotions take over and we can't help ourselves. We act totally out of character."

She sensed he was no longer talking about Lara and Reese. "That sounds more like Gloria and Alan," she said, searching for some way to defuse the situation. "They're certainly an odd couple."

"What about you?" he asked. His voice was low and incredibly sexy. "Haven't you ever felt that way?"

Of course she had. She felt that way right now, but she wasn't going to tell him that. She moistened her lips with the tip of her tongue, and his eyes instantly dropped to her mouth. All the searing heat and the undercurrents they'd been trying to avoid seemed to swirl around them, bursting into life.

"What do they say?" Sean continued in that same low, husky voice, his gaze locked with hers. "Truth is stranger than fiction."

The intensity of his gaze made her pulse leap, and she knew he wanted to kiss her. She was never so sure of anything in her life. And, God help her, she wanted him to kiss her, too.

Kiss me, she wanted to say, but the words stuck in her

throat. However, if she leaned forward slightly… As if her body had a mind of its own, she felt it move toward him. His mouth drew nearer. Her eyelids closed—

"Sean, you've got to—"

Hailey felt as if she'd been doused with a bucket of cold water as their heads simultaneously swiveled in the direction of the sound. Through passion-filled eyes, an image of a tall, blond-haired man dressed in blue jeans and a navy blazer registered in her mind.

Sean's voice was husky as she heard him say, "It's Mac." She looked into black eyes that were as dazed as her own.

"Uh, I'm sorry to interrupt, but I thought you might want to see this."

"Sure, come on in," Sean said, waving him in. "I want you to meet Hailey Monroe. Hailey, this is Mac Warren."

"Ms. Monroe." He nodded vaguely, then turned his attention to Sean. "This just came in. I thought you ought to take a look at it." He handed Sean several pieces of paper, then quietly walked out of the room, closing the door behind him.

She watched him as he read. He closed his eyes for a second, then drew a deep breath. Whatever it was, it wasn't good news.

"What's wrong?" she asked.

"We just got the results from the FBI on the money from your dad's safe-deposit box." He hesitated then said, "The money from your father's safe-deposit box was part of the ransom money."

Hailey recoiled as if he'd struck her. She shook her head. "No, there must be some mistake."

He handed her the report so she could see for herself. "I'm sorry. I'm really sorry. I know you'd hoped for a different outcome." He raked a hand over his hair in frustration. "Hell, this is a rotten way to find out about your dad."

"That's got to be the understatement of the year."

Sean swallowed. He didn't know what to say. He wanted

to take her in his arms, tell her that it was going to be all right.

"So that's the end of it? The investigation is over?"

"There's nothing further to investigate. It's pretty clear your father was involved in the kidnapping."

"There's got to be some other explanation for the money. We just have to look for it."

His heart went out to her. "Hailey, don't do this to yourself."

"What do you want me to say? That I believe my dad was a kidnapper? I won't."

"You've got to accept it."

"I don't have to accept anything," Hailey snapped. She threw the report at him, spun on her heel and stalked to the door.

"Hailey, wait!" He quickly scooped up the papers, laid them on the desk, then tore off after her. He reached the bank of elevators just as the doors of the one she'd entered closed. Damn! He pressed the elevator button. There were three elevators, but according to the plate above each, they were all several floors away. It would be faster to take the stairs.

By the time he reached the street, Hailey was nowhere in sight. He stood on the sidewalk, peering up and down the dark street. Finally, he spotted her. She was midway up the block, and he sprinted after her.

When he reached her, he grabbed her arm and held her. "We need to talk," he said.

"What more is there to say?" she snapped, pulling her arm from his grip. "I think you've made your position crystal clear." She started to walk away.

"Hailey, will you listen to me?"

She kept walking.

"At least let me take you home."

"I'll take a cab," she retorted over her shoulder.

He watched in frustration as she continued up the street. She was hurt, angry, upset and in no mood to listen to anything he had to say right now. He'd go out to the estate tomorrow morning. Maybe by then she would have calmed down and she'd be ready to listen.

Sean turned and was headed to his office when he noticed the car. He would scarcely have noticed it except for one thing—its windows were tinted. Not that tinted windows were all that unusual. This was Los Angeles, after all. Lots of his clients drove big cars with tinted windows. But this one was moving very slowly. He frowned as a niggling thought tingled in the back of his mind. Something wasn't right. But what—then it hit him like a ton of bricks. *The car's headlights were off!*

He whirled. The car was nearing the intersection at the end of the street. His eyes darted about, searching for Hailey. He spotted her as she stepped off the curb. In that instant, the car's headlights flashed on, the engine roared to life, and the car leaped forward in a burst of speed…and headed straight for Hailey!

Chapter Nine

"Hailey, look out!" Sean shouted.

Hailey whirled and found herself caught in the blinding headlights of an oncoming car. For one terrifying second, she stood there, frozen, paralyzed by shock and fear, then instinct took over. She flung herself out of the path of the oncoming car. But not in time to prevent the car from clipping her on the hip before roaring away.

She hit the pavement hard, the fall knocking the breath from her.

Sean was by her side instantly. "Don't try to move," he said. "Just lie still." His hands moved over her quickly, checking for signs of injury.

"I'm all right." She brushed his hands away and tried to stand up. She made it to her knees before sinking to the pavement as a wave of nausea and dizziness washed over her.

"You're not all right," Sean said. "I'm taking you to the hospital."

"I'm not going to any hospital," she said stubbornly. "I'm fine. Really." For a moment she thought he was going to argue with her, but her expression must have told him she meant it. She was silently congratulating herself when she found herself being lifted.

"You don't have to carry me," she protested weakly. "I can walk."

"Sure you can." He kissed her forehead. "But carrying you makes *me* feel better. So just lay back and enjoy the ride."

She looped her arm around his neck and complied with his request. She had to admit it felt good to be carried, good to be held. The warmth and strength of his lean, muscled body were very soothing to her shattered nerves.

He set her in the passenger seat of his car, then climbed in next to her. She leaned against the headrest and closed her eyes. She didn't open them until the car stopped in front of a fashionable apartment building.

"Where are we?" she asked.

"This is where I live. Since you refuse to go to the hospital, I thought I'd bring you here. My next-door neighbor's a doctor. I'm going to see if I can get him to take a look at you." His voice allowed no argument.

He swept her into his arms and carried her up the walkway. The doorman got the door for him and signaled for the elevator. He carried her straight to the living room, somehow managing to flick the light switch on the wall, and lowered her onto the couch as if she were made of fine crystal. She felt the cushions sag as he sat beside her. "Does anything hurt?" he asked anxiously.

"My leg, a little. I think I fell on it."

"Let me see." He dropped to the floor and knelt in front of her.

He lifted her leg and began kneading her ankle, then her calf, checking for signs of injury. She was totally focused on the feel of his hand as it glided gently up and down her leg, his touch as soft as a caress. And if his hand went a little higher than was necessary, to the soft inside of her thigh, Hailey couldn't bring herself to object. His hand felt so good.

"Nothing seems broken," he said in a slightly strained voice, straightening. "But I'd feel better if Jim had a look."

"I'm okay. I don't need a doctor."

"Let's just be on the safe side." He reached for the telephone on the table next to the couch and punched in a number. Briefly, he explained the situation to his friend. She noted, however, he described her near brush with death as an accident.

Did he really believe that? she wondered. She wouldn't be surprised if he did. It was hard enough for her to believe what had happened. But all she had to do was close her eyes, and it all came rushing back—the car barreling down on her, the twin headlights rushing at her.

Someone hated her, wanted her dead. They'd tried before. This time they'd almost succeeded. If Sean hadn't followed her, seen the car coming and shouted a warning, she would be dead. She pushed the disturbing thought out of her mind and tried to focus on Sean's conversation with his friend. A moment later, she watched him lower the receiver into the cradle, then cross the room and sit opposite her.

"Jim will be over in a minute," he said. "In the meantime, I think we should talk about what happened."

"It wasn't an accident."

"No, it wasn't," he said quietly. "Whoever was driving that car was trying to kill you." He massaged his temple. "I should have checked down by the lake more thoroughly after the shooting. Maybe if I'd gone back earlier, I'd have found something—"

"You can't think that way," she said firmly. "You did everything you could."

Sean looked at her, his expression bleak. "It doesn't make sense. Why would anyone want to harm you?"

"I can make a wild guess." She gave him a pointed look. "So can you."

"You think this is connected to the kidnapping?"

"Don't you? I never had anyone try to kill me until we began this investigation."

"So we're back to Gloria, Reese and Paul," he said grimly.

"I don't know about Reese, but both Gloria and Paul have

reason to want me out of the way, especially Paul. He has a lot to lose if it turns out I'm Susan.''

Sean was silent as he pondered her words.

She looked at him sharply. "You can't still think my father was involved in the kidnapping. Not after what happened tonight.''

Sighing, he raked his hand over his hair. "I don't know what to think anymore. About your dad, about Paul or Reese, about anything. All I know for sure is what I saw tonight.'' He stood and began to pace. "It's possible the attempts on your life have nothing to do with the kidnapping.''

"You don't really believe that.''

He issued another sigh. "No, I don't. I'm afraid what happened tonight is tied into this whole bloody mess. What I don't understand is why the prospect that you might be Susan Palmer is so terrifying to someone.''

"I do.'' She swallowed. "I think it's because someone believes I can identify him or her.''

He paused in his pacing and stared at her. "But you can't, can you?''

MAC WARREN took a sip of coffee and stared across the cocktail table at Sean. "How's Hailey?''

"My neighbor checked her over and gave her a clean bill of health. She has a number of bumps and bruises and will probably be a little sore for a day or so, but luckily no broken bones. Jim gave her a sedative to help her sleep.'' He glanced in the direction of the living-room doorway. "We'll have to keep our voices down. I don't want to wake her.''

Mac stared at him, surprised. "She's still here? Why didn't you take her home?''

"Jim didn't want her to make the long drive to the estate tonight.''

Mac took a sip of coffee. "How did Alan take it?''

"Just the way you would imagine. He was beside himself. It took all my powers of persuasion to convince him not to drive here tonight.''

Mac frowned. "He's really getting emotionally attached to her. What are you going to do if it turns out she isn't Susan?"

Sean leaned into the sofa cushions and wearily rubbed his face. "To tell the truth, Mac," he muttered, "at the moment that's the least of my problems."

"Oh?"

"I thought I had everything all figured out, but things are happening that just don't make sense."

Mac looked at him curiously. "Like what?"

"What happened tonight, for one. Yesterday someone takes a shot at her, today she's nearly run down, and then there was that incident in Chicago. One brush with death would be suspicious enough, but three?"

Mac looked at him sharply. "Sounds like you don't believe what happened tonight was an accident."

He shook his head. "I don't. There's more going on here than meets the eye. If I wasn't sure before, I am now."

"You aren't reading too much into this?" Mac asked.

"He was headed straight for her. I saw it. As soon as Hailey stepped off the curb, he hit the gas."

Mac's eyebrow lifted. "He? I thought you didn't see the driver."

"I didn't. The car had tinted windows, but I did get a portion of the license plate number. And I know it was a big car, dark color, black, maybe dark blue."

Mac gave him an approving look. "You make a pretty good witness, Sean. I had Kevin at the Department of Motor Vehicles run a check on the license number. The car is registered to a guy out in Century City. However, he reported it stolen earlier today. The police found the car, abandoned, a couple of blocks from your office. They dusted for prints, but the preliminary report suggests it was wiped clean."

Sean pulled on his lower lip, thinking. "A stolen car, no prints," he said half to himself. "He made damn sure we couldn't trace him."

Mac shook his head. "I see where you're headed, but I

don't think we should rule out the obvious—that the driver was some kid out for a joyride or hopped up on drugs."

"Mac, I know what I saw. He was out to kill her."

Mac set his cup down and looked him in the eye. "And what are you out to do?"

Sean looked at him, surprised. "The same thing I always want to do—get to the truth."

Mac slanted him a sideways glance. "Are you sure that's all you're interested in?"

"What do you mean?" Sean asked, shifting uncomfortably under his friend's scrutiny.

"Oh, I don't know, I thought you might also be interested in Hailey Monroe."

Sean raked a hand over his hair. "I'd be lying if I said I wasn't attracted to her, but that doesn't mean I can't be objective," he added quickly.

"I think you'll try to be, but, Sean, it's bound to affect the way you handle the case. Look at you. You're second-guessing yourself and looking at this case, I think, too much from Hailey's point of view." He paused, then added, "This case has consumed a great deal of your life. I don't want you to do something that you may later regret."

Sean issued a weary sigh then nodded. "You and me both. I was just so sure Jack Monroe was involved in the kidnapping, but now…"

"You don't think that's the case anymore?"

"I'm not saying that, but other names, other motives have started cropping up—Gloria Falcon, Reese Tyler and Paul Keegan, for instance." He spent several minutes laying out what they'd found.

"I see what you mean," Mac said when he was done. "And I agree, this information should be checked out, but I don't think we can just disregard the mountain of evidence we have against Monroe."

Mac was right. It was too soon to eliminate Hailey's dad. "Okay, have Vance continue investigating Monroe, but I want you, Dennis and Trevor to follow up on the others. I want you to focus especially on their finances. Specifically, I want to know if any of them came into a large sum of money around the time of the kidnapping. I also want to know their whereabouts when these attempts were made on Hailey's life."

Mac whistled. "You don't want much, do you? Seriously, this is going to take some time."

"Pull Gordon and O'Brien off the Lindley case. Have them help you."

Mac nodded, then said, "Let's say, for the sake of argument, that someone is trying to kill Hailey. Isn't it possible it might be for a reason that has nothing to do with the kidnapping?"

"It's possible, but I don't think so. None of these accidents occurred until *after* Jack Monroe sent Alan that letter."

Mac thought about his words. "I understand that, but it still doesn't make sense. Hailey can't identify this guy Sarge. In going after her, he takes the risk of exposing himself. Why?"

Sean shrugged. "We must have rattled someone's cage. And I'd bet anything it's one of the people we interviewed."

Mac set his coffee cup on the cocktail table and stood. "I'll get on this right away. I'll see what I can do about helping you keep your woman safe."

"She's not my woman."

"Right." Mac grinned. "And the Pope isn't Catholic."

They talked for several more minutes, then Mac left Sean alone with his thoughts. He walked to the bar in the corner of the room and poured himself a drink. He was too keyed up to sleep. He began the investigation believing that Jack Monroe was a kidnapper. Now he wasn't sure what he believed. The only thing he was sure of was how close he'd come to losing Hailey tonight. Suddenly, he felt an urgent need to see her, to assure himself that she was all right.

He downed his drink in a single gulp, then headed down the hallway to the guest room. He slowly opened the door and stuck his head inside. Hailey was sound asleep. Her raven black hair was tousled around her face, and sleep had brought a delicate flush to her cheeks. Her breasts moved up and down in a slow, deep rhythm. A sharp longing went through him. He'd give anything to hold her in his arms. An image of them entwined together shot through his mind. That image stayed with him, and when he finally fell asleep, his dreams were filled with delicious images of the two of them making love.

The last thing he expected was to be jolted awake by her bloodcurdling screams.

HAILEY BOLTED UPRIGHT in bed, her hands flailing, trying to dislodge his hold. But he tightened his grip on her arm as he dragged her across the room. She bucked, kicked, tried to get away, but the hand tightened. She was close to the edge. Then she was falling—

"Hailey, wake up!"

Her eyes flew open, and she found herself looking into Sean's concerned face. For a moment she just stared, then she threw her arms around his neck.

"It's all right, sweetheart." He pulled her to a sitting position, holding her, rocking her. "It's all right. I'm here."

The feel of Sean's arms around her brought a sense of warm security. She clung to him, and he held her as if he might never let her go.

"You okay now?" he asked softly as she gradually became calmer.

"Yes." She nodded shakily. "It was just a bad dream." She slumped against him, resting her head against the wall of his chest. "Why do I keep having this dream? What does it mean?"

He brushed a lock of hair from her face. "Susan's doctor said she'd been traumatized by her mother's death." He paused, and she sensed he wanted to say something more but didn't know how. She was about to ask what was wrong when he said, "The doctor tried to get you to talk about it, but you were too young."

Her eyes flew to his face. He'd referred to her and Susan as one and the same. A thread of joy coursed through her. With that simple statement, she felt he'd not only accepted that she was Susan, but also that they had taken a giant leap in their relationship.

"You didn't have the words," he said, "but the feelings were there—locked in your subconscious mind."

"And they've haunted me ever since," she added shakily.

"Maybe it would help to talk about the dream. Talking about it might release the emotions that are locked inside you, causing you to have the dream. Do you feel up to talking about it?"

"I think so," she whispered.

"Okay, start at the beginning," he said, then punctuated his words with a reassuring smile.

She drew in a steadying breath, then began, "The dream is always the same. There's the lady in white, who I now know is Lara. She's in this pristine white room—"

"That's the bathroom of the Palmer estate," Sean interjected. "She was getting ready for bed."

"Lara falls to the floor. I'm about to run to help her, when I see him—" she swallowed "—the monster. I try to get away, to hide, but he finds me." She shuddered and Sean's arms tightened around her. "He drags me across the room. I'm terrified, and then I feel myself falling. That's when I wake up."

"Is this the way the dream has always been?"

She nodded. "Pretty much, why?"

"It's not a very accurate account of what happened that night. You sure it hasn't changed?"

"I'm sure. I used to have it all the time as a child, but it stopped. It came back right after my parents died."

He nodded slowly. "No doubt the trauma of losing your adoptive parents brought it back."

She looked at him. He was so patient and understanding. He made her feel all kinds of things—safe, protected, desire...most of all desire. It was then that she realized he was only wearing briefs. He'd been asleep when he'd heard her scream. She could almost hear the snap inside herself as her senses awakened. Her breathing seemed loud and ragged.

"You must think I'm such a coward. Afraid of a silly nightmare." She gave a shaky little laugh.

"Fear isn't a bad thing. It keeps you on your toes. Take tonight, for instance. Seeing a car barreling down on you had to be terrifying, but you didn't panic. You handled that incident just fine. I'm proud of you."

She met his gaze. His eyes arrested her, stripped her of all coherent thought. The expression she read in the dim golden light was dark with concern...and wanting.

Reason told her to move away, that if he touched her, she was lost. But instinct and need held her still. His fingertips traced the line of her jaw, then he cupped her face in his hands. Her eyelids fluttered closed. Need swelled inside her like a living thing, flexing and stretching, awakening with it a sharp, aching hunger.

He lowered his mouth to hers. She remained still, her back against the headboard. Hot and hungry, that was the only way to describe his mouth as it moved over hers, mingling desire with something nameless. A wild surge of pleasure racked Hailey's body. She felt her breasts swell, and their sensitive peaks tightened as she burned with desire. But this was wrong.

She dragged her mouth away. The taste of him lingered, potent as wine.

He raised his head, but remained where he was with his hands cupping her face.

"We shouldn't do this," she whispered.

"Why not?"

She could think of a million reasons. The timing was wrong. She didn't go in for casual affairs. But, more important, they were involved in an investigation, and while they shared a common goal—identifying the kidnapper known as Sarge—they differed on who the evidence pointed to. Despite what had happened tonight, she sensed Sean still considered her dad a suspect. And yet...

He felt so good. God, she wanted him, wanted him to make love to her more than she'd ever wanted anything in her life.

She averted her eyes, afraid to look at him, afraid he would see the hunger in her eyes.

"You're right," he said, "we can't do this." He dropped a light kiss on her lips, then made a move to stand. "Try to get some sleep. I'll see you in the morning."

"Don't go. Could you stay with me for awhile? I don't want to be alone."

Sean hesitated only a moment before slipping into bed beside her, gathering her into his arms. "Go on, go to sleep. I'll stay with you."

Her eyes fluttered closed as she luxuriated in the feel of his arms. Her last thought as sleep overtook her was, if she wasn't careful, she could fall in love with him.

Sleep, however, was the farthest thing from Sean's mind. He was fighting a feverish desire to make love to her. The memory of the erotic dream he'd been having moments before she'd woken him certainly didn't help matters.

He swallowed a moan when she snuggled closer, bringing her firm, flat stomach and full breasts against him. His fingers itched to lift up her T-shirt and explore every inch of her delectable body.

He closed his eyes, trying to halt the images that were forming in his mind, to bring his thoughts under control. It didn't do a damn bit of good. If anything, it made things worse.

He opened his eyes and stared up at the ceiling. Tonight was going to be a long night. A very long night.

CONSCIOUSNESS slowly penetrated Hailey's mind, and her eyes gradually opened. Sean was lying next to her, asleep. His hand was resting on the curve of her hip, and her head was cradled against his shoulder. She could feel the taut hardness of one of his legs, the one that was thrown over hers.

She lay perfectly still as memories of her dream and what preceded it came flooding back. The last thing she remembered was falling asleep in Sean's arms.

She tilted her head and looked up at the man who held her securely in his warm embrace. God, he was beautiful— not just on the outside but the inside as well. He was kind and gentle. She had never felt so safe, so special, so alive as she did in his arms. She snuggled closer.

Sean stirred slightly. His eyes suddenly flickered open and held hers. The emotion in them jolted Hailey, making her heart take a perilous leap and igniting a heated sensation in the pit of her stomach. He continued to stare at her, his gaze like a soft caress. She could feel the touch of that gaze and tried to halt the dizzying current racing through her, but it was too late.

Desire, the likeness of which she'd never known, rose in her like the hottest fire, clouding her mind and heating the core of her body. It was as if his eyes were casting a spell on her, bewitching her senses. She felt the emotional barriers she'd erected crumble. Feelings long denied burst forth, and she faced the truth. She wanted to make love with him, wanted it more than anything in the world.

As if she'd voiced her thoughts aloud, Sean leaned over and kissed her. He kissed her softly at first, a series of slow, shivery kisses. Gradually, the kisses increased in intensity, becoming harder, deeper. She had never before realized kissing could be so varied, so wonderful. She reveled in it, gloried in it, surrendered to it.

His hands sought the hem of her oversize T-shirt, and breaking the kiss, he gently pulled it over her head, then quickly resumed kissing her.

Hailey moaned when his fingers caressed the sensitive skin of her stomach before slowly moving toward her breasts. His hands tenderly cupped their fullness. Then his tongue replaced his fingers on her breasts, bringing their dark tips to crested peaks.

She uttered a cry of pleasure, then another. His hands were on the move again, gliding over her, as though obsessed with knowing every line, every curve of her body. He stroked her back and shoulders, her hips, her waist and thighs. When his hand moved lower to the very essence of her, little whimpers of pleasure escaped her throat, only to be captured by his mouth.

Hailey's mind was whirling. Sensations she'd never felt before tore through her body. All she could think about was the feel of his sensual mouth and hands on her, making her tremble with need.

"I want you. Please tell me that you want me, too."

Each word he spoke sounded like a caress, an erotic stroke. Hailey wanted him, too. She couldn't deny she was aching with a need to be possessed by him.

"Tell me, Hailey. Tell me what you want."

"I want you to make love to me," she whispered.

"Oh, Hailey," he groaned, then captured her lips in a mind-shattering kiss. He tore his mouth from hers. "I'll be right back."

"Sean?" she said, rising on one elbow. He was already of the room. Was something wrong?

A moment later he was back. He held up a small foil packet. "Now we're ready," he said huskily.

He placed the packet on the nightstand next to the bed, then stepped out of his briefs. He stood before her, completely naked, his rich brown body totally male, totally splendid and, at the moment, totally aroused...for her.

He rejoined her in bed and pulled her to him. "I've wanted you for so long, Hailey. From the moment I saw you in David Forbes's office, I wanted you," he whispered hotly against her ear. "Maybe even before then."

Moving between her knees, the potency of his arousal evident, he paused and smiled down at her. His chest swelled with a ragged breath, and she reached for him. He took her hands, interlaced his fingers with hers, and held them against the bed near her temples. He rubbed his cheek against hers before taking her mouth in a fierce and hungry kiss.

Hailey caught her breath as she felt his strong thighs nudge her thighs apart and his hardness probing at her feminine core, pressing downward and slowly penetrating her. She sucked in her breath at the sheer size of him.

"Are you all right?" he asked tenderly, giving her body time to adjust to him.

In response, she moved her hips in a slow rotating motion.

"Oh, Hailey, you feel so good," he said, his voice full of passion. Then he slowly and gently began moving within her, setting an erotic rythym.

Hailey wrapped her legs around him, pulling him closer. At her lead, gentleness fled, chased by white-hot, consuming desire. Sean burrowed deeper and deeper inside her. She couldn't stop her cry of pleasure at the resulting sensation. The feeling was so exquisite, the heat so intense. It was almost torment. Her heart pounded violently against her ribs. She clung to him with desperate hands, feeling as if she was spiraling out of control. Her eyes closed. Her neck arched. Her head thrashed on the pillow.

"Please, please," she whimpered, begging for release.

"I can't get enough of you," Sean groaned. He pushed harder and deeper into the moist, clinging heat of her. "Baby, you're driving me crazy."

Warm sensations began to spiral up through Hailey's middle and radiate outward until her fingertips and toes began to throb. Perspiration ran from her hair and her forehead into her eyes. Her breathing was ragged and shallow. She gripped his shoulders and dug her nails into his skin, feeling his muscles strain and tighten against her hands. Each hard, powerful stroke into her body was intense, complete. And the more he plunged into her, then withdrew, the deeper he plunged the next time, until the beauty built inside her, leaving her breathless with wonderment, whimpering with joy.

The fire he'd built inside her grew hotter, raging out of

control, until their passion encompassed them. Together they scaled the heights of ecstasy, becoming one in body and soul.

SEAN WAS THE FIRST to awaken. He found his arms wrapped around Hailey, his face buried in the sweet-smelling strands of her hair. She was curled on her side, the satiny skin of her back pressed against his chest. The memory of their lovemaking was so vivid, he felt his body respond with automatic desire. And why not? Hailey was life and lust and honeyed warmth. She was everything a woman should be—everything he'd ever wanted in a woman.

But this was not the time to start a relationship. Not in the middle of the investigation, not when her father was still a prime suspect. He should have thought about that last night. Well, he was thinking about it now. And his conscience was giving him fits. It wasn't fair to Alan or Hailey. He needed to back up, take things slow.

He pulled away and sat up. Morning light shone through the window onto her pillow. She looked so damn sexy that despite his resolve to take things slow, he was tempted to pull back the sheet, wake her and make love to her again.

Before he could act on his impulse, he left the bed and went straight to the shower. He stepped into the stall and let the hot water pour over him. He was washing her magical spell away, he thought. Washing away the desire, his craving for Hailey. She was like a sickness in his blood, making him lose control, making him do insane things.

Like last night, for instance.

He'd been so hot for her, he hadn't given any thought to the investigation. His entire focus had been on satisfying his overpowering hunger for her. He groaned as he felt his body harden at the memory of their lovemaking. He switched the water to cold, trying to cool his overheated body as well as his wayward thoughts. A few moments later, he shut off the water and returned to the bedroom.

He watched her sleep as he dressed. With each layer of

clothing he felt more protected, less vulnerable. But when she stirred, opened her eyes and smiled at him, he realized how thin his emotional armor was.

"How are you feeling this morning?" he asked softly.

"Much better, thanks," she answered. She pulled the sheet to her shoulders.

There was a silence. The smile that had played on her lips faded, and her face took on a guarded, wary expression. She was pulling away, retreating into herself. But wasn't that what he wanted? To put some distance between them? Yes. No. Hell, he wanted Hailey.

"I'm going to make breakfast," he said, breaking the silence. "What would you like?"

"Nothing. I'm not hungry."

He started to turn away, then turned back. "Hailey, I think we should talk about what happened last night."

"Let's not." She sat up, hugging the sheet to her chest. "We slept together. No big deal."

"It was a lot more than a roll in the hay for both of us, so don't try to pretend otherwise."

"What do you want me to say? That you're the best thing that ever happened to me? Declare undying love?"

"No, but I want to tell you how I feel. I want to know how you feel."

"Don't, Sean," she said flatly. "Last night was a mistake, we both know it. I think we should just put it out of our minds and pretend it never happened."

He stared at her, his expression bleak. "Maybe you can do that, but I can't."

Chapter Ten

Despite her words, Hailey was having a hard time pretending they hadn't slept together. All she had to do was look at Sean's handsome face, and it all came rushing back. The way he held her, loved her. Like she was the most precious thing in the world to him. And it hadn't all been on his part, either. Never in her life had she given herself so completely to another human being.

But no matter how much she might desire him, there was still the investigation and the question of her father's guilt. It didn't matter that Sean was looking at other people—her father was still a suspect. That fact lay between them like the widest chasm, and until it was resolved, there could be no relationship.

She glanced toward the window. Sunlight filtered through the slits in the shade, promising another hot, humid day. It would be like so many others. The continuity, the sameness, would prevail. But Hailey seriously wondered if she would ever be the same again after being so totally touched by another human being.

"You're thinking about last night, aren't you?"

Sean's husky voice sent a ripple of heat through her. She slowly turned. He stood in the doorway, staring at her. His dark eyes were enigmatic, and Hailey regretted that she hadn't learned to mask her feelings better.

"You can't forget it any more than I can," he said, moving into the room.

"Well, it's not every day someone tries to kill you," she answered, pretending to misunderstand his words.

His lips parted as if he were about to say something, but at that moment the doorbell rang, and he went to answer it. A moment later Alan burst into the room, Gloria on his heels. He made a beeline for Hailey.

"My dear, are you all right?" Alan asked, taking her hands in his. His eyes darted over her, searching for signs of injury before coming to rest on her face.

"I'm fine," she said, then reinforced her words with a smile.

"Thank God," he breathed then wrapped her in his arms. She could feel his heart hammering in his chest. He'd really been afraid. "What did the emergency room doctor say? Do you have to go back for a check up?"

"I—I didn't go to the hospital."

"What!" Alan turned on Sean, eyes blazing. "I can't believe you didn't take her to the hospital. She could have internal injuries—"

"Alan, my next door neighbor is a doctor. He checked her out and gave her a clean bill of health."

"Nevertheless, I think I'll have my doctor—"

"Alan, for heaven's sake," Gloria snapped. "She's fine."

He let out a deep sigh then slumped on the living-room sofa. "I know you all think I'm being overly protective, but I can't help it. Now that I've found my daughter, I'm not going to let anything happen to her."

"That's makes two of us," Sean said. He gave Hailey a possessive look.

She swallowed as a wave of wanting heated her innards. From the corner of her eye, she saw Alan assessing them with an intense look. She wondered if he suspected they'd slept together, but when he spoke, it seemed his mind was on an entirely different matter.

"Now that I know Hailey is fine," he said, "I'd like for you to tell me what really happened last night."

Hailey stiffened. They'd agreed not to tell Alan about the attempts on her life. It would just cause him to worry.

"I don't know what you mean," Sean began. "I told you, Hailey was nearly—"

Alan held up a hand, halting Sean's words. "I know you're trying to protect me, but frankly, I'm getting damn tired of everyone treating me with kid gloves. I know there's something you're not telling me. I could hear it in your voice. Now why don't you tell me what it is?"

Sean looked at Hailey, then at Alan. "It wasn't an accident. Someone deliberately tried to run Hailey over."

"But why? Why would anyone want to harm Hailey?"

"They wouldn't," Gloria insisted. "I think you're both making too much of a silly accident."

"I wish that was all it was." Sean raked his hand over his hair in frustration. "I didn't want to say anything until we had something concrete, but..." He hesitated, as if searching for the right words. "It's possible I was wrong about Jack Monroe being involved in the kidnapping."

Hailey's heart skipped a beat. That was the first time Sean had said he thought her father might be not be involved. Thank God.

"There's a possibility the third man may have been someone in your inner circle."

"One of my friends? A family member?" Alan shook his head, rejecting the idea. "That's impossible."

"I'm afraid it's not only possible but highly probable," Sean said, his expression grim.

Alan swallowed. "And you think the person who tried to run Hailey down is the same person." His voice was little more than a whisper.

"Yes, I do."

For a moment Alan didn't say anything, then he erupted in fury. "My God, you're telling me that the person who kidnapped Hailey has been a guest in my home, eaten at my table—'' His voice broke as he fought for control. ''Do you have any leads?''

''A couple, but like I said, I don't want to start pointing fingers at anyone until I have something concrete.''

Alan's eyes blazed with anger. ''Damn it, Sean, I have a right to know who's behind this.''

''And I'll tell you as soon as I have some hard evidence.''

''Don't spare any expense. I want this man caught.''

Sean looked at Hailey. ''That's a promise,'' he said.

''I also want you to beef up security around the estate. I want a man assigned to Hailey—''

''What? I don't need a bodyguard.''

Alan threw her an anxious look. ''My dear, be reasonable. An attempt has been made on your life. We have to take precautions.''

''I agree,'' she said. ''But a bodyguard isn't necessary. Whenever I leave the estate, I'm either with you or Sean. I think that's ample security. Besides, I can't help Sean with the investigation if I've got a baby-sitter tagging along.''

''Hailey, I don't think you appreciate the risk you're taking in not having protection.''

''I do. I just don't think a bodyguard is necessary.''

Alan threw a pleading look at Sean, who shrugged. ''It's her call,'' Sean said.

Alan let out a deep sigh, then nodded. ''All right, I'll go along with your wishes—for now. Sean,'' he said, standing, ''why don't we step into the kitchen? There's another matter I'd like to discuss with you. Please excuse us. We'll just be a minute.''

Hailey watched as the two men walked out of the room. Alan was being awfully secretive. Had he picked up on the sexual tension that swirled around her and Sean? She wouldn't be at all surprised. He was very astute.

''You know what I think?''

Hailey blinked and looked at the woman seated across

from her. She'd forgotten that Gloria was there. "I beg your pardon?"

"I think if Lara had been alive, I'd put my money on her being Ryan's accomplice," Gloria said smugly. At Hailey's look of surprise, she added, "Alan thought she was so wonderful, so sweet, but she was nothing but a two-timing whore."

Gloria had Hailey's full attention now. "She was unfaithful?"

"Well, I don't know that for a fact," Gloria admitted grudgingly, "but she certainly exhibited all the signs of a woman having an affair. She was secretive, restless and constantly having Ryan drive her into L.A. for supposed luncheons and shopping trips." She gave Hailey a knowing look. "Who's to say those little junkets weren't simply a ruse to hide her affair with him?"

"No one," Hailey answered smoothly. "Just as who's to say it wasn't you who was having the affair with Ryan."

"Wh-what?" Gloria spluttered. "That's ridiculous."

"Is it? It wouldn't be the first time, or have you forgotten about your affair with Paul?"

Gloria licked her lips. "That was a long time ago and has nothing to do with anything."

Hailey shook her head. "On the contrary, I think it has everything to do with the kidnapping. You hated Lara. It probably stuck in your craw that Alan preferred her over you. Then Lara died and you found yourself competing with a dead woman's child. What did you do? Seduce Ryan into helping you with the kidnapping? Or did you tell him you'd split the money with him?"

"That's crazy. Everyone knows there were only two people involved in that kidnapping—Ryan and his friend Denny Hanson. You're just trying to throw up a smoke screen to divert attention from the fact that your father was trying to extort money from Alan."

"The way you used Ryan to divert attention from yourself? What happened? Did he get greedy? Is that why you killed him?''

Gloria shot to her feet. "How dare you! Don't think for a minute that I'm not going to tell Alan about your ridiculous allegations.''

"Go ahead. You can also tell him about the loan you made to Paul. Or should I?''

Gloria's face took on a cornered, desperate look. "You can't tell him. Please don't.''

"That depends on you. I want to know why you loaned Paul the money, and I want the truth.''

For a moment Gloria didn't say anything, and when she spoke, her voice was a whisper. "H-he was blackmailing me.''

"Why? What did he have on you?''

Gloria drew a weary sigh and sank onto the sofa. "He knew I'd embezzled money from the company.''

Hailey had thought of a number of possible reasons, but that hadn't been one of them.

"It started right after Alan married Lara,'' Gloria continued. "I was angry. I wanted to hurt him the way he'd hurt me.''

"So you stole money from Palmer Publishing?''

Gloria nodded. "I regretted it and did everything I could to make amends. I thought I was careful, that I'd covered my tracks, but somehow Lara knew. She was my administrative assistant,'' she explained, "but it seemed to me she was always snooping around. Well, anyway, she must have told Paul, because after she died he had money problems, and he threatened to tell Alan what I'd done if I didn't give him three hundred thousand dollars.''

"So you gave him the money?''

"What else could I do?'' Gloria cried. "For the first time, Alan was looking at me like a woman, not an employee. A woman he wanted. I couldn't lose that. So I gave Paul the money. But I swear I had nothing to do with the kidnapping.''

IT WAS ALMOST two hours later that Hailey and Sean were alone again. And during that two-hour period, Sean had seen a side of Alan he had never seen before—the over-protective father. Alan had taken him into the kitchen and told him point-blank that he wouldn't tolerate him toying with Hailey. Sean had assured him his intentions were strictly honorable, but Alan had still seemed a little wary.

Maybe he should have been more candid, told Alan just how strong his feelings were for Hailey. But then, he hadn't told Hailey. He looked at her and his pulse quickened. She was seated on the sofa next to him. He was glad she'd stayed. Even though it was ostensibly to tell him about her conversation with Gloria, a part of him hoped it was also because she wanted to be with him as much as he wanted to be with her. It had also saved him the trouble of having to come up with some bogus reason for her to remain. Until this killer was caught, he didn't intend to let her out of his sight.

"So what do you make of her story?" Hailey asked when she'd completed her narrative.

He shook his head. "Gloria may be a thief, but she's not the person who's been trying to kill you. That phone call I had to take a few minutes ago was from Mac. Gloria's alibi checks out. She was hosting a charity function in Bel Air last night. Her alibi also checks out for the other times."

"So we can eliminate Gloria as a suspect. What about Paul?"

"That's a different story. He says he went for a drive, alone, but no one can vouch for his whereabouts. And he doesn't have an alibi for the two other occasions when someone tried to kill you. The same is true for Reese."

She cleared her throat, and her gaze dropped from his. "Did…um…you mean what you said about my dad not being a suspect anymore?"

"Yes, I did," he said softly. "I was wrong about him. I don't know how he came across those things in his safe-deposit box, but I don't believe he's Sarge. Sarge and the person who's been trying to kill you have to be one and the same.''

Hailey nodded. "So it comes down to Paul or Reese?''

"That's the way it looks. But how we go about proving which one it is, I don't have a clue. All we have are theories, suppositions, but no hard evidence that directly links either man to the kidnapping.''

"If only I could remember what happened,'' she said in exasperation. "Why is my only connection to the past a dumb dream?''

Sean nodded slowly. "I was thinking about that. Would you mind telling me the dream again?''

She looked at him, surprised. "Why? You said yourself it's not an accurate account of what happened the night Lara died.''

"I know, and that's what puzzles me,'' he said thoughtfully.

"Sean, it's a dream. It's not supposed to be accurate.''

He shook his head. "That's not entirely true. Your dream is the memory of an actual event, an event that you've never been able to confront consciously. I wonder if the dream is jumbled because you've confused it with another equally traumatic incident.''

She looked at him, surprised. "The kidnapping?''

"Why not? Two traumatic events following so closely in time could have gotten confused in your mind and somehow merged together into a single event. That might explain some of the discrepancies between what you remember and what really happened that night—for instance, the presence of the monster, hands grabbing you, the falling. It seems to me those things might be memories of the kidnapping. And if you're dreaming about the kidnapping, by analyzing the dream we may get lucky and find a clue to the third man's identity.''

She slanted him a sideways look. "I think you're grasping.''

He grinned. "Hey, it's the only thing we got.''

"When you put it that way," she said, returning his smile, "I guess we have nothing to lose."

He moved to the cocktail table and sat on the edge. "Okay, lie back on the couch and close your eyes."

She gave him a wry look but did as he requested.

"Now take a deep breath and relax." He watched her chest move up and down. Before he could stop himself, an image of her glorious breasts flashed before him. Suddenly, all he could think about was their lovemaking the night before.

"Sean?" Hailey said.

"Sorry," he said, shaking off the fantasy. "Tell me what you see."

"I'm in a white room," she began. "Lara's there. She's dressed in a long white dress." Hailey's lovely mouth curved into a smile. "She looks like an angel."

So do you, he thought, but aloud asked, "What is she doing?"

"Talking. She's gesturing with her hands and walking back and forth real fast. I remember that I'm not supposed to listen to adult conversation, but they're talking so loudly, I can't help but hear."

"What are they saying?"

Her forehead puckered into a frown. "I don't know. The words don't make sense."

"What happens then?"

"Lara falls to the floor. I'm about to run to help her when I see him, the monster."

Sean leaned forward. *This is where the dream changes,* he thought.

"I'm afraid." She wrapped her arms around herself. "I run down a corridor into another room, but it's really the same room. I don't like it here."

Was this a memory of her time at Hanson's house, maybe even Sarge's? He tried to stem his growing excitement. "Tell me about the house," he said.

"It's scary. Everything is red. It's everywhere, on the

wall, the floor, even on Lara. I want to leave, but it's too late. He's coming. I hide behind a big chair, but he sees me.'' She shuddered. ''He's dragging me across the floor. I try to get away, but he's too strong. I keep trying, then suddenly the floor disappears and I'm falling. That's when I wake up.'' She opened her eyes and sat up.

Sean thought for a moment. ''It's pretty jumbled,'' he said. ''Let's see if we can take it apart and make some sense of it. The police report said Lara slipped on some water on the bathroom floor, then hit her head on the side of the sunken tub and fell in. The police surmised that you woke up, saw her in the water and fell in trying to save her.''

Hailey nodded. ''The part about Lara and the bathroom is consistent with what happened, but the monster and everything after that don't seem to fit.''

''Not in relation to what happened that night,'' he said slowly, ''but maybe that part of the dream is about the kidnapping.'' He leaned forward. ''Let's go back to the monster. What does he look like?''

She shrugged. ''I don't know. I have the impression he's big and scary-looking. The only thing that stands out is his hands. They're huge, but that could be because he's wearing gloves.''

''Gloves?'' Sean frowned. ''Vanover wasn't wearing gloves. That's why the police were able to connect the kidnapping to him. They found his fingerprints on Susan's swing. And there would be no reason for Hanson or the third man to have worn gloves.''

Hailey looked at him and shrugged.

''What do you remember about the room you ran into after you left the bathroom?''

She gave him a pointed look. ''I'm still *in* the bathroom. It just looks different.''

''Are you sure you're in the bathroom?''

''Yes, I'm sure. I can hear the sound of running water.''

He shook his head. ''That's not right. The water wasn't

running. Lara had already filled the tub. The faucet was off.''

Hailey gave him an exasperated look. "I'm sorry, but that's the way I remember it."

He could hear the impatience in her voice and decided to drop that line of inquiry. "Okay, anything else?"

She thought for a minute, then looked at him. "Lilacs. I could smell lilacs. That's how I knew he was coming. Now I remember. Lara put it in the bath water. It must have gotten on his clothes."

Sean frowned. "Hell, this doesn't sound like it has anything to do with the kidnapping. None of it does."

She shrugged. "It was a good try. But I think the dream is just a confused version of what happened the night Lara died—part fact and a lot of fantasy."

He expelled a deep sigh and nodded. It probably was the events of the night Lara had died, but all confused. Or was it? He had a sudden thought. What if it wasn't her memory of that night that was faulty, but the police's construction of what had happened? Maybe they were the ones who had gotten it wrong. That would mean—

His head snapped up as realization dawned. "That's it! God, I've been so stupid. Why didn't I think of it before?"

"Think of what?"

"The dream. We've been looking at it all wrong. You're not dreaming about Lara's accident. You're dreaming about her murder!"

"Murder!" Hailey was reeling from Sean's revelation.

"God, it all makes sense." He paced back and forth, clearly agitated. "Don't you see, that's why you were kidnapped. It never had anything to do with money or revenge. It was to keep you from telling what you saw that night. The night Lara was murdered."

"Sean, it's just a dream," she insisted. "We can't go around accusing someone of murder simply on the basis of a dream."

He shook his head. "Not on a dream, but on what you saw that night."

"How can you be so sure that's what I saw?"

"It's the only explanation for why your memory of what happened that night doesn't square with the official report. You were with Lara when she died, but what you remember isn't what happened, at least not according to the official police report. The police report said she slipped and hit her head on the edge of the bath as she fell in, but I think you saw someone kill her. You didn't fall into the water. Lara's killer pushed you in. He tried to kill you to keep you from telling what you saw. The only thing that kept you safe was the fact you'd been severely traumatized by the event and didn't remember what happened. But then you began to recover. That's why he arranged for the kidnapping."

He believed what he was saying. And so did she, she realized with a shiver. "If you're right, how do we go about proving it?"

"We review everything we've learned, but this time we look at things from the perspective of who had a reason to kill Lara."

They spent the remainder of the morning reviewing their notes. Then they went to LAPD headquarters. There, they got lucky. Sean's friend, homicide detective Tate Wells, had located the old police file on Lara Palmer's accidental drowning. They reviewed the autopsy report, studied the photos taken of the bathroom as well as the adjoining master bedroom. They sifted through the statements the police had taken from everyone who had been at the house that night, and compared that list against the people who had been interviewed in connection with the kidnapping. They quickly eliminated everyone except Paul and Reese.

"It always comes back to them, doesn't it?"

Sean pursed his lips, thinking. "Yeah, but if I were a betting man, I'd put my money on Reese. I don't think Paul is capable of killing his own sister."

"Maybe he didn't mean to kill her," Hailey pointed out. "Maybe it was an accident, but I think he did it."

Sean smiled. "You think he's guilty because you like Reese better than Paul. But both men had motive and opportunity. However, what we need is some hard evidence."

"Then I think we'd better start trying to get it. Where do you want to start?"

"Unfortunately," he said somberly, "the best place to start is with the man who knew Lara best—Alan."

IT MIGHT BE the best place to start, but how did you tell a man that his wife's death wasn't an accident, but murder? It would be hard to break that kind of news to anyone, but in Alan's case it was doubly hard. He had loved Lara more than life itself.

Alan slumped against the sofa cushions, his face deathly pale, his right hand clutching his chest. For a moment, Sean thought he was having a heart attack.

"My God, why would anyone kill Lara?" Alan's voice was little more than a whisper. "Everyone loved her. She didn't have an enemy in the world."

"She had one," Sean said grimly, "the person who killed her."

Alan shook his head as if he was having difficulty taking it in. "How can you be so sure that Lara was murdered?"

"Because Hailey was there. She saw the whole thing."

Alan stared at her. "You saw it?"

"Not the way you're thinking," Hailey replied quickly. "I saw it in a dream." Then Sean explained how they'd reached their conclusion.

"Your whole premise is based on a dream?" Alan asked incredulously.

"Not just a dream," Sean said quickly, "but on Hailey's recollection of what happened that night. It's just come through to her in a dream state. Remember, Susan's doctor said that could well turn out to be the case."

"Yes, but couldn't you be mistaken?"

"We could," Sean conceded, "but we don't think so. It all fits. Granted, it's not enough to get the LAPD to reopen the case at this stage, but it's enough for me. I think our strongest point is the fact that Hailey is starting to remember. It's just a matter of time before she remembers the rest, and then she can tell us who she saw."

Suddenly, Alan looked every one of his sixty-two years. "Lara was murdered. I didn't lift a finger to help catch her killer, and because of me, he was able to kidnap Hailey." He buried his face in his hands and began to sob.

"Alan, it's all right," Hailey said, stroking his back, trying to comfort him. "You didn't know. No one did."

Sean broke the deadly silence that had descended over the room. "Can you think of anyone who may have had a vendetta against her?" he asked.

Alan looked up, his brown eyes awash with tears. "The killer had to be a stranger. Somehow he must have gotten into the house that night."

Sean shook his head. "It couldn't have been a stranger. The police report said there were no signs of a break-in. Whoever it was had to know his way around the house, had to know the location of your private quarters, as well as where the nursery was located and Lacy Anderson's routine. We have to be looking at someone intimately connected with this household." He paused, then added, "Someone who was at the house that night."

Alan frowned. "But the only people that were here were a few close friends and family members. None of them could have done such a thing."

"Not only did one of them kill Lara, but they also tried to kill Hailey. And when they failed, they arranged for her kidnapping."

"But who? Who could have done such a thing?"

Sean had known this question was going to come up. He'd gone over his response a thousand times in his mind, but it was still hard to verbalize. "Alan, the investigation seems to indicate that either Paul or Reese would have to be involved."

Alan stared at him, horrified. "Come on, Sean. You expect me to believe that one of the people I love most in the world could have murdered my wife, arranged for the kidnapping of my child?" His voice broke. "No...no, I refuse to believe that."

"Believe it." Sean didn't want to hurt him, but Alan had to accept that someone in his inner circle was a killer. "Reese and Paul both had reasons to hurt you and Lara." He ticked the points off on his fingers. "Reese was angry and out for revenge for your marrying Lara. Paul had money problems, and Lara had cut him off. They could have argued about money. He may not have meant to kill her, but in the heat of the argument he may have lost his head."

"I can't deal with this," Alan said, passing a shaky hand over his face. "Please, excuse me. I—I think I'd like to be alone."

Sean's heart went out to him as Alan hurried from the room.

"What if we're wrong?" Hailey asked, wiping tears away.

"We're not. The killer has to be either Paul or Reese." He pushed away from the desk he'd been leaning against. "Let's see if we can't narrow it down to one. Let's talk to Hanson again."

"CAN YOU THINK of anything about Ryan Vanover or the kidnapping that you didn't tell us before?" Sean asked.

"No, I can't," Hanson said, emphasizing his words with a shake of his head.

"Let's go over it again, but this time instead of focusing on the kidnapping, tell us about Ryan."

Hanson gave them a sour look, but complied. "I met Ryan about a year before the kidnapping. He was a big talker. He was always talking about striking it rich as a rock singer, and if he wasn't talking about that, it was the Vietnam war. How the American people didn't appreciate the Vietnam vet.''

That's right, Hailey thought, Ryan would have been part of the generation that had gone to Vietnam.

"He felt he'd been given a bum rap," Hanson was saying. "He'd served his country, but instead of being treated like a war hero, he'd come back to antiwar protesters.'' Hanson took a drag on his cigarette. "That was a sore point with him. Myself, I'd gotten a deferment and didn't serve, but I sympathized with him.''

He's rambling, Hailey thought. She looked at Sean, signaling that they ought to try to get the conversation back on track.

"He was part of the Tet Offensive, you know?" It was a rhetorical question. Hanson didn't really expect an answer. "He was part of an army division that got trapped at this Vietnamese village called Hue.''

Hailey's head snapped up. "He was at Hue? Are you sure about that?''

"Yeah, I'm sure. He said he'd been having nightmares for years about what had happened there. The Viet Cong had them pinned down, the city was surrounded—''

She closed her eyes. She'd heard that story—how several combat units had gotten pinned down. They'd had to fight their way out of the city…street by street, building by building.

"—and the American soldiers that had died. It had taken a week and they'd sustained heavy casualties.''

Hailey's hand flew to her mouth. "Oh, no," she moaned, rocking back and forth. "Oh, God, no.''

"What is it?" Sean asked. She could hear the concern in his voice.

She shook her head, unable to speak. As if in a fog, she heard him thank Hanson for his time. Then he was hustling her out of the room, the building, to his car. Once they were inside, he wrapped his arms around her and held her.

"Hailey, tell me what's wrong. Are you sick?"

"Yes, I'm sick. I'm sick of the lies, the deceit." She started to laugh, a high-pitched hysterical sound that ended on a sob.

"Stop it!" He gave her a little shake. "You're not making sense. Just calm down, sweetheart, and tell me what's wrong."

He stroked her back and hair. Hailey pulled away. "I was stupid, that's what's wrong." She didn't know that tears were brimming in her eyes, running down her cheeks.

"What are you talking about?"

"I don't know why I didn't think of it before," she said, her voice little more than a whisper. "The time frame, the service rank of sergeant." She looked at him, her expression bleak. "Don't you understand? Sarge is my uncle!"

Chapter Eleven

Sean had hoped Hailey's suspicions about her uncle would prove groundless, but a search of Frank Roberts's war and VA hospital records had failed to rule out the possibility. Although they'd served in different branches—Frank Roberts in the army and Ryan Vanover in the marines—both men had been in Vietnam and both had been at Hue. He hated to admit it, but it looked as if Hailey might be right about her uncle being Sarge.

But, without a doubt, questioning Frank Roberts was going to be one of the most difficult things he had ever done—made even more so by Hailey's presence.

He hadn't wanted her to come with him to Chicago, hadn't wanted her to be present during the interview, but she'd insisted. He doubted if she realized how hard the interview was going to be on her, on all of them. He glanced at her. She was seated across from him and next to her uncle on the sofa. Her hands were clasped tightly in her lap. She hadn't spoken more than a dozen sentences since they'd gotten there.

"You sure I can't get you anything?" Frank Roberts asked. His nut-brown face and sharp, dark eyes looked from Hailey to Sean.

Sean shook his head. He couldn't help but wonder what the other man was thinking. He would have to be as thick as a brick not to notice the tension that emanated from

Hailey. Despite his attempts to engage her in conversation, she'd been distant and uncommunicative since their arrival. But the only outward sign he'd given that he was aware something might be amiss was a slight tremor in his voice when he'd shown them to their seats.

"I'm sorry to bother you, Mr. Roberts," Sean began. "I know the past few weeks have been difficult for you, but there are several items we need your help in clarifying."

"It must really be important for the two of you to come all this way just to talk to me. Not that I'm not happy to see Hailey." He threw her another warm smile, which she didn't return.

He looked at her, frowning. "Hailey, is something wrong?"

"You tell me." Her voice was flat, devoid of any emotion.

Sean cleared his throat, as much to cover the awkward moment that followed as a way to open the conversation. "As you know," he continued, "we've uncovered evidence that suggests that Hailey is Susan Palmer."

Frank Roberts looked at his niece, then nodded slowly. "Yes, Hailey told me."

"You also know that when we began this investigation, we were working under the assumption that the third man was Jack Monroe. Then, later, we thought it might be someone within Alan's inner circle. However, we recently came across information that cast doubt on that being the case." He glanced at Hailey and felt a twinge of conscience at what he was about to do. There was no easy way to say it, so he plunged right in. "We have reason to believe the third man was someone Vanover met when he was in Vietnam."

Roberts sat up. "Oh?"

"You were also in the service, weren't you? Even served in Vietnam."

Roberts shifted slightly, as if he wasn't entirely comfortable with the question. "Ah, yes, that's right."

"And you moved to Los Angeles after you left the service, around '73."

"That's right," Roberts answered cautiously.

"Mr. Roberts, this isn't an easy question for me to ask, but did you know Ryan Vanover?"

Frank Roberts shot from his seat like a ball propelled from a cannon. "No, of course I didn't know him."

Sean sighed. He'd hoped Roberts wouldn't make things any more difficult than they were already. "Mr. Roberts," he said gently, "that's not true. You and Vanover were friends. You met in Vietnam."

Roberts whirled, his eyes flashing with anger. "That's a lie! I've been patient with you, but that's it," he snapped. "I'd like for you to leave."

Hailey looked at her uncle. Her face was etched with pain. "For heaven's sake, tell the truth!"

Roberts was visibly shaken by her words. He dropped onto the sofa and draped his arm around her. "Hailey," he said. "This is all just a dreadful mistake."

She shook off his arm and pinned him with a pained look. "How dare you sit there and lie to me!" she cried. He recoiled as if she'd struck him. "Don't you think I know what the three of you did? Lies, it was all a bunch of lies."

Frank Roberts swallowed. "I—I don't know what you mean."

"Stop it! Just stop it!"

Sean looked at Hailey, then at her uncle. "Are you saying it isn't true?"

"Of course it isn't true!"

"What part of it isn't true? You didn't know Ryan Vanover or you didn't help him kidnap Hailey?"

A gamut of emotions ran across Roberts's features—shock, confusion, fear...most of all, fear.

"Why did you do it? For the money? Was that the reason?" Sean asked.

"No, no!"

"Then why did you cover for Vanover? Why did you take Hailey and leave California?" Sean asked.

"I—I…" Roberts looked like a caged animal. His mouth worked but nothing came out.

"Mr. Roberts, I know this is unpleasant, but you're going to have to answer my questions, either here or at police headquarters. It's all going to come out. We checked with the Defense Department. We know you and Vanover crossed paths at a little village in Vietnam called Hue. You were seriously injured during the battle there. We also know Vanover was awarded the Purple Heart for saving a number of lives during that battle. Were you one of the men he saved?"

Roberts didn't say anything.

"You're the only person who knows the truth. I'll ask you again, did you or your brother-in-law aid Ryan Vanover in any way in the kidnapping of Susan Palmer?"

When Roberts still didn't say anything, Sean lost it. "For God's sake, man, look at your niece. You've put her through hell. Don't you think she deserves the truth?"

Frank Roberts closed his eyes and nodded faintly. "Yes," he whispered.

Sean let out a sigh of relief. Now they were getting somewhere. "You're Sarge, aren't you?"

"No, I…" Roberts began, then looked at Hailey, and the denial died on his lips. He slowly nodded. "But I didn't have anything to do with the kidnapping. Neither did Jack," he added quickly. "It was Ryan and Denny Hanson."

"How did you get involved?"

He issued a weary sigh. "Ryan came by my apartment one evening with this little girl. He said she was his niece. I had no reason to disbelieve him." He looked at Hailey and swallowed. "He said his sister had taken ill suddenly and had to be hospitalized. He needed a place for the little girl to stay for a few days, since he couldn't keep her in his room in the servants' quarters at the Palmer estate. He said he thought of me because of my background in child welfare.'' He looked at Sean, pleading for understanding. ''I didn't want to.''

''Why did you agree?''

''I didn't have any choice,'' Roberts said, his voice laced with pain. ''I owed him. You were right, Ryan saved my life, saved me from a sniper's bullet when we were in Nam. You've got to believe me. I didn't know who she was. It was only when the story broke the following evening that I learned Hailey's true identity.''

''Why didn't you go to the police?''

Roberts rubbed his temple. ''I was afraid. Put yourself in my place. I had Alan Palmer's child. Who was going to believe me? The police were going to think I was one of the kidnappers and had gotten cold feet.'' He drew a deep breath. ''I called Ryan at the estate at least a half dozen times before he returned my call. He didn't deny that she was Susan, but he refused to come and get her. He told me if I went to the police, he'd tell them I was involved. But if I'd just sit tight and keep my mouth shut, he'd come and get her in a day or so.''

''Why the delay?''

''He said he couldn't take Hailey until he'd found another place to stash her. When I asked when that would be, he started yelling at me to get off his back. Then he muttered something about if he had any sense, he'd just do what he'd been hired to do, kill her and be done with it.''

Sean sat up straight. ''Vanover was *hired* to kidnap Hailey?''

''That's what he said. He'd been hired to kidnap *and* kill her, but he couldn't go through with it, which is why he'd left her with me in the first place.'' Roberts's mouth twisted in a bitter smile.

That's why Vanover had wanted the sweater. He'd needed to prove to the man who hired him that Susan was dead. ''Did he say anything about the person who hired him?''

"No, but I got the impression it was someone close to Alan Palmer. The conversation ended with Ryan saying he'd come by in a few days for the little girl, but he didn't show—that week or the next."

Sean nodded. Vanover hadn't showed because he was dead.

"And then I received a package in the mail from him. It contained five thousand dollars in cash. I was sure it was part of the ransom payment."

"Why didn't you just pin a note to Hailey and leave her in the corridor of the nearest police station? Why did you run?"

"I was terrified. Hailey's picture was all over the news. Someone was bound to recognize her. It was just a matter of time. So I took her to my sister's in Chicago."

"How did you get your sister and brother-in-law to help you?"

Roberts dropped his head. "I lied. I told Jack and Abby pretty much the same story Ryan told me, and they agreed to look after Hailey for a few days. Then I returned to Los Angeles and tried to contact Mr. Palmer, but he misinterpreted my attempt. He thought I was one of the kidnappers. The next thing I knew, the police were on my tail, so I cleared out and returned to Chicago. By then, Jack and Abby knew the truth, but they were also terrified of going to the police. They were afraid I'd be arrested." He swallowed. "Maybe they were right to have been."

Sean frowned. "I still don't understand why you didn't just drop her off at a police station."

"It was too risky. Ryan was dead. Probably killed by the man who had hired him to kidnap and kill Hailey. And according to Ryan, that person was close to her father. It seemed to us that returning her was tantamount to signing her death sentence. We didn't know what to do. We were between a rock and a hard place."

"So you did nothing," Hailey said coldly.

Frank Roberts shook his head vehemently. "That's not

true. Over the next couple of months, Jack and I made several attempts to contact Mr. Palmer, but we were unsuccessful. In our last attempt, Jack came within a hairbreadth of being apprehended. After that, we were afraid to try again.'' He paused and looked at Hailey. ''Jack and Abby had also become emotionally attached to you.'' He closed his eyes. ''God help us, we didn't want to give you back. Hailey, I'm sorry. I never meant to hurt you. None of us did.''

For a moment, no one said anything. Then Frank Roberts stood and walked to the desk in the corner of the room. He took a large white envelope out of a drawer, walked across the room and handed it to Hailey. ''This is for you. It's your dad's letter.'' His throat worked. ''You couldn't find it because I took it. I was afraid Jack was going to tell you the whole story.''

Sean watched as she opened the envelope with shaky hands and pulled out a three-page letter. Her eyes filled with tears as she read. When she was done, she handed it to him. He took it and quickly skimmed the pages. The letter confirmed Roberts's story and explained the cryptic language Jack Monroe had used in his letter to Alan. He'd been trying to warn him about a possible threat to Hailey from someone in his inner circle.

It was an emotionally charged afternoon. The only comfort he could draw from the confrontation was the knowledge that they had gotten answers to a number of questions. They knew that Frank Roberts was Sarge. They also knew he had not been involved in the kidnapping. Nor, for that matter, had Jack Monroe. They knew the killer, the person who had masterminded Hailey's kidnapping, was someone close to Alan. They knew a lot more than they had known before coming here, but they were still a long way from having an answer to their most immediate question—who killed Lara Palmer and arranged for the kidnapping of her young daughter?

"HAILEY, we need to talk about what happened today."

She didn't say anything. Sean frowned. She'd been sitting on the living-room sofa for the past hour. She hadn't uttered a single word since he'd brought her to her apartment. He hadn't pressed her to talk. He wanted to give her time to absorb the shock, but as she continued to just sit there, not saying anything, it was beginning to trouble him. She'd experienced a devastating loss—the loss of trust of one of the people she loved most in the world. He knew from personal experience how painful that could be and that it was probably best to talk about it. Yet she was holding everything inside, the way she'd always done.

"Do you want me to make you something to eat?" he asked. He sat in one of the leather armchairs across from her, fighting the urge to pull her into his arms.

"No," she said, wrapping her arms around herself, staring into space.

He knew she was hurting, and he wanted to chase away the pain, tell her it would be all right—that she should talk about it, not hold the pain inside to fester and grow.

Yet nothing he said seemed to get through to her. But as he examined her ashen face, he knew he had to continue to try. She needed to get it all out so she could move on.

His eyes followed her as she stood, walked to the window, stared out.

"Hailey, for God's sake, say something!"

She didn't respond, just continued to stare blankly out the window.

"Talk to me. Scream, yell, cry. Do something, but for heaven's sake, don't hold it in."

She still didn't reply. He forced himself to continue. "You've had a terrible shock. You need to talk about what happened...get it out." He paused. "You have every right to be hurt and angry. What your uncle did was wrong. I don't know what kind of relationship the two of you will have in the future. Maybe none. Now you're thinking only of the hurt and pain he caused you, but don't forget the good times. He loves you very much. And remember this—his silence was prompted by his love and concern for you.''

For a long time Hailey didn't say anything, then she finally blurted, ''How could they have lied like that—not just Uncle Frank, but Mom and Dad, too? They all lied. Oh, I know, not in so many words, but in deeds.'' Her voice sounded as hurt and bewildered as a small child's. ''Everything I've ever thought about them, about myself, has been a lie.''

Sean let out the breath he'd been holding. ''No, it wasn't,'' he said gently. ''It wasn't a lie that they loved you and wanted what was best for you. They may have gone about it the wrong way, but they did the best they knew how. They all did. Your uncle loves you very much, and he made a mistake.''

''But he lied,'' Hailey said in a low, tortured voice. ''Not just in the past, but he continued to lie. He lied repeatedly. He knew Dad wanted me to know the truth, but he stole the letter. So much of what happened over the last month didn't have to, if he'd just told the truth.''

''And he's paid a heavy price for his silence.''

Levering himself out of the chair, he crossed to where she stood and enfolded her in his arms. For a moment she resisted. Then, with a tiny sound that was half sigh, half sob, she turned and slumped against him.

She pressed her head against his chest, and he could feel the beat of his heart thumping against her cheek. After a while he lifted her into his arms, then sat with her in his lap, cradling her protectively. But he didn't press her to talk.

Long moments later she began on her own.

He didn't say anything. Just let her talk. She told him all about her life with Jack and Abby Monroe—the birthday parties, Sunday dinners, family vacations, all the family things they had done. The words were fierce, but he held her tenderly, rocking her in his arms, kissing her hair and her forehead, giving her all the comfort he could. When the words stopped, the tears began. He blinked back his own tears and held her close, trying to absorb her pain.

After a few moments she stopped crying, but she kept her face hidden against his chest. He wished he could take away the hurt, the pain, promise her that everything was going to be all right. But things were far from over. There was a killer still out there.

Chapter Twelve

"What do you mean take a break? We still have a lot of material to go through." Hailey looked at the stack of documents on the conference table in Sean's office, then at him.

"Yeah, but we don't have to go through all of it now." Sean leaned back in his chair and looked at her. "Why don't you call him?"

Hailey looked to the side. She didn't need to ask who he meant. She knew he was talking about her uncle. A week had passed since they'd returned to L.A. Uncle Frank had called several times, but she wouldn't take his calls. She couldn't, not now, not when her emotions were so raw.

She was still struggling to come to grips with the role he and her parents had played in her kidnapping. It was too much for her to deal with, so she'd elected to focus on the investigation.

"You know you're going to have to talk to him eventually," Sean said, breaking into her thoughts. "If for no other reason than to give closure to the situation."

"I know," she said quietly. "I just need some time."

Sean leaned over and gave her hand an affectionate squeeze. He always seemed to understand what she was feeling, and her appreciation of him grew. "I hate to admit it, but we're back to where we started," she said for want of something to say.

Sean looked at her and frowned. "That's not entirely true. We've made a lot of progress. We've eliminated your dad as a suspect. We know money wasn't the motive for the kidnapping, that it was to cover up Lara's murder. We know the killer is someone closely connected to Alan—which brings us back to Paul and Reese."

"That's still a long way from knowing which one killed Lara." She sighed. "If only I could remember who I saw that night."

"That's just it. You do." He tapped his forehead with his finger. "It's there in your subconscious, but as a child it was too difficult for you to deal with, so you repressed it."

"But not completely," she added. "That's why I have the nightmares."

He nodded slowly. "I think it's significant that the dream came back when you learned the Monroes weren't your parents. And each subsequent dream has been stronger and more intense than the last. Like I told Alan, I believe it's just a matter of time before it all comes back. But since there's no guarantee you're going to remember who you saw any time soon, we're going to have to rely on good, old-fashioned investigative work to identify Lara's killer." He grinned and threw her a file. "Let's get to work."

They worked for close to two hours, reviewing the background check Mac had completed on Paul and Reese, looking for holes or inconsistencies, anything that might connect either man to Lara's murder or the missing ransom money. A little after one, Hailey heaved a weary sigh, then leaned into the sofa cushions.

"I swear if I read one more page, I'm going to scream," she said.

Sean grinned. "Why don't we take a break. I'm losing my concentration, too."

He crossed the room, dropped on the sofa next to her, and began to rub the back of her neck. "You're awfully tense," he said as he gently kneaded the muscles between her shoulder blades and the base of her neck.

"Mmm, that feels good," she sighed.

"Turn around so I can massage your back."

Hailey turned slightly so she faced away from Sean. His hands began to move slowly up and down her spine—stroking, caressing. A moment later she felt his hands slip beneath her sweater and unclasp her bra.

Hailey's breath caught in her throat.

"Just relax," he whispered.

Then his glorious hands were moving on her back, skin against skin, kneading, stroking her tense, tired muscles. She let out a low sigh of contentment and started to relax. His hands were deft and sure, touching each tired spot. With each stroke, her sweater moved higher until it was pushed up to her shoulders, allowing him full access to her back.

Her skin tingled everywhere he touched her, and as much as she tried to control her reaction, her delighted body betrayed her. A moan escaped her lips when his hands moved from her back to her sides, up and down, stroking, caressing. But when his hands moved from her sides to the sensitive skin of her stomach, a wave of heat washed over her as he pulled her snugly against him.

"What are you doing?" Hailey asked shakily.

"Making you a bit more comfortable." He spoke in a soft, husky voice. His hands were making small circles on her stomach. "I don't know about you, but I'm feeling better already."

Her eyes closed as warm pleasure began to fill her. "You are?"

"Damn right." He brushed her hair to the side and lightly kissed her neck. "Are you certain you don't feel better, too?"

She swallowed. "Maybe we should get back to work."

"That's not what you want to do."

"Y-yes, I do," she said, but she couldn't stop the sigh that escaped from her lips.

"Liar." The feel of his warm breath on her neck was doing incredible things to her. She moaned and leaned against him as he made a necklace of small, biting kisses along her neck.

One moment Sean's hands were moving down her sides, then the next they were sliding over her stomach and upward. She caught her breath when she felt his hands lightly brush against the undercurve of her breasts, then cup them gently. She moaned as his thumbs stroked her nipples. His hands felt so good. A wave of heat washed over her as she gave herself up to the pleasure of his mouth, his hands, his touch.

"Just what I thought," he murmured, nibbling her earlobe. "Your nipples are hard."

"They are?" she gasped.

"Yes, and they're not the only thing."

Her eyes flew open. She had to call a halt to his lovemaking before things got out of hand. Abruptly, she stood. Pulling her sweater down, she walked across the room. Sean followed. He stood behind her, not saying anything, just running his hand slowly, sensuously up and down her arm. She shivered.

"Am I making you nervous?"

Of course he was, but she wasn't about to admit it. "Not at all."

"Good." He continued stroking her arm and snaked his other arm around her waist, pulling her against him. He swayed with her, his hips slowly pressing against her. He held her like that for a moment before turning her to face him. "I want you." His voice was soft, low and husky with passion.

"Sean…" she began breathlessly, only to lose the thought on a sigh as his arms wrapped around her, holding her close.

He kissed her neck and moved his mouth to her ear, the

tip of his tongue barely touching inside. She shivered, tilting her head back. Eyes closed, she clung to his hard, muscled shoulders.

He ran his hands down her back, grabbing her behind, squeezing. She could feel the hard muscles of his thighs through the thin material of her slacks as he backed her against the wall, pressing into her. The heat emanating from Sean's rugged frame seemed to cover her in a cloak of warmth that heightened her passion as she moaned deep in her throat.

His hands were everywhere. He pushed her sweater up, kneading her breasts, stroking her nipples until they stood up hard against his hands. One hand slid to her waist, and his fingers opened the top button of her slacks.

She felt the zipper inching slowly down. She tried to move away, yet a part of her was enjoying this—his mouth on hers, his hands on her body, his hardness pressing against her responding flesh. She raised her arms to push him away and found herself embracing him. He was kissing her, his tongue in her mouth moving with a life of its own, sliding, sucking, teasing, drawing her out. She couldn't breathe.

"I want you," he sighed into her mouth. "Now."

Hailey twisted away, feeling his fingertips below her navel, moving down, inching along her skin to the lacy border of her panties. "No, Sean," she moaned. "Someone could come in—"

His fingers slid beneath the lace.

No words were spoken. There were only the low, aching moans of need. They were both breathing so hard, so fast, that her ears were filled with the sound...and she scarcely heard the telephone ringing. Only when it had rung again and again did her feverish brain register what it was.

It took all her willpower to swim against the flood of desire. She struggled to pull her mouth away. "Th-the telephone—"

"Let it ring." His mouth slid down her throat, scorching

her flesh with his lips. His face burrowed through the thick strands of her hair to press hungrily against her neck. His hands gripped her waist as if he was afraid she'd pull away. Her whole body was aching for him.

But the ringing continued, unrelenting, nagging with a sense of urgency.

"Sean," she whispered breathlessly. "You'd better answer it. It could be important."

Groaning, he wrenched himself free. She watched as he leaned over the desk and picked up the receiver. She stared at him, aware of her hot tingling mouth—and her hot tingling body—aware of just how badly she wanted him.

"I told you I didn't want—" he began, then stopped. "Okay, put him through."

He didn't say much, just listened then finally nodded. "We'll be right over."

Something in his tone made her look at him sharply. Suddenly, her heart began to pound. "What is it?"

He returned the receiver to its cradle, then looked at her. "That was Dr. Price. He has the results of the DNA test."

HAILEY HAD KNOWN this moment would come, and yet she felt totally unprepared for it. With a sense of dread, she followed Sean down the sterile white corridor to the bank of elevators.

"Don't look so nervous."

"That's easy for you to say," Hailey said. "Your whole future doesn't change with the results of a test."

He paused and turned her to face him. "And neither does yours. You don't need a DNA test to tell you who you are, and neither do I. You're Hailey Monroe, Alan Palmer's daughter."

"I know," she said quietly. "It's just that once Alan is given the results, there'll be no turning back. I'll really be Susan Palmer."

"It doesn't matter what your name is. You'll still be the

same person you've always been. Hey, Alan is going to be ecstatic.''

"Alan is going to be ecstatic that *Susan* is alive, but I'm not Susan. I'm not some four-year-old. I can't give him back the years he's lost, the memories. I'm not even sure how I feel about him.''

"Don't you think he knows that?''

"I'm not sure. Sometimes when he looks at me, I don't think he sees me—Hailey Monroe. He sees Susan, or what he thinks she ought to be like.''

"Don't sell Alan short. He needs some time. You both do.''

Just then, the elevator came to a quiet stop and the doors opened. She followed him off the elevator to the reception area.

A young, perky blonde looked up and smiled as they approached.

"Sean Cassadine and Hailey Monroe to see Dr. Price.''

"Dr. Price is expecting you. His office is the last door at the end of the corridor. Just go right in.''

Sean took her arm. They proceeded down the corridor and stopped outside the office. He looked at Hailey. She gave him a reassuring smile.

Sean twisted the knob, pushed open the door and recoiled.

Next to him, Hailey stifled a scream.

Dr. Price lay face up on the carpeted floor, his arms outstretched, his legs partially hidden behind his desk.

"Stay here," Sean said, moving across the room. He knelt next to the body and placed two fingers on the doctor's neck, checking for a pulse.

"Is he—" Hailey's voice failed.

Sean nodded slowly. "Yeah, he's dead. Looks like he was shot at close range." He gave the body a cursory glance, noting its position, then he proceeded to go through Dr. Price's pockets.

"Shouldn't we call the police?"

"In a minute. I want to look around." He stood, crossed to the desk and began going through the drawers.

Hailey frowned. "What are you looking for?"

"The results of the DNA test," he said. "I'm not sure, but my guess would be that's why he was killed. From the look of his clothes, whoever killed him went through his pockets. But his credit cards and money are still in his wallet, so robbery wasn't the motive." His eyes scanned the room. "This office has been searched."

It was then she noticed the condition of the room. Papers were strewn about the desk, several file cabinet drawers were partially opened, and the chairs facing the desk were ajar.

She turned to Sean. He was checking beneath the desk blotter. "Nothing," he muttered. There were two books on the desk, *Gray's Anatomy* and *The Physician's Desk Reference*. He fanned the pages of both, but there was nothing hidden there. He looked at the file cabinets and bookcase along the back wall, then at Hailey. "It would take too long to search them. I guess it's time to call the police."

Sean had concluded his call when Hailey noticed a small brown object on the floor near the front of the desk.

"What's that?" she asked.

He walked to where she stood. "It's a cigar butt." He pulled a handkerchief from his pocket, knelt, picked it up and studied it. "The end has been cut, not chewed off, like some cigar smokers do."

Hailey's hand flew to her mouth. "Paul Keegan clips the end of his cigars. You think he killed Dr. Price?"

IF SEAN SEEMED to have doubts about Paul's guilt, homicide detective Tate Wells didn't. Sean explained the reason they were in Dr. Price's office and told Tate about the missing DNA results and finding the cigar butt. Dr. Price's distraught secretary claimed to have seen a black man with white hair leaving the doctor's office about twenty minutes before Hailey and Sean arrived. That was enough for Tate to call the district attorney's office to request a search warrant. Then he made a beeline for Paul's office. He balked at the idea of their coming along and only relented when Sean offered to share the information they'd collected during the investigation.

Tate was apparently one of those cops who believed in the element of surprise. When they reached the reception area outside Paul's office, he didn't bother to knock, just barged right in.

Paul was bent over his desk, poring over some papers. He looked up, blinked twice, then stood.

"What's the meaning of this?"

"Mr. Keegan, I'm Detective Wells." Tate flashed his badge and shield. "I have a warrant to search your office and your home." He handed a copy of the warrant to Paul, then nodded at the two detectives who accompanied him. They went to work.

Paul looked from the detective to Sean and Hailey. "What the hell is going on?"

"We're investigating the murder of Dr. Clifford Price. You know, the guy who was doing the DNA test for your brother-in-law."

"I know who he is," Paul snapped. "What do you mean you're investigating his murder?"

"Someone put a bullet in him earlier today."

"That's terrible, but what does his death have to do with—" Paul's eyes widened as he watched a police officer pick up an expensive vase from his desk. "Put that down!" He turned to Tate, his jaw clenched. "Your cops break anything, you're going to pay for it. And trust me, it's going to be a hell of a bill."

Tate gave him a sour look but instructed his men to be careful.

"Paul, did you know Dr. Price?" Sean asked.

"Of course not. I never met the man."

Sean frowned. "Then why did his secretary think she

saw a man matching your description leaving his office earlier today?''

"How would I know what some damn secretary thought or why?" he snapped. "I'm not a mind reader."

"Paul, where were you—''

"Sean, if you don't mind," Tate barked, "I'll ask the questions. Mr. Keegan, where were you this afternoon, say between the hours of one and three?"

"I was at a meeting across town. It began at noon and lasted until four."

"Can anyone vouch for you?"

"My brother-in-law, Alan Palmer, was also there."

"And what time did you get back here?"

He shrugged. "I guess about four-thirty."

"And you've been here ever since?"

"That's right. If you don't believe me, you can check with my secretary. She'll tell you I was here."

"Don't worry, we will. Is that your briefcase?"

"Yes."

"You want to open it?"

Paul swore under his breath but complied with the detective's request.

Inside there was a yellow legal pad, a fountain pen, an appointment book and a checkbook. Tate lifted the appointment book and flipped through the pages. A small white envelope bearing the name and logo of Genetic Laboratories fell out.

Paul visibly paled at the sight of it. "I—I don't know how that got in there."

Tate gave him a disgusted look then extracted the letter from the envelope. It was the lab results.

"I tell you I don't know how it got in there."

"Mr. Keegan, I'd like you to come downtown with us."

Paul turned to Sean, his eyes pleading. "You've got to help me. Tell him I didn't have anything to do with this murder. It's a setup."

If he was acting, Hailey thought, he was good.

"I think the best thing you can do is call your lawyer and have him meet you at the station."

"Yes," Paul said vaguely, "that's what I'll do."

While Paul was on the phone with his lawyer, Hailey asked to see the test results. There were a lot of statistics and scientific mumbo jumbo. The only thing she saw was the last line of the typed letter. *DNA blood testing has determined with a 99.9% probability that Alan Palmer is the biological father of Hailey Monroe.*

Just one simple sentence containing words that Dr. Price had, no doubt, uttered hundreds of times before, but this time those words had cost him his life.

TATE WELLS leaned back in his chair in Sean's office and regarded him thoughtfully. "You don't think Paul Keegan killed Dr. Price, do you?"

Sean shook his head. "It doesn't add up."

Tate sighed. "We're getting a lot of heat," he said. "The press is claiming that Keegan is being treated differently because he's rich, that we're dragging our feet."

"Dr. Price was only murdered a week ago."

"The mayor thinks that's a week too long. He wants to know when we're going to make an arrest—"

"Remind him how long it took to crack the Ennis Cosby case," Sean said dryly.

"Yeah, but the public thinks this one's a lot simpler."

"It's not simple. There are a lot of things that are not simple about this case," Sean countered.

"Try explaining that to Councilman Quinn. He's another one who thinks it's simple. He thinks finding the cigar butt and the results of the DNA results in Keegan's briefcase makes this one pretty open and shut."

Sean frowned. "Were you able to get any prints off the cigar butt?"

Tate shook his head. "Nothing that was usable."

"What about the test results?" Hailey asked. "Any prints on the paper or the envelope?"

Tate shook his head again. "No, but we got lucky at Price's office. We lifted a clear set of Keegan's prints off the corner of the doctor's desk, which means he lied about never having been there. We can place him at the scene."

"What about his alibi, didn't it check out?" Sean asked.

"He attended the meeting, all right, but so did fifty other people. He could have slipped out once the session started, jumped in a cab, killed the doctor and made it back in time for cocktails, and no one, including Palmer, would have been the wiser."

"Sean, you have to admit the case against Paul is pretty strong," Hailey pointed out.

"That's just it. It's *too* strong. Paul is not stupid, but if you believe the evidence, he left his cigar butt in the middle of the floor, right out in plain sight. Instead of destroying the DNA results, he carried them around in his briefcase and left his prints all over Dr. Price's desk."

Hailey shrugged. "He slipped up, or maybe he heard someone coming and had to get out of there fast."

Sean massaged the back of his neck. "Maybe. I just don't know."

"Tell me something, Sean," Tate said. "Why don't you think he whacked the good doctor?"

He shrugged. "It's a gut reaction. Paul may be capable of a lot of things, but one thing I don't believe he's capable of is killing his own sister. I believe whoever killed Dr. Price also killed Lara Palmer and arranged for Hailey's kidnapping."

Tate pursued his lips. "It could be that the two cases are unrelated."

"They're related. I'd stake my life on it. By all accounts, Dr. Price was a quiet, unassuming man who didn't have an enemy in the world. The only reason he was murdered was the DNA results."

"My point exactly. Keegan had the most to lose if Palmer learned the results of the test. He killed Dr. Price because he wanted to keep the results quiet. I rest my case."

"That doesn't make sense. Killing Dr. Price wouldn't have gained him anything. All anyone would have to do is perform the test again."

"Maybe he was hoping to buy himself some time. You said there have been several attempts on Hailey's life. Maybe he hoped to have her out of the way before another test could be performed."

"I suppose." Sean said, unconvinced. "But Hailey's death wouldn't prevent another test from being performed. In fact, quite to the contrary, it would most likely ensure that police investigators would follow up with one. Tate, you might also want to question Reese Tyler."

Tate whistled. "Senator Tyler? You think he's involved in this?"

"That's what I've been trying to find out."

Tate pushed his lanky frame from the chair and stood. "I'll make some discreet inquiries. Senator Tyler has a lot of powerful friends and he knows how to use them."

Sean nodded. "One more thing. Could you hold off on an arrest for a while? Paul's not going anywhere."

"I'll give you a couple of days, but after that..." Tate opened the door and almost bumped into Mac. The two men exchanged pleasantries.

Mac dropped into the chair Tate had vacated in front of Sean's desk. "I thought you might want to know we completed the financial checks on Lacy, Gloria, Paul and Reese," he said. "Lacy's money is all from fencing stolen goods, and Gloria doesn't have any. As for Paul and Reese, they've both had money problems over the years. Reese with various political campaigns, and Paul due to a couple of poor investments. But we couldn't connect either man to the ransom money. It doesn't mean the connection isn't there. It's just hard to find complete financial records going back twenty years."

Sean nodded. That's what he'd been afraid of.

"Oh, yeah," Mac said, "Gloria Falcon called."

Sean was quietly alert. "What did she want?"

Mac chuckled. "To let you know that she'll do whatever she can to aid in the investigation."

Sean frowned. "She said that?"

Hailey smiled. "She said pretty much the same thing to me yesterday. Then she started telling me about what a hard life she's had, how much she loves Alan. That he's the best thing that happened to her. It was weird. She's been nasty and unpleasant to me for weeks, and now she wants to be my new best friend."

Sean chuckled. "The lady's not stupid. She knows which side her bread is buttered on."

Mac nodded. "Sounds like your investigation is making a lot of people nervous and unhappy."

He nodded slowly. "I don't doubt it."

"Well, one person is happy—Alan." Hailey grimaced. "He wants to throw a party. To introduce me to his friends, so to speak."

"A party?" Sean's mouth slowly curved into a broad smile. "I think that's a wonderful idea."

Mac and Hailey looked at him as if he'd suddenly grown two heads. "Are you nuts?" Mac roared. "That's the last thing we ought to agree to. You might as well just sit Hailey on Wilshire Boulevard and place a sign around her neck saying, 'Come and get me.'"

"That's exactly what I'm going to do—that is, if Hailey is game." He looked at her and gave her a reassuring smile. "The killer is going to have to make a move soon. I'd rather that move be on my terms. What better place to give him his chance than at a party?"

Chapter Thirteen

The party was in full swing. If Hailey could gauge from the noise level or joviality, then the party was a huge success. Alan had gone all out, sparing no expense. There were two buffet tables loaded with stuffed mushrooms, boiled shrimp, raw oysters, cheese cubes and crackers, cubed cantaloupe, whole strawberries, olives, pickles and salad peppers. Two standing rib roasts were presided over by two chefs in tall white hats wielding carving knives the size of machetes. There were four bars, but for those who didn't wish to stand in line, waiters moved about the crowd with glasses of champagne.

The guest list was a venerable who's who in the world of business and politics, from the mayor of Los Angeles to the CEO of Microsoft. The entertainment industry was also there in full force—Quincy Jones, Steven Spielberg, Bill and Camille Cosby and Will Smith, just to name a few. It seemed that everyone who was anyone was there. And why not? It was the social event of the year. The introduction of Alan Palmer's daughter to society. No one wanted to miss that.

Hailey was torn between fascination and a distinctly uneasy sensation. Everyone looked so innocent, but somewhere in this room—among the rich and famous—was a killer. And that thought brought her up short, marring what should have been a happy occasion.

She glanced around the room. There was no reason to be nervous. She was in a house full of people, and security was tight though unobtrusive. While the bulk of the security was stationed outside, a few people had been placed inside the house in the guise of guests and waiters to monitor Paul and Reese's movements, as well as the crowd in general.

She'd been more than a little surprised that Sean had been able to convince Alan to invite Paul, and even more that he'd actually shown up. Speaking of which, where was Sean? She'd seen him briefly before Alan had whisked her away to stand next to him in the receiving line.

She scanned the crowd. It took her a moment to locate Sean. He was standing on the opposite side of the room, talking to a stunning redhead—or maybe she ought to say, with a redhead draped around him. Hailey's eyes narrowed slightly as she took in the scene. The redhead was dressed in a designer gown that Hailey guessed cost more than she made in a month and that showed her ample bust and figure off to perfection.

For a moment Hailey felt a twinge of jealousy, until she remembered the look in Sean's eyes when he'd seen her that evening. She'd dressed with special care, selecting the strapless, buttercup-yellow sheath because it complemented her tawny-brown skin and raven-black hair. He'd looked her over from head to toe. He'd made her feel beautiful and desirable. Just thinking about his heated gaze made her feel a warm glow. It had given her the added poise and confidence she'd needed to stand in the receiving line next to Alan, bestowing gracious smiles and brief handshakes as his friends and colleagues came forward to be introduced.

That was Sean's first impression of Hailey—a beautiful, confident woman on the arm of one of the most powerful and respected men in the country. He broke off his conversation with Pamela Voss and stared at Hailey. Sean was convinced there wasn't a man in the room who hadn't scurried over to be introduced or just plain slobber. One idiot actually kissed her hand. He'd overheard another ask if she was a model, a third invited her to dinner, lunch or breakfast, whatever she preferred. Sean stood it as long as he could before marching over to where she stood.

"Alan, I'm going to borrow Hailey."

"Just be sure to bring her back," Alan teased.

He took Hailey's arm and moved through the crowd, not stopping until he reached a slightly secluded spot. "How are you holding up?" he asked.

"I'm okay, but I'll be glad when this evening is over."

"So will I."

Hailey tilted her head. "You still think the killer is going to make his move tonight?"

"My gut feeling is that he's getting desperate. He's going to have to make a move soon. Tonight would be perfect."

"It might be too perfect. He may suspect that it's a setup."

"Yeah, but if he's as desperate as I think, it might just be too tempting to pass up. Just stay close to me."

"Don't worry about that."

"I saw you talking to Eric earlier. What did he have to say?"

Her eyes widened in mock surprise. "The way that redhead was draped all over you, I'm surprised you could see anything."

His face broke into a broad smile. "You're jealous."

"Of that amazon? Why would I be jealous?"

"You tell me." When she didn't answer, he asked, "So what did Eric have to say?"

"Not much. He was just making nice-nice for Alan's benefit."

"Don't look now," Sean said, "but Reese is headed this way."

"Sean, Hailey," Reese said graciously. He leaned over and kissed Hailey on the check. "May I say how lovely you look." Again, she was struck by his charm.

"Would you honor me with a dance?"

Hailey ignored the warning look in Sean's eyes as she let the senator lead her to the dance floor.

As they danced, he told her several hilarious stories about his early days in politics. She didn't believe a word of his outrageous tales and she told him so. Aside from telling tall tales for humor's sake, he seemed like such an honest and sincere person, and she found it impossible to believe he was a killer.

"Mind if I cut in?" Sean drawled from behind her. Hailey faltered and missed a step as a rush of excitement slithered across the surface of her skin.

"Not at all. Thanks for the dance," Reese said with a smile, handing her into Sean's waiting arms.

Sean drew her close—so close, her body felt welded to his from her thighs to the tip of her head. In time to the slow, soulful strains, their bodies moved as one with perfect fluidity. She rested her head against the curve of his shoulder and closed her eyes, unaware of the faint sigh that escaped her lips.

This was heaven, the one place she wanted to be. In the arms of the man she...

Her eyes flew open. Exactly what *did* she feel for Sean? Friendship? Affection? Sexual attraction? She turned the question over in her mind, but she suspected if she were honest with herself, she already knew the answer. As much as she tried to fight it, she was in love with him. But how did he feel about her? She knew Sean liked her and enjoyed being with her, but whether or not his feelings ran any deeper, she just didn't know.

The next two hours were a blur as she wrestled with that question and her mounting tension. Too many sleepless nights were catching up with her. She was feeling tired and headachy and couldn't wait for the evening to end.

"Look happy." Sean's voice came from her behind her. "This is your party, remember."

"I know," she said, then rubbed her forehead. "I was wondering where you'd gone. I couldn't see you in the crowd and I was afraid—'' She broke off uneasily, glancing around. But no one seemed to be paying any attention.

She felt his arm go around her waist. "Why are you rubbing your temple?" he asked. "You okay?"

"I'm fine. It's just a headache."

"You sure? You look a little frayed around the edges."

"That kind of flattery could turn a girl's head," she said dryly.

"You know what I mean." He lifted his hand from her waist and brushed a lock of hair behind her ear. "I know this has been hard, but just hang in there. It's going to be over soon. And as for the way you look, you're the most beautiful woman here," he said quietly.

She looked at him, and her breath caught in her chest. He had a hard, intense, hungry look on his face. Time suddenly seemed to stand still all around them. People faded from her consciousness, and the noise and music were muted. Her blood throbbed through her veins slowly, powerfully.

They were utterly alone in the middle of the crowd. Her body quickened, her breath coming fast and shallow, her breasts rising as if to his touch. The ache of wanting him was so intense she thought she would die. "Don't look at me like that," she whispered.

He didn't reply. Instead his gaze moved slowly to her breasts, lingered, and she knew her nipples were visibly erect. A muscle twitched in his jaw.

A loud voice suddenly broke through their fantasy. "I would like to make a toast."

Slowly the chatter of voices stilled, and everyone turned toward Alan as he stood in the center of the room.

The spell that had held Hailey and Sean in its grip was broken, and Hailey shuddered as they turned to face Alan.

"To my daughter," Alan said clearly, lifting his glass of champagne to Hailey. "I'm the happiest man in the world now that you are back." He turned, making a sweeping motion with his free hand. "I also want to thank all of you for your support and prayers through the years. As a token of my appreciation to you and the people of Los Angeles, I've purchased a parcel of land on Veterans Parkway to be used as a park for the children of the city. It will be called Hailey's Playhouse in honor of my daughter.''

All around the room glasses were lifted to Hailey, champagne was drunk, and a chorus of ''welcome home'' filled the room.

She plastered a smile on her face and kept smiling until she thought her face would crack.

''What's wrong?'' Sean whispered.

''I don't like the idea of a park being dedicated in my honor,'' she whispered back. ''I haven't done anything to deserve that kind of recognition.''

He nodded. ''I understand, but try convincing Alan of that.''

''I don't think I could even broach the subject with him. I'm afraid he would take it as a sign that I'm rejecting him as a father.'' She ran her hand over a stomach that could only be described as queasy. ''What a mess. And if that isn't bad enough, I think I'm coming down with the flu.''

Sean leaned toward her. ''Maybe we should call a halt to the evening. If you're not feeling—''

''Come on, Sean, you can't monopolize all of Hailey's time.'' She looked into the face of a tall, distinguished man Alan had introduced her to earlier. Immediately, he began asking about her stay in California. Once they'd exhausted that topic, he began quizzing Sean about his security company. She was only half-listening to the conversation when she happened to glimpse the profile of a waiter's face as he passed. There was something about him that was faintly familiar.

She continued to study him as he moved about the room passing out drinks. He looked to be in his mid-thirties. From the pockmarks on his face, she guessed he'd once suffered from severe acne. But the scars didn't detract from his appearance—on the contrary, they added character to his face. While he couldn't be classified as handsome, exactly, there was something about him—an air of danger—that some women might find... Suddenly, she remembered where she'd seen him. It had been on the train platform in Chicago. He'd been in the crowd. The cop had told him to move along. Now he was *here*.

She grabbed Sean's arm. "That's him," she whispered. "The man who's been trying to kill me. That's the man who pushed me off the train platform in Chicago."

"Where?" Sean's head whipped around, searching the crowd.

She nodded in the direction of the doorway. "That's him. The tall, dark-haired waiter who just left the room. I think he was headed for the kitchen."

"Stay here." Sean signaled to Mac, then started out of the room after the man. Hailey was right behind him. She saw Mac speak into a two-way radio, then head toward the front door.

When they entered the kitchen, the man was nowhere in sight. The only persons in the room were Niles, several household workers and the caterer.

Sean swore. "Are you sure he came this way?"

Before she could answer, the door to the pantry swung open, and the man she'd fingered stepped into the room.

For a split second he stared at them, then he turned and ran.

Sean was right behind him. The man wrenched open the back door and ran down the steps. Sean took a flying leap and tackled the man. He came up swinging. Sean ducked, then, like a prizefighter, caught the left side of the man's face. He pivoted and hit him again. But the punch didn't stop the man.

He lunged at Sean, who blocked the blow and hit him again, sending the man sprawling to the ground. With lightning-fast reflexes, the man reached into his pocket and pulled out a gun.

Sean was quicker. His left leg shot out in a karate kick,

knocking the gun out of his hand to the ground. Sean kicked it toward Hailey, and she picked it up. It felt heavy and alien in her grasp. A moment later, Mac was there taking the gun from her.

Sean grabbed the man by the collar, yanked him up and led him toward the storage shed next to the stables. Once inside, he was plopped into a chair.

"Lock the door," Sean ordered. Hailey found the knob and pushed the button.

"Now we don't have to worry about being disturbed while we talk."

"You might as well save your breath," the man growled. "I'm not telling you anything."

"We'll see about that." Sean nodded to Mac, who drew a length of rope from his pocket then tied their prisoner's hands behind his back. Once that was done, Mac went through the man's pockets.

"His driver's license says his name is Ben Gilman," Mac said, "and he lives in Palm Springs."

"Who hired you?" Sean asked.

"Like I said, I'm not telling you anything."

"What did you do with the waiter you took that uniform off of?"

Gilman just smirked.

Sean shrugged. "Suit yourself. Mac, he's all yours."

Gilman sat straighter. "Hey, wait a minute. I know my rights. You have to call the cops—"

Mac backhanded him hard across the face. Before the other man could recover, Mac grabbed him by the throat. "I don't want to hear anything from you but an answer to my question," Mac snarled. "Got it?" He released Gilman and waited until the man stopped making choking noises.

Gilman swallowed. He was visibly afraid, but still defiant. "I'm not telling you a damn thing."

"Wanna bet?" Mac pulled a switchblade out of his pocket and flashed it in front of their terrified captive's face.

"This baby cuts through flesh like a knife through butter," he said. "You want to see?"

"Wh-what are you going to do?" Gilman sputtered.

"I believe you're about to find out," Sean said dryly. "Hailey, gag him."

"No! No!" he screamed.

She took the handkerchief Sean offered her and tied it over Gilman's mouth.

Gilman cringed as Mac pushed his head back, turned his face to the side and slid the blade slowly down his cheek then alongside his throat. He had Gilman's full attention. The man's eyes bulged as he followed the progress of the knife. Through his gag, he was desperately trying to say something.

Ignoring his grunts, Mac began to slice the buttons off Gilman's vest, then his shirt. He pulled the ruined shirt open and pressed the blade of the knife against Gilman's chest. "Hailey is going to remove your gag, and if you make any sound that isn't an answer to one of our questions, you're going to find yourself minus an organ or two."

Who would have thought Mac could sound so fierce, Hailey mused as she removed the gag.

Sean's eyes burned into Gilman's. "Who hired you?"

Gilman shook his head. "I don't know." The words were barely more than a hoarse croak.

"That's not the right answer." Mac pressed the blade against the man's perspiration-soaked chin. Then, with a flick of his wrist, he nipped the tip of Gilman's nose.

"Stop," Gilman pleaded as a trickle of blood ran from his nose to the corner of his mouth, "you've got to believe me. I don't know the guy's name. I never talked to him face-to-face. I got my instructions over the phone."

Sean's eyes narrowed. "You expect me to believe you accept snuff jobs from a voice over the phone?"

"I...yeah. That's my policy. Always has been. For security. That way, the client can't finger me, or vice versa."

"How do you get paid?"

"The money is wired to my bank in the Cayman Islands. The client pays half up front and the balance when the job is done."

"I want the name of the bank, the account number and the name on the account."

Gilman hesitated, but when Mac pulled his head back and placed the blade of the knife against his throat, he complied.

"Now I want to know about this job," Sean said.

"I got a call about a month ago. The guy offered me a hundred and fifty thousand dollars to kill Ms. Monroe, and only Ms. Monroe. I didn't have anything to do with the murder of that doctor."

"So you admit it was you that pushed Hailey off that train platform, and it was you that shot at her and tried to run her over?"

"Yeah, it was me."

"So what did you have planned for Hailey tonight?" Sean asked.

Gilman's eyes shifted anxiously from Mac to Sean, and then, in a barely audible voice, he said, "I—I slipped something into Ms. Monroe's drink."

Hailey gasped. Her symptoms weren't the flu. She'd been poisoned!

THE DOCTORS SAID Hailey was lucky to be alive. Gilman had slipped a deadly poison into her drink. The first symptoms weren't supposed to appear for an hour after ingestion, but because of her small stature, the poison had moved quickly through her system so the symptoms had appeared earlier. If they had gotten her to the hospital just fifteen minutes later, the outcome might have been drastically different.

Alan was livid when he learned Sean had used Hailey as bait to smoke out the killer.

"That's it," he said as the paramedics wheeled Hailey out on a stretcher. "I'm calling a halt to the investigation."

"Don't you want to know who killed Lara?" Sean asked.

His head swiveled in Sean's direction, and his eyes flashed with anger. "What kind of question is that? Of course I want to know, but not at the expense of losing my daugh—" He never got to finish his sentence. With those words, he clutched his chest and crumpled to the floor.

The paramedics wanted to take him to the hospital, but Alan refused. Sean instructed Gloria to call his doctor, then he accompanied Hailey to the hospital. When he called a few hours later to give an update on Hailey's condition, he learned that the doctor had given Alan a clean bill of health but insisted that he remain in bed for a few days.

Sean swallowed and stared at Hailey as she lay on the narrow hospital bed. She'd almost died, he thought bleakly. He would never forgive himself for putting her in such danger.

Her eyes slowly opened. "Hi," she said, giving him a little smile.

He eased down on the side of the bed, careful not to jar her.

"I'm sorry." His voice was low and laced with pain and self-reproach.

"It's not your fault," she said softly. "I knew what I was doing. Alan was just upset. He didn't mean what he said."

He gave her a wry smile. "I'm glad you can be so forgiving, but I have to live with what I did to you."

She cupped his face in her hands. "What you did was apprehend a man hired to kill me," she said firmly.

He turned his face in her hand and laid a tiny kiss in her palm. A deep shudder shook him. God, he loved her.

"It's all right," she said, stroking his face, his hair. "And don't worry about Alan. He'll come around. By the way, how is he?"

"He's fine. I know he's anxious to talk with you. Do you feel up to talking to him?"

"Sure." She gave him a wan smile.

He dialed the number for her then handed her the receiver. She talked just long enough to assure Alan that she was all right, then she handed the phone to Sean.

"Now I'd like to talk to my uncle," she said. "Could you dial his number?"

He smiled. "I think that's a great idea."

Again, her conversation wasn't very long, but Sean was glad she was willing to give her uncle a chance, and he told her so.

It was also time to tell her how he felt about her. He was about to do so when Tate Wells came in and tiredly settled himself into one of the two chairs in the room. Sean remained close to Hailey's side.

"Well, you're looking a sight better than the last time I saw you," Tate said to Hailey. "How do you feel?"

"Like I just had my stomach pumped," she said, and he laughed.

"I want to ask you a few questions, if you feel up to it."

"Of course."

"I took Sean and Mac's statements last night. I just want to know if you remember seeing Gilman talking to Paul Keegan."

She shook her head. "I'm afraid not."

"What about Reese Tyler or Gloria Falcon?"

She shook her head again. "The first time I remember seeing him was when he passed by Sean and me. I don't recall seeing him before then."

"That's okay," Tate said. "It was a long shot."

"You find out anything about our hit man?" Sean asked.

"Gilman is an alias. His real name is Andrew Bennett. We ran his prints through the FBI computer. He's got a rap sheet a mile long. Seems the FBI, Scotland Yard, Interpol and a number of other law enforcement agencies have been after him for years. He's suspected in the murders of at least nineteen people.''

Sean gave a low whistle. ''Any chance of getting anything out of him?''

Tate shook his head. ''I doubt it. He's hired himself a hotshot criminal lawyer. A guy out of New York. He's not about to let him say 'Boo.''' He sighed and got to his feet. ''I'll check back with you, Hailey. Maybe you'll remember something later. Sean, can I see you outside?''

Sean gave Hailey a reassuring smile, then followed the detective out of the room. He and Tate strolled down the hall toward the elevators. ''We followed Gilman's trail through the woods to the edge of the estate,'' the detective said. ''Just like you figured, we found Gilman's car parked there. It looks like he waylaid one of the caterer's people for his uniform. Once inside, it was easy enough for him to blend in with the rest of the caterer's staff.''

''What about the missing waiter? You find him?''

''Yeah, we found his body in the woods, near Gilman's car. He was dead.''

They had reached the elevators, but Tate didn't punch the button to call it. He and Sean strolled to the end of the hall, out of earshot of anyone.

''We questioned Paul Keegan, as well as Gloria Falcon and Reese Tyler. They all claim not to know Gilman. And with Gilman's claiming not to know who hired him…well, we don't have much to go on.''

Sean ran his hand over his hair in frustration. ''This hit man puts a different slant on things. Gloria, Paul, Reese— their alibis don't mean anything now. God, I feel so damn helpless. One of them is a killer, and I don't have any idea which one it is.''

''We're doing all we can,'' Tate replied gruffly. They turned and walked toward the elevators. ''How's Palmer doing? I heard he collapsed when he heard about Hailey.''

''He's resting at the estate. The doctor said he just

fainted, but with his heart condition, he wanted Alan to stay in bed for a few days.''

Tate shook his head. ''Poor guy. He's been through a lot. Just goes to show, money can't buy happiness.'' They reached the elevators, and this time he punched the button. ''Call me if Hailey remembers anything.''

Sean remained in the corridor, which is where Mac found him.

''Sean, we got a line on Gilman's money. It was transferred to his account in the Cayman Islands from a bank right here, Commerce National.''

''Can the money be traced?''

Mac shook his head. ''It was all in cash. Only the banks know the account holder's identity, and they aren't talking.''

Sean chewed his lip. He'd call Tate, tell him what they'd found. Tate could get the district attorney to subpoena the local bank's records, but the bank was likely to resist any kind of disclosure of the account holder's identity. They could be tied up in court for who knows how long.

Grim-faced, Sean said firmly, ''I want the name on that account, and I don't care how you get it.''

''IT'S SIX-THIRTY. Everyone is gone. Why are you still here?'' Hailey asked, poking her head into Sean's office.

He looked up, then did a double take. ''Damn it, Hailey,'' he yelled. ''What are you doing here? You're supposed to be home in bed, resting.''

She threw him a sour look before setting the picnic basket she carried on the floor, then sinking into the chair in front of his desk. She didn't know who was worse, Sean or Alan. She'd been released from the hospital the day before, but both men had fretted and fussed over her until she thought she would scream.

''I was going crazy at home,'' she explained. ''I thought I'd come and help you with the investigation.''

''I don't need any help.''

"That's not the way it looks to me," she said, glancing pointedly at the documents on his desk.

"Never mind the way it looks. Does Alan know you're here?"

"I left him a note," she answered dismissively. "I told him I was coming here and that you would bring me home later."

Sean shook his head. "No, you're going home now."

"Come on, Sean," she coaxed. "Be reasonable. There's nothing for me to do there."

"I thought you were going to help Alan plan the dedication ceremony. It's just a couple of days away."

"It's Sunday. And Alan won't let me do anything. I can't even see the park until Saturday afternoon. That's when he's going to give me a private tour of the grounds and let me see the plaque. By the way, you're also invited. Come on, Sean," she coaxed, "let me stay. I brought dinner." She picked up the picnic basket and placed it on his desk. "Niles made your favorite—fried chicken with wild rice and snow peas, a tossed salad and a bottle of Alan's best white wine."

He eyed her for a moment longer, then sighed. "Well, I guess it wouldn't hurt to let you stay. This way, at least I'll know you're out of harm's way."

She hid a smile. "So what are you working on?" she asked, pointing to the documents on his desk.

"I'll tell you after we eat." He stood, picked up the picnic basket and headed for the conference table on the other side of the room. He moved with such pantherlike grace, she thought, as she followed him to the conference table. Oh, how she loved him, needed him, but she was afraid to tell him how she felt. This was not the time for her to find out that he didn't return her feelings.

"God, I'm starving," he said, looking into the basket. "I missed lunch."

He settled into a chair across from her and placed his hand palm up on the table. Hailey looked at him questioningly, then lifted her hand to place it in his. He stared at her slender fingers and stroked them gently with his thumb before raising his dark eyes once more to gaze at her warmly.

"I'm sorry I yelled at you," he said. "I'm glad you're here."

"So am I," Hailey said, smiling. A rush of joy swept through her.

Hailey could feel the tension ebbing from her body as they ate. Sean asked her endless questions about her childhood. She told him about her life in Chicago, and he told her about growing up in southern California. It was a sharing time, a special time.

Hailey was amazed at how quickly the next few hours slipped past. By the time she and Sean had polished off the bottle of wine and eaten the last of the chicken, night had descended.

"We'd better get started on that stack of documents," she said.

He shrugged. "There's really nothing to do. I was just killing time going through Reese and Paul's financial statements while I waited for Mac to call. He thinks he's got a line on a guy at Commerce National Bank who will give us the name on the account."

"How soon will you know?"

"I'm hoping Mac calls tonight."

"That quickly?" She eyed him suspiciously. "Just how is he getting this information? Sean, you aren't doing anything illegal, are you?"

"Let's just say, if you're willing to shell out enough money, there are people who will sell out their own mother." His eyes met hers evenly. "And I'll do whatever I have to do to keep you safe." He got up and came around the table, took her hands in his and pulled her to her feet.

"You mean everything to me," he said softly, then lowered his mouth to hers. She wound her arms around his neck, and he pulled her closer to him.

Minutes passed, and nothing existed beyond the passion of their kiss. They clung to each other, their tongues thrusting together, deeply, wildly. When he unzipped her dress and let it drop to the floor, she barely noticed. She was burning up. She felt as if she was standing in front of a raging fire that grew hotter and hotter.

He quickly unclasped her bra and dropped it to the floor. He groaned and slid his hands under her rib cage, and with his thumbs slowly caressed the rosy peaks. He squeezed her breasts gently, erotically, as he stared at her.

"Your breasts are so beautiful," he whispered. "So firm and golden. I love looking at them, touching them."

Hailey gasped and ran her hands through his dark hair as he bent his head and opened his mouth wide, taking a tip of the tiny bud into his mouth. She cried out at the hot, wet pressure, the friction of his teeth against her sensitive flesh. A moment later he repeated the ritual on her other breast. Her knees buckled and she would have fallen if he hadn't wrapped his arms around her waist as he continued his devastating assault.

Just when she thought she couldn't take any more of his sweet torture, his mouth once again claimed hers. At the same time, his hands explored her back, then ran up and down her sides and reached around to the outer swell of her breasts. One hand curved around a breast and gently fondled the soft fullness. She moaned against his ardent mouth as he slowly massaged the mound. With his other hand, he pulled her closer, drawing her between his legs and pressing her hips upward to meet the hard evidence of his arousal. She clung to him, hot with desire and dizzy from a barrage of emotions so intense she could barely breathe.

"Oh, Sean," she gasped, going nearly limp in his arms.

"I want you," he whispered, his voice hoarse with desire. "I want you so very much."

"And I want you," she said, and walked with him across the room. Gently he eased her onto the sofa. He came down on top of her and gathered her close. Then his mouth claimed hers, and his hands were everywhere. Wave after wave of heat washed over her as she gave herself up to the pleasure of his mouth, his touch.

Afterward she was never sure when he stripped off his jeans and shirt. What she did remember with aching clarity was the fire he'd built inside her until she'd trembled with need and longed to be joined with him.

She caught her breath as she felt his strong thighs nudge hers apart and his hardness poised on the brink of her feminine core. Then he slowly entered her and paused deep inside.

After a moment he began to move. Slowly at first. Then harder, faster, deeper as her body instinctively matched his rhythm. She felt the impact of him throughout her body, hot, demanding, deliciously overpowering. He was like a flame burning into her. She gasped but couldn't stop to catch her breath, the feelings were so intense.

I love you, she said silently. She ached to speak the words aloud, but sensed the time was not right. Instead, she held him close, stroking his head, his back.

When the electricity coursed through her body, warning of the impending climax, she heard herself cry out his name, then his answering cry, as if from a distance. Then he pulled her close and told her how much he needed her, wanted her.

His loving words sent her spilling over the edge, and before the delicate convulsions had rippled completely through her body, he was following her, huskily shouting his own release. Clinging together, they drifted back to earth as their bodies cooled and their breathing returned to normal.

Sean pulled her against his side, resting his lips on her forehead. Again, Hailey wished she could tell him how much she loved him. But instead, she contented herself with curling into his strong, protective arms. They lay there for precious long moments, entwined in each other's arms in the warm afterglow of love, until a shrill ringing brought her to reality.

It took her a few seconds to realize she was hearing the telephone.

She glanced at the clock on his desk. Ten-thirty. No one called at this time of night unless something was terribly important or wrong. Her heart slammed against her chest as she watched Sean pick up the receiver. "Yes?"

He didn't say anything, just listened. Hailey saw his mouth pull down into a frown. A moment later he lowered the receiver, then looked at her. "That was Mac. He got the name on the account."

"Who is it?"

"Paul. The money that was wired to Gilman came from Paul Keegan."

Chapter Fourteen

Sean still had doubts about Paul's guilt. Paul's lawyer had gotten him released from jail on a four-hundred-thousand-dollar bond, and the public-relations firm he'd hired was working overtime putting their spin on the story. He'd appeared on "Larry King Live" and several other popular talk shows proclaiming his innocence. But Tate was confident they had their man. Alan had congratulated him on a job well done. Everyone considered the matter closed.

Sean knew he should, too. Instead of spending Saturday afternoon cooped up in his office, going over his notes, he should be with Hailey. They hadn't had a moment alone since Paul's arrest. There was so much he hadn't said but needed to say to her. First and foremost he needed to tell her how much he loved her, respected her and wanted to spend his life with her. That's what he should be doing, not second-guessing the outcome of the case. He knew that. He couldn't shake the feeling he'd missed something—but what?

He leaned back in his chair, steepled his hands, rested his chin on the point and looked at the investigative report spread out on his desk. He'd read it three times, and it always came out the same. Paul was guilty. Case closed. He just found it hard to believe Paul could kill his own sister and try to kill his niece. But if Paul hadn't done it, then who had? Both Gloria and Reese had been eliminated as suspects, and Lara hadn't been the kind of person who had enemies. She had been loved and well-liked by everyone. There were no skeletons in her closets, nor, for that matter, in Alan's. And they'd had a good marriage. No, Paul had to have killed her, killed her for the money he thought he'd inherit. Tate had an airtight case.

And yet, he couldn't help the feeling something wasn't quite right. Once again his thoughts turned to Reese. Maybe it was the fact that Reese had tried to downplay his anger over Alan and Lara's marriage. But he'd been extremely angry. So angry, in fact, it had taken him three years to get over it. Or had he? Over the years Reese's name had been linked to a number of prominent and well-to-do women, even a starlet and a model, but he had never married. Could it be he'd never gotten over Lara? It was possible, Sean thought. That kind of love could generate powerful emotions. Negative emotions. It was not unheard of for a person to resort to murder when his or her affections weren't returned. He picked up the file on Reese and began to read.

He'd only read a few pages when Mac stuck his head in the doorway. "Hell, Sean, what are you doing here? I thought you were going to spend the afternoon with Hailey, then later the two of you were going with Alan to check out the dedication site?"

"Yeah, that's the plan," he said without looking up. "I just wanted to go over my notes on Paul one more time."

"Why?" Mac asked, plopping into the chair in front of his desk. "The police seem to have a pretty strong case against him."

"Maybe I should have dug a little deeper into Lara's background," Sean said absently. "After all, she did carry on a hot and heavy love affair with Reese for over a year."

"So, she had a sex life before she married Alan. I had one, too, before this case," Mac added morosely.

Sean's head came up. "I want you to see if you can locate an old girlfriend of Reese's—Gwendolyn Levin. He dated her right after Lara dumped him. I'd like you to get on it right away.''

Mac groaned. ''This is Saturday. My day off. I came in to pick up my laptop, not to get an assignment.''

''I guess it can wait till Monday,'' Sean replied gruffly.

''You know, Sean, this case has ruined your sense of humor. And my social life.'' Getting no rise out of him, Mac frowned. ''Seriously, Tyler's a powerful man. He's got a lot of money and support behind him. There's talk of his running for governor. You're not going to tie him to a twenty-year-old murder.''

Sean frowned. ''But it always comes back to him. He had motive and opportunity to kill Lara.''

''True, but he didn't have any reason to kill Dr. Price, and most likely whoever killed Lara also killed Price. Paul fits the bill on both counts.''

Sean pursed his lips. ''So everybody keeps telling me.''

''Maybe you ought to listen.''

Sean leaned back in his chair, then let out a deep sigh. ''I don't want to be the cause of an innocent man going to prison. I just need to have this question answered to my satisfaction.''

Mac stared at him, perplexed. ''I don't understand what your problem is. We can place Keegan at Dr. Price's murder scene.''

Sean slowly expelled his breath. ''This just doesn't feel right. I'm missing something.'' He braced his elbows on the desk and ran his hands over his face. ''This is driving me crazy.''

''You're wound up tighter than a coil spring. You need to relax. At least, take the rest of the day off.'' Mac glanced at his watch. ''If you hurry, you may be able to squeeze in a romantic carriage ride with Hailey before lunch. Frankly, for a man who wants to convince his lady to move out here, you're not doing a very good job. You ought to be plying her with liquor, showering her with flowers.''

"All right," Sean grinned, "you've made your point. I'll finish this report then head out of here."

And he'd really meant to go, but once he got into Reese's file he couldn't put it down. There had to be something in this file that he'd overlooked. He read it three more times. Then, he read Lara's file, then Reese's file again before it hit him. Sean stared at the dates on the paper in front of him. It was so obvious. Why hadn't he thought of it before? If he was right... Suddenly, he had an urgent need to talk to Reese.

He picked up the phone and dialed Reese's home number. His maid answered. She told him he'd just missed the senator; that he'd gone down to his office to work.

Sean punched in the number to Reese's direct line and got his answering machine. He left a terse message advising that he was on the way over. For a moment he considered running by Genetic Laboratories, but a quick glance at his watch told him he didn't have time. He slipped on his vest and jacket and went out the door.

Fifteen minutes later, he stepped into the lobby of the Palmer Building and took the elevator to the seventh floor. He stepped out of the elevator, took a left and went through the double doors to Reese's suite of offices. He listened for the sound of voices or activity as he moved down the corridor, but heard nothing.

The reception area was vacant. It was just as well, he thought. This wasn't a conversation he wanted to have overhead. He skirted a large trash bin apparently left by a janitor and continued down the corridor to Reese's office. At the door, he paused, drew a deep breath, then knocked. There was no answer.

He turned the knob and pushed the door open. "Reese?"

The lights were off, but he could see the outline of a man standing at the window, his back to him.

"Reese, we need to talk."

"I know," he said, then he slowly turned around.

Sean didn't see the hand that came out of his pocket or the gun until it was too late. "What the—"

The first bullet hit Sean in the shoulder.

The second one hit him in the chest.

Searing pain ripped through his body. He slumped to the floor. He could feel blood, his life force, seeping from his body, soaking his shirt, his jacket, the floor beneath him. He was distantly aware of movement around him, motion and light. His life flashed before him—images of Hailey, regret for the things he hadn't done. Most of all he regretted he never told Hailey that he loved her. For a moment her image was bright before him, then it began to fade. He tried to hold onto it but everything was getting darker.

Then there was nothing.

WHERE WAS SEAN? Hailey paced in the living room of the Palmer estate, alternating between wondering what was keeping him and worrying about what she would say once he got there. They had a lot to discuss. And somewhere in that conversation she planned to tell him how she felt about him—that she was in love with him. She thought he was also in love with her, but what if she was wrong?

She pushed the troubling thought aside and glanced at her watch. He should have been here hours ago. He'd missed their lunch date, and now he was on the verge of missing the tour of the park and the dedication site. Where could he be? She had called his apartment and the office several times, but had gotten no answer. Nor had she been able to reach him on his cellular phone or pager. She'd tracked Mac down, but he hadn't had any idea where Sean could be.

She nibbled her lower lip. Any moment now Alan would be coming to collect her. Alan had been late getting to the house and was cloistered in his study on a conference call. She didn't want to go without Sean, but it was getting late.

"Where's Sean?" Alan asked the moment he stepped into the room.

"I don't know," Hailey said. "I've been trying to reach him all afternoon. We were supposed to have lunch together, but he never showed or called."

Alan frowned. "That doesn't sound like Sean." At her pensive look, he added, "Something must have come up. I bet he'll be coming through that door any minute, all apologies."

She nodded. "I'm sure you're right."

Alan smiled. "I know you'd like for him to come with us to check out the site, so why don't we give him a little more time?" He walked to the bar in the corner of the room. "Can I get you anything?"

"No, nothing," she said. "By the way, where's Gloria? Isn't she coming with us?"

Alan shook his head. "She called me at the office. She said she had a prior engagement and wouldn't be able to accompany us, after all."

That's odd, she thought. She was surprised Gloria didn't jump at the opportunity to show Alan she accepted Hailey. She said, "So tell me about tomorrow's ceremony."

She'd said just the right thing. For the next few minutes Alan talked about the ceremony. "There'll be about a hundred people in attendance," he said. "The mayor, Reese and a few other local politicians, as well as a number of people from the business community. There'll be a few speeches and a couple of musical selections. The ceremony will run about an hour." He leaned forward excitely. "I know you've had reservations about having this park dedicated to you, but I think you're going to be pleased. The park covers five city blocks. It's going to have slides, swings and a sandbox for the younger kids and a basketball and tennis court for the older kids, as well as a swimming pool."

It sounded wonderful, and she told him so.

He smiled. "And I hope you like the plaque. It stands two feet by two and a half feet. It's made of granite and sits in the northwest corner of the grounds." Alan looked at his watch, then frowned. "It's eight o'clock. It's going to take at least twenty-five minutes to drive out to the site. I'm afraid if we don't leave soon it'll be too dark to see anything."

Hailey was torn. She was worried about Sean, but she also knew how important it was for Alan to give her this private tour. "I guess we'll have to go without him." She tried to keep her disappointment out of her voice, but Alan must have heard it.

"I doubt if I can make up for Sean, but I'll try." He took her arm and led her to the car. As he drove, he told her about the remaining work to be done, the landscaping and the designation of a bike and hiking trail.

The car drew to a stop in front of a slightly wooded area. It appeared to be bounded on all sides by a twelve-foot chain-link fence. Just inside the fence, she could see the construction trailer that served as the base of operation for the architect and project manager.

She stepped out of the car and followed Alan to the security guard's station outside the fence. The guard was nowhere in sight.

"He must be making his rounds," Alan said. She watched as he fished a key out of his pocket and unlocked the huge padlock on the gate, then stepped aside so she could enter.

"It's going to be dark soon, so we'll have to forgo the grand tour," he said, "and just head over to the dedication site. The plaque is being housed in a large canvas tent on the other side of those trees."

As they walked, Alan pointed out where the various playground equipment and tennis and basketball courts would go. In the distance, she could see the canvas tent.

Alan was telling her about his plans for making the park wheelchair accessible when he paused. "Did you hear that?"

"What?" Hailey asked.

His eyes scanned the area, then he shook his head.

"Never mind. I thought I heard something, but I guess I was wrong."

They were only a few feet from the tent when Alan paused again. "That's strange."

"What?"

"The lights are off out here." He looked around. "I told them the lights are to come on as soon as the sun sets. If they're not on out here, then they're probably out in the tent, as well. There's no point in our stumbling around in the dark. Stay here. I'm going to see if I can find the security guard or at least the light switch." He headed toward the construction trailer.

She watched him until he rounded the bend and disappeared. She wrapped her arms around herself as she surveyed the area. She had to admit it was a great location. The park would be a bright spot in the heart of the inner city. She walked to the tent, pulled back the flap and stepped inside. It took her eyes a moment to adjust, but even in the dim light she couldn't have missed the pickup truck and the huge granite plaque sitting on the tailgate of the truck. It hadn't been erected. The hole had been dug— she could see that, as well as the mountain of dirt that would be used to fill it. The ropes and the pulley to lower the plaque were all there.

How could this be? she wondered. Everything was supposed to be in place for tomorrow's ceremony. God, Alan was going to explode when he saw this. She walked to the truck to get a better look at the plaque. She didn't know what made her look down as she passed the hole, but she did…and what she saw made her heart stop.

Sean was lying at the bottom of the hole. She dropped to her knees and leaned over as far as she dared as she called desperately to him. "Sean! Sean! Can you hear me?"

He didn't answer or, for that matter, move. As her eyes adjusted to the fading light, she could see blood on his shoulder, his chest. He was hurt. Maybe even dying. Terror filled her heart.

She had to get down there. It was about a five-foot drop, she estimated. She could go down, but how would she get him out? She couldn't lift him. She looked over her shoulder, searching for Alan. What was keeping him? "Alan," she screamed. "Help! Help!" But there was no sound of running feet or movement from outside.

Her eyes darted about the tent, searching for a ladder, a rope, anything she could use to get Sean out. Other than a couple of wooden planks lying near the mouth of the hole, there was nothing. She bit back both tears and terror. What was she going to do? Sean could be dying. *Calm down. Think.* There had to be some way to get him out. She moved about the tent, frantically looking for something, anything she could use.

When she was about to despair, she heard footsteps and her name being called. Thank God! It was Alan! She drew a sigh of relief and ran to the opening in the tent. "I'm in here!" she called, then ran back to the hole.

Alan appeared in the doorway. "Alan! Over here!" she called. "Sean's down in the hole. He's hurt."

Alan didn't say anything. He stood there, looking at her. Hailey jumped up and ran to where he stood. "Did you hear me?" she screamed, tugging on his arm. "Sean's down there. He's hurt. We've got to get help."

Alan looked at her, then at Sean.

"What's wrong with you? What are you waiting for? Come on. We've got to get help."

"I don't think so," Alan said slowly. "After all the trouble I went through to get him in there, getting him out would defeat the whole purpose."

Hailey fell back a step. "What?"

"You heard me. I put him there. And in a few minutes, you're going to join him." He drew a gun out of his pocket and aimed it at her.

Shocked, Hailey looked from the gun to Alan's face.

"Really, my dear, don't look so surprised. You and Sean did a marvelous job of investigating Lara and Dr. Price's murder, identifying their killer. Unfortunately, Paul isn't your man."

She stared at him. She couldn't believe it. Alan—her father—was the monster from her dreams, the killer! He had killed Lara and Dr. Price!

"I'm sorry. I wish it didn't have to be this way," he said, "but it's gone too far. I can't back out now. Turn around."

"Alan," Hailey urged, trying to reason with him. "You can't do this. Sean is your friend. You're my father."

He laughed, a bitter angry sound. "But that's just it," he said. "I'm not your father."

"But the DNA test. It was positive."

"Was it?" Alan shook his head. "That's why I had to kill Dr. Price. He called me right after he finished the test. He told me I wasn't your father. I offered to pay him for his silence. Even though he accepted, I knew I couldn't trust him. The moment I was out of the office, he called you and Sean. He didn't know, but I was in the corridor, listening."

"But the police found Paul's fingerprints on his desk, and what about the cigar butt?"

"I planted that stuff. Just like I slipped that bogus DNA result into Paul's briefcase. I also made sure Dr. Price's secretary saw me leave his office. Since I was wearing a white wig, I knew the police would assume the man she saw was Paul."

Hailey frowned. "But how could you know..." Realization dawned. "You knew, didn't you? You knew all the time that you weren't my father."

"Yes," he said, his voice devoid of emotion. "Lara told me that night. She was leaving me and taking you with her. But I couldn't let her go."

"So you killed her."

"It was an accident," he said quickly. "I loved her. I

would never have done anything to hurt her. She was just so damn adamant about leaving. And for what? The possibility that she and Reese might get back together.''

''Reese?''

''Oh, yes, Reese.'' Alan's voice was laced with bitterness. ''I should have never let him back into our lives. Lara said seeing him again had rekindled her love. And she was sure he still loved her. But even if he didn't, she was convinced he'd marry her.'' He looked at Hailey. ''You were her ace in the hole. That's when she told me that I wasn't your father, that Reese was.''

Hailey stared at him, stunned. ''Reese is my father?''

Alan nodded. ''Lara thought if she told him you were his child, he'd do the right thing and marry her. I told her it didn't matter, but no amount of threats or pleading would make her change her mind about leaving. We argued. I pushed her. She fell and hit her head against the edge of the bathtub. Unfortunately, you saw the whole thing. You turned and ran and…I panicked. Before I realized what I'd done, I'd pushed you into the bathtub.''

Hailey shook her head. ''You didn't push me,'' she accused. ''You threw me in. How could you harm a small child? Didn't you feel anything for me?''

''I told you I panicked,'' he snapped. ''And—and maybe there was a part of me that always suspected you weren't mine. I tried, but I never bonded to you, the way a parent should.''

Hailey didn't buy it. More likely, she thought, he was so obsessed with Lara, there was no room in his heart for anyone else. Which also meant he'd have no qualms about killing her and Sean.

''You must have been relieved when you learned I didn't remember anything,'' she said.

Alan nodded. ''But I was also afraid one day you might remember what you saw, who you saw. So I hired Ryan to kidnap and kill you. Unfortunately, I killed him before I realized he lied about going through with it.''

Hailey swallowed. "The notes and calls from my dad and uncle, that's what tipped you off, isn't it?"

He nodded. "I knew then you were alive. From that moment on I lived in constant fear one day you'd show up at my door. And you did, didn't you?"

"You didn't have to respond to my dad's letter."

"Yes, I did. I wanted you out of the way, but after Gilman's blunder in Chicago, I wasn't sure if he was the man for the job. That's why I leaked the story to the *National Banner*. So I'd have an excuse to invite you here. That way, if I had to, I could kill you myself."

The hair on the back of Hailey's neck stood up at his words, but she tried to keep her fear at bay. "I understand why you feel you have to kill me, but why Sean?"

"I'm really sorry about that, but it was just a matter of time before he figured out I was the killer. I had planned to lure the two of you here, but after I intercepted a call from Sean to Reese earlier today I had to speed things up." At her look of confusion, he added, "I had Gilman bug Reese's home and office phones. And it's a good thing I did. Otherwise I wouldn't have heard Sean's message to Reese. I was already at Palmer Publishing. All I had to do was take my private elevator to Reese's office and erase the message. I told the guard in the lobby to intercept Reese and tell him there was an emergency at his house. Then I went to his office and waited for Sean."

She took a step back and almost stumbled on a wooden plank. "You'll never get away with this."

"That's where you're wrong." Alan smiled. "You see, my dear, everyone is going to think that after killing Doctor Price and framing Paul for his murder, you and Sean ran off together."

"No one is going to buy that."

"I think they will when they see the real DNA results, proving you're not my daughter." He shook his head. "You were quite the temptress. You seduced Sean into helping you steal a quarter of a million dollars from me.

When I found out what the two of you had done, you skipped town to prevent prosecution. I'm afraid the police are going to be too busy looking for the two of you to focus on me.''

He was right, she thought. He had played his role perfectly. He was the grieving and loving husband, the devoted father. He'd been above suspicion. "You thought of everything, didn't you?''

"I tried to, but I'm afraid I'm going to have to cut this discussion short," he said. "I've got of lot of work ahead of me. I've got a plaque to erect." He took a step closer. "Turn around.''

A tremor spread through Hailey's body. She had to keep him talking. "So the park, the plaque, they were just a means to an end. A tidy way of disposing of us.''

Alan nodded. "Actually, I thought it was quite an ingenious idea. Who would ever think to look for you here, beneath your plaque? Naturally," he added, "the wording will have to be changed.''

"You…you can't shoot me. The guard will hear. Or did you forget about him?''

Alan smiled. "No, I didn't forget about him. He went off duty an hour ago. When I left you earlier, I double-checked. It's just you and me.''

At that moment, a faint rustling sound came from the hole. Alan's eyes swiveled in the direction of the sound. It was for only a second, but it was enough. Hailey swept her right hand down on the hand holding the gun. It spun from Alan's outstretched hand to the ground. With her right foot, she stamped on his instep.

Alan was a big man, powerfully built, but Hailey's strength came from the surge of adrenaline coursing through her body and the element of surprise. She bent, picked up a wooden plank and slammed it into his stomach. Alan's head snapped sharply to the side, and his arms flew out. His legs wobbled, but he didn't go down.

He righted himself and lunged at her. Hailey hit him

again. His eyes seemed to float upward and disappear into the top of his head. Then he slumped to the ground. Hailey drew a ragged breath, stumbled to the edge of the hole and dropped to her knees. Sean was still unconscious.

"Hang on. I'm going for help." She was about to move away, then she turned back. "Sean, I love you. Please, don't leave me."

"HE'S GOING TO BE FINE," the doctor assured Hailey as he finished bandaging the gunshot wound to Sean's shoulder.

She barely heard the doctor's words. Her eyes were riveted on Sean as he sat on the examination table in the hospital emergency room. He was going to be all right. Thank God.

"I wish you'd consider staying in the hospital overnight," the doctor said. "A concussion, no matter how mild, shouldn't be taken lightly."

"I'll take care of him, Doctor," Hailey said. Sean's eyes met hers, and what she saw in the depth of his eyes made her heart melt.

The doctor issued a few more instructions then left the room.

She touched the side of Sean's face, her eyes bright with tears. "I thought you were dead."

"I would have been if I hadn't being wearing my vest." He pointed to the bulletproof vest the doctor had removed in order to take out the bullet in his shoulder. "Lucky for me Alan didn't know that I sometimes wore one. I must have hit my head on the doorjamb when I fell."

"God, I've never been so scared in my life," she said shakily. "Seeing you lying there, bleeding, and not being able to do anything." Hailey shivered.

"It's all over now," he murmured, pulling her against his good shoulder. "Alan can't hurt you or anyone else." His hand stroked her hair, then her back. "Are you sure you're all right?"

"I'm fine." She sighed and burrowed closer. "It's still hard for me to believe he killed Lara and Dr. Price."

"I know, Sean said. "I've known him all my life, and I would have never thought he was capable of committing such crimes. He was obsessed with Lara."

Hailey lifted her head to stare at him. "What's going to happen to him?"

"He's facing at least two counts of murder, two counts of attempted murder, conspiracy and probably a host of other charges. But don't think about that."

She swallowed. "H-he also said Reese is my father."

"I guessed as much," Sean said gently. "While I was reviewing Lara's file I noticed that you were a seven-month baby. I began to wonder if it really was a case of premature birth, or if Lara had in fact been pregnant when she married Alan. That would explain why Dr. Price was murdered. A DNA result that excluded Alan as the father would have made him a suspect in Lara's murder."

"Is that why you went to see Reese?"

"Yes. I wanted to confirm my suspicions before I confronted Alan." He looked at her, noting the uncertainty in her eyes. "You are going to tell Reese, aren't you? You aren't going to let him find out from some tabloid newspaper?"

"I don't know. I don't even know how I feel about it."

"I understand," he said. He tipped her chin, and she stared at him. "Reese likes you, and you like him. It's a start."

"Will you go with me?"

His face broke into a broad smile. "Try and pry me away from you. Baby, I'm afraid you're stuck with me."

"I—I think I can deal with that," she said, returning his smile.

"I'm glad," he said, then covered her mouth with his. They kissed for precious long minutes. When he drew his mouth away, he held her close. "I was afraid tonight, too.

But, more than anything else, I was afraid that…" His voice faltered.

"Yes?" she prompted softly.

"I was afraid I wouldn't get to tell you that I love you."

"You do?" Gray eyes searched his face hungrily.

"Yes. I love you more than life itself." He drew a deep breath, then released it in a long sigh. "Hailey, I love you and I want to share my life with you."

Her face broke into a brilliant smile. "Oh, Sean, I love you, too."

He loved her. Warmth expanded in her chest, trickled into her shoulders and arms, rushed through her legs. It made her feel strong, weak, invincible, vulnerable, full and empty all at the same time. And very, very happy.

"Will you marry me?" he asked, drawing her into his arms again.

"Yes, oh, yes, Sean!" Hailey said. "I love you so much." Tears began spilling down her cheeks. When she wrapped her arms around his neck, he bent to meet her kiss, his mouth hungry and tender. The kiss grew longer, deeper, weaving a magic spell that spoke of love and commitment…forever.

CANCELED

RETURN TO SENDER

RETURN TO SENDER

Sometimes the most precious secrets come in small packages...

What happens when a 25-year-old letter gets returned to sender...and the secrets that have been kept from you your whole life are suddenly revealed? Discover the secrets of intimacy and intrigue in

#478 PRIORITY MALE
by Susan Kearney (Aug.)

#482 FIRST CLASS FATHER
by Charlotte Douglas (Sept.)

Don't miss this very special duet!

Heat up your summer this July with

Summer
Lovers

This July, bestselling authors Barbara Delinsky,
Elizabeth Lowell and Anne Stuart present three
couples with pasts that threaten their future happiness.
Can they play with fire without being burned?

FIRST, BEST AND ONLY
by Barbara Delinsky

GRANITE MAN
by Elizabeth Lowell

CHAIN OF LOVE
by Anne Stuart

Available wherever Harlequin and Silhouette books
are sold.

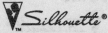

MEN at WORK

All work and no play?
Not these men!

July 1998

MACKENZIE'S LADY by Dallas Schulze

Undercover agent Mackenzie Donahue's
lazy smile and deep blue eyes were his best
weapons. But after rescuing—and kissing!—
damsel in distress Holly Reynolds, how could
he betray her by spying on her brother?

August 1998

MISS LIZ'S PASSION by Sherryl Woods

Todd Lewis could put up a building with ease,
but quailed at the sight of a classroom! Still,
Liz Gentry, his son's teacher, was no battle-ax,
and soon Todd started planning some
extracurricular activities of his own....

September 1998

A CLASSIC ENCOUNTER
by Emilie Richards

Doctor Chris Matthews was intelligent, sexy
and *very* good with his hands—which made
him all the more dangerous to single mom
Lizette St. Hilaire. So how long could she
resist Chris's special brand of TLC?

Available at your favorite retail outlet!

MEN AT WORK™

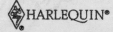

Look us up on-line at: http://www.romance.net   PMAW2

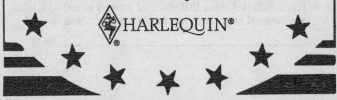

Presents
Extravaganza
25 YEARS!
It's our birthday and we're celebrating....

Twenty-five years of romance fiction
featuring men of the world and captivating women—
Seduction and passion guaranteed!

Not only are we promising you three months of terrific
books, authors and romance, but as an added **bonus**
with the retail purchase of two Presents® titles,
you can receive a special one-of-a-kind keepsake.
It's our gift to you!

Look in the back pages of any Harlequin Presents® title,
from May to July 1998, for more details.

Available wherever Harlequin books are sold.

HARLEQUIN®

FREE BOOK OFFER!

Dear Reader,

Thank you for reading this *Harlequin Intrigue*® title! Please take a few moments to tell us about the role that mystery plays in your fiction reading. When you have finished answering the survey, please mail it to the appropriate address listed below and we'll send you a free mystery novel as a token of our appreciation! Thank you for sharing your opinions!

1. How important is the mystery/suspense element in a series romance paperback?

   1.1 ❑ Very important   .3 ❑ Not very important
   .2 ❑ Somewhat important   .4 ❑ Not at all important

2. Which of the following types of paperback books have you read in the past 12 months? (check all that apply)

   2 ❑ Espionage/Spy (e.g. Tom Clancy, Robert Ludlum)
   3 ❑ Mainstream Contemporary Fiction (e.g. Patricia Cornwell)
   4 ❑ Occult/Horror (e.g. Stephen King, Anne Rice)
   5 ❑ Popular Women's Fiction (e.g. Danielle Steel, Nora Roberts)
   6 ❑ Fantasy (e.g. Terry Brooks)
   7 ❑ Mystery
   8 ❑ Science Fiction (e.g. Isaac Asimov)
   9 ❑ Series Romance Fiction (e.g. Harlequin Romance)
   10 ❑ Action Adventure paperbacks (e.g. Mack Bolan)
   11 ❑ Paperback Biographies
   12 ❑ Paperback Humor
   13 ❑ Self-help paperbacks

3. How many mystery novels, if any, have you read in the past 6 months?

   Paperback _____ (14, 15)   Hardcover _____ (16, 17)

4. If you indicated above that you read mystery paperbacks, what are the most important elements of a mystery book to you?

   _____ (18, 23)

5. If you enjoy reading mystery paperbacks, which of the
   following types of mystery fiction do you enjoy reading?
   (check all that apply)
   24 ❏ American Cozy (e.g. Joan Hess)
   25 ❏ British Cozy (e.g. Jill Paton Walsh)
   26 ❏ Noire (e.g. James Ellroy, Loren D. Estleman)
   27 ❏ Hard-boiled (male or female private eye) (e.g. Robert Parker)
   28 ❏ American Police Procedural (e.g. Ed McBain)
   29 ❏ British Police Procedural (e.g. Ian Rankin, P. D. James)

6. How do you usually obtain your fiction paperbacks?
   (check all that apply)
   30 ❏ National chain bookstore (e.g. Waldenbooks, Borders)
   31 ❏ Supermarket
   32 ❏ General or discount merchandise store (e.g. Kmart, Target)
   33 ❏ Borrow or trade with family members or friends
   34 ❏ By mail
   35 ❏ Secondhand bookstore
   36 ❏ Library
   37 ❏ Other _____ (38, 43)

7. Into which of the following age groups do you fall?
   44.1 ❏ Under 18 years
     .2 ❏ 18 to 24 years
     .3 ❏ 25 to 34 years
     .4 ❏ 35 to 49 years
     .5 ❏ 50 to 64 years
     .6 ❏ 65 years or older

*Thank you very much for your cooperation! To receive your free
mystery novel, please print your name and address clearly and
return the survey to the appropriate address listed below.*

Name: _____

Address: _____ City: _____

State/Province: _____ Zip/Postal Code: _____

In U.S.: Worldwide Mystery Survey, 3010 Walden Avenue,
P.O. Box 9057, Buffalo, NY 14269-9057
In Canada: Worldwide Mystery Survey, P.O. Box 622,
Fort Erie, Ontario L2A 5X3

098 KGU CJP2   WHID982

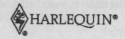
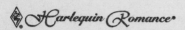

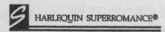